LIPSTICK AND LIES

LIPSTICK AND LIES

Lesley Grant-Adamson

Hodder & Stoughton

British Library Cataloguing in Publication Data

Grant-Adamson, Lesley
Lipstick and lies
I. Title
823.9'14 [F]

ISBN 0 340 71317 8

Typeset by Palimpsest Book Production Limited,
Polmont, Stirlingshire
Printed and bound in Great Britain by
Mackays of Chatham plc, Chatham, Kent

Hodder and Stoughton
A division of Hodder Headline PLC
338 Euston Road
London NW1 3BH

For Alisoun Gort

CHAPTER ONE

I know what I'll say when they come for me. I'll tell the tale that protects me from trouble. It's as familiar as the truth and with cach repetition it grows more real. But it isn't the truth.

Each year I keep three anniversaries: the date of the murder, the date of the hanging and Sandy's birthday. I keep them involuntarily, jolted into remembrance by, perhaps, a glance at a calendar or the act of writing the date on a cheque. Without these cruel anniversaries it might have been possible to bury the truth.

I don't mark them in my diary. Look, my pencilled notes are only for appointments, shopping to do and bills to pay. There's nothing to startle anyone who peers over my shoulder.

Two more days. To the anniversary of the murder, I mean.

Oddly, I'll be spending it at the scene of the crime. Well, no, not exactly but close, visiting a cousin of mine who's settled in the town. June's older than me, lame now and clinging onto family, always begging visits. How could I refuse without her wondering whether my reasons were less to do with enjoying a busy life than with repugnance at long-ago death? Deaths. Two of them, remember: the slaughter and the hideous legal retribution.

This year it so happened it was June who alerted me to

the anniversary, in a telephone conversation hingeing on her increasing isolation. She ended a good-natured grumble by saying: 'Anna, you never allow enough time, dear. Come for a weekend and then we'll really have time to talk. How about the end of March?'

And there it was, the fatal date, falling this year on the final Saturday of the month. The murder itself took place on a Tuesday.

Without quibble I replied: 'Yes, I'll come then.'

I wrote diagonally across the space for two days on the diary page: *See June*. As I scribbled I imagined her sitting by her telephone, triumphant. Because she looks frail I underestimate her. If I were to forget how gaunt her body is and concentrate on the determined line of her jaw, which is plain now she's taken to commanding her steely hair with combs and drawing it into a knot on the nape of her neck, I'd give way less frequently. When I'm annoyed I've done so I tell myself she's selfish. We are on the whole, I think, a selfish family.

Since June's call the anniversary has hung around in my head, an impending tribulation that's all the worse for being anticipated. If only I could be sure June isn't aware of it, too. Of course, there's no means of checking without giving away what's on my mind, so I'll just have to turn up on Friday evening and hope for the best.

I could be lucky. She hasn't talked to me about the murder for ages, except for a few cautious remarks when I first went to visit her. She'd been living in the town – a run-to-seed sort of place, all history and no future – for a couple of months by then and it would have been peculiar if neither of us had commented on her coming full circle, back to what was once her parents' home and also to the town where the family drama was enacted. Every one of us had moved away in the intervening years. June's parents, too, had let their house and gone.

'The last batch of tenants were awful,' she said, and we smartly set off along the landlord-tenant byway which meant murder was kept off the agenda.

2

Perhaps she attempted to revive it before I left an hour or two later. Yes, I'm sure she did, but I'm adept at dodging and I had the perfect excuse for slipping away: I faced a long journey home. Presumably she registered my reluctance because she hasn't mentioned it again, not even, I think, indirectly.

Reminiscing with June is curious. As she's ten years older than me her perspective has always been different. What I saw as a child, she viewed with the sensitivities of a girl on the brink of womanhood. All the events and characters we refer to are remembered from quite different angles.

'Auntie Patch was my favourite,' I admitted once. 'I was really sad when she went to the States.'

June's face lit with humour. 'But Patch was so mean, Anna. Don't you remember what she did to Nella?'

Nella had seemed to me a dull, locked-in personality. I raised an eyebrow in query and June told me the tale of two sisters. The story didn't amount to much, not unless you were the aggrieved sister, but it justified the opinion June held. I couldn't argue with her because she was looking at it from the vantage point of her extra ten years.

'Good heavens,' I said, showing the required surprise. Privately I was sure there was bound to be another interpretation, one that favoured Patch. Bias, like beauty, is in the eye of the beholder.

On one of the other occasions that we went in tandem down memory lane I sensed June holding back rather than contradict me. It would be very easy for all our conversations to turn into mild arguments which she's bound to win because of the superiority those ten years grant her. She remembers lots of things I don't and lots more about the things I do, or so she says.

Do you know, I don't especially remember June herself when I was young. Although I struggle for a recollection of a gawky big girl, I can never bring her into focus. I recall her parents and her rather dashing brother more clearly. Naturally, I haven't said this to June because it's a distancing kind of thing and she needs, very obviously needs, to feel close to someone who's family.

We have little in common apart from a few genes. She's a retired civil servant who's led a risk-free life in the lower ranks of the Ministry of Something or Other. She's a spinster who's never, as far as I know, been tempted to change her status. Her taste runs to understated jersey suits with German labels; holidays where one learns about art, opera or cookery; the *Daily Telegraph*; and scarifyingly dry sherry. I'm not like her. My life isn't like hers. That scattering of genes is the magnet that attracts her to me and I, dutifully, respond.

No doubt we had more in common when we were young, living in the same town and making Sunday afternoon outings to see the same set of grandparents. We were at the same family events, such as christenings and weddings. Not funerals, though. The family excluded children from funerals. I remember the exclusion, remember being curled on a deep bedroom window-sill and watching a black car pull away down the street, and I remember the silence in the house because everyone had gone to be sad somewhere else. But I don't know how old I was or whose funeral it was or who, precisely, was in the car. I'm left with a sensation, a symbol rather than an entire event.

To me childhood is another place, one peopled by strangers. In my mind's eye I see the little girl on the window-sill and I call it 'me', but only because it's my memory or my imagining. I have feelings about that moment she lived through, but I doubt they can be her feelings. No, I'm investing the scene with a pathos she can't have experienced because she was *in* the picture and I'm merely looking at it, interpreting it. Sometimes, at odd remembered moments in her young life, I identify with her and accept her without question as me. But it doesn't last. It's rather like recognising a friend across a street and finding, as you hurry towards them, you're facing a cold-eyed stranger.

People talk about children blossoming into adults, and

they use rosebuds as sentimental symbols of innocent childhood, but to me the imagery seems inadequate. A gentle
unfurling of petals doesn't describe the metamorphosis that
separates babe in cradle from child, and child from adult.
We're reinvented in a series of different forms before we're
completely developed, and it's as hard to find the child in
the adult as it is to see the caterpillar in the butterfly. The
butterfly drinks nectar and doesn't know why the caterpillar
chewed on the leaf. When we leave childhood behind, we
lose a language and a system of reasoning, and there's no
way back.

The child that was me and the big girl that was June
are both strangers to me now. I can't put myself into the
pictures June's memory paints, although I often pretend to
because repeated rejections would chafe away at the weak
strand that binds us.

I should say we seldom hold matching views of current
events, either. For instance, I'm convinced she exaggerates
when she complains about her neighbours and their garden
fires and noisiness. Although I've been to her house a
number of times I haven't caught a whiff of smoke or
heard a peep.

And then there's this business of her local shopkeepers,
who deliver groceries and meat and vegetables, even a
decent bottle of wine, and appear to me to be a blessing
most housebound folk can only envy. June, though, knows
the worst about them: overcharging, giving short measure,
gossiping about her to all and sundry.

Once, irritably, I started to say: 'Cancel them, then. You
don't have to bring them to the house if they cause you so
much upset.'

Just in time I bit my tongue because she has no choice
but to rely on them, and it's her reliance which is her real
hurt. I expect she extends the resentment to me, too, because
I'm the only member of the family who visits regularly. I'm
more or less certain of that. To begin with she made it sound
as though several of the others came, and I believed it simply
because they live nearer. Now I suspect they each made a

single visit, calling on her soon after she moved in, drawn by curiosity to see her parents' old house once more. What did they talk about, I wonder? Probably the things she doesn't talk about to me.

She isn't truly old although you might be thinking so from what I've said. No, she's in her early sixties. But I notice she's behaving old, as though having a lame leg is affecting her attitude. This surprises me because the family prides itself on stoicism – or used to although I doubt any of them have said it in a long time, stoicism having gone out of fashion. Who cares about stiff-upper-lippery these days? People prefer to bare their breasts and share their suffering, wouldn't you say?

Sometimes I catch myself wondering where June and I will be in ten years' time. Will she, as she insists, be destitute and totally crippled? Will I be the only one who visits and, willy-nilly, becomes responsible for her?

But it's too soon to worry. Besides, June is most unlikely ever to be destitute and she'll come to the top of the waiting-list and have an operation one of these fine days. After that, who knows? Salsa dancing? Mediterranean cruises? A walk to the butcher and the grocer?

When we meet, June and I, we gently ruffle a few leaves of memory, swap stories of times long past, discuss her troublesome present and her fears of the future. We don't, if we can help it, dwell on murder.

Yet I feel it drawing closer, the moment when the matter becomes unavoidable. They'll come for me, you see, and I'll have to tell them something. Oh yes, I'm confident I know what's best to say. All that's required is the story that's always been my salvation. But having found me there's a chance they'll go to the old house, too, and then they'll encounter June and I don't imagine she has a story that fends off questions.

You see my difficulty? I'd like to warn her to expect questions but I'm stuck because I can't do anything without discussing the murder.

6

CHAPTER TWO

June put me in the big front bedroom for the weekend.

'I can't say it's snug,' she said, 'but it has a lovely view of the park. Well, you know, don't you? I hardly have to tell *you* that.'

And she laughed at her slip, confusing me with a near stranger and forgetting how I'd run in and out of the room when I was little and played, notoriously, with the perfumes and powders on her mother's dressing table.

I carried my bag upstairs alone. The stairs are a trial to June and her awkward left leg. She sleeps in a downstairs back room herself and uses a small shower-room on the ground floor instead of the spacious bathroom on the mezzanine. I wondered how frequently she goes upstairs and what effort it cost her to prepare a room for me.

Pausing on the landing, I put my head into the bathroom. It needs a face-lift which I'm confident it won't get. The house also needs people which it won't get, either. Before I'd opened the door to my bedroom I was feeling like a guest in an otherwise empty hotel. That was curious because the house is compact by the standards of Edwardian suburbs. After all, there are only three bedrooms and it has no more than two floors unless you count the cellar and a cramped attic.

The impersonality is what does it. June's furniture from her city flat is sparsely dotted around and it's not the sort of stuff you'd choose for rooms of these proportions, anyway. The extra pieces she's bought, a few chintzy things, do look right but the result is an uncomfortable mix. Impersonal. Small-town hotel. Unsuccessful venture. Not a comfortable place to be.

Not entirely comfortable for June, I should say, being pushed back into this corner of her youth and finding it no longer fits. I ought to ask her why she didn't sell the house when she inherited instead of attempting to make a home of it.

The bed looked brand-new. I poked it with one hand and approved its firm resilience. Well, if nothing else I could look forward to a decent night's sleep. Then I hung up a couple of garments, on the back of the door rather than trust them to a vaguely musty wardrobe.

Before you notice my vanity for yourself, let me confess I care about being well-groomed. That's an old-fashioned expression but I can't better it. My clothes are stylish and expensive, and I don't resist paying for a top hairdresser and fine-quality make-up. It's probably unfashionable to say so but I derive great satisfaction from knowing I'm looking my best.

Abandoning the rest of the unpacking, I crossed to the bay window. The park stretched away, more or less as remembered although smaller. Three boys, wearing scaled-down versions of a first division FA club strip, were kicking a black-and-white football. Their goalposts were two trees. I tried to recall whether the trees used to be there. I don't know about trees, not the various types and not their rates of growth.

The path is where I expected to see it but the flower-beds have been torn up and grassed over. Regretting the flowerbeds, I stirred a memory of intense lavender scent and towering hollyhocks. Heaven knows if it was ever true. I mean, *can* you smell lavender and see hollyhocks on the same day or are they different stages of summer? I'm no

8

better at flowers than I am at trees, and I hesitate to trust my memory.

'The flowerbeds have gone,' I protested to June a few minutes later. We were in the big front sitting-room sipping her favourite sherry. She was looking well, wearing the soft green jersey suit that especially flatters her pale skin. Seated, the clumsiness of the strong flat shoes she's forced to wear nowadays isn't so obvious.

She exonerated the town council in a word. 'Cost.'

I pulled a face. 'How can you put a price on the pleasure a flower brings?'

'The displays were expensive to maintain, partly because people were spiriting plants away to their own back gardens.'

We shared a grumble about the dismal state of affairs when people stoop to such behaviour.

'In our day, crime was . . .' she began, and then took a sip of sherry, giving herself time to change tack.

I chipped in, pushing the forbidden topic aside. 'Did I tell you my neighbour had to call the police twice to sort out those girls from the terrace?'

June looked startled. '*Girls*? I didn't realise they were girls.'

'Oh yes, there are five of them. The oldest is nineteen.'

'When you said drug dealing . . . and fighting . . . You don't expect it of girls, do you?'

I'd told her the tale on previous visits but she'd been too involved with her own worries to take it in properly. In fact, I'd only ever mentioned it to distract her, to demonstrate there were more alarming problems than a grocer suspected of adding three pence to a shopping bill. Obviously, it hadn't worked.

'Violence!' she said, shocked now she understood. She reached for the sherry bottle, and muttered 'girls' in varying degrees of incredulity as she topped up our glasses.

Two rings on her right hand were so loose they clinked

against the bottle. I realised they were her mother's wedding and engagement rings, and was sure I hadn't seen them on her before. She doesn't have good hands for jewellery. They're long but too angular for elegance. The rings slid around but were held safe by her prominent knuckles. June fiddled with the rings while we talked, convincing me they were unfamiliar and she would have preferred to take them off.

Food soon, I hoped. Promising smells were coming from the kitchen along the hall and I was hungry. June is an excellent cook, so I'd skipped lunch and resisted nibbling during the car journey, but she likes to tease and won't say what's in the offing. Ever since I arrived and caught the first whiff I'd been silently guessing.

She was reading my mind. 'A good twenty minutes to go, Anna. You have plenty of time to enjoy your sherry.'

I paid her one of those compliments cooks like to hear and she replied with a grateful smile. When June smiles you see her slightly crooked front teeth. Just as I was thinking that she's a shade too old for the flaw to have been corrected in childhood as a matter of course, she spoke again. What she said was totally unexpected.

'Anna, I'm afraid I've some rather unsettling news. I've had a visit from a researcher who wanted to know what I could tell her about Rita's murder.'

All I could manage was 'Oh.'

'Yes, I'm sorry. I didn't want to tell you, I know how you hate talking about it, but I don't really have a choice. As she's tracked me down, she'll find you, too. I decided I should warn you.'

I mumbled agreement, saying it was best to be forewarned and so forth. 'Did she . . . ?' Unable to shape a useful question I left it hanging.

June said: 'She was very polite. Her name's Gillian Spry.'

A question turned up. 'Did she leave her card?'

June reached into her jacket pocket for it, revealing to

me how carefully she'd prepared for this conversation. I leaned across to take the card from her.

```
                    Gillian Spry
                    RESEARCHER

                         CJI

Woodbridge House
18 Wessex Road              Tel. 0171 340 1449
London NW1                  Fax 0171 340 8565
```

So they hadn't come for me first, they'd gone to June and I'd left her unprepared. I breathed a mute sigh. Here I was at the scene of the crime and on the anniversary of it, and June was telling me CJI were getting involved. Well, I'd known they would, of course. For weeks it had bothered me that they were bound to come. All I'd got wrong was their sequence. And now . . . Anxiety welled up. I fought against it. Mustering a few questions, I struggled to show a normal degree of interest.

'This Gillian Spry, when did she call?'

'Tuesday morning.'

There was a hiatus while we both considered June's reasons for not telephoning me with the news straightaway. Correctly, she'd guessed I would have made it an excuse not to come.

'Did she explain what they're planning?'

June frowned. 'No, I don't think she said precisely. To be honest, I was so taken aback I didn't absorb everything she said.'

Miss Spry, I assumed, was skilled at saying little herself and coaxing others to do the talking. While not wishing to sound cynical, I should think she went away from the interview fairly satisfied.

'June, what did you tell her?'

She became flustered, fussing with her rings. 'More than I should have chosen. But she took me unawares, you see. I mean, if she'd written or phoned first . . .'

Naturally that's why they don't. I murmured sympathetically and encouraged her to tell me everything that had happened.

June said: 'Well, she began by asking whether I was a member of the Foley family. She wasn't sure Foleys still lived here, you see. When I said yes she told me what it was about. The murder. I was caught off guard but I started saying I preferred not to discuss it and, in any case, I wasn't a witness because I'd been on holiday at the time.'

Reliving the conversation made her groan with embarrassment. 'Oh, heaven knows *what* I said, Anna. She was just standing there letting me ramble, only popping in a word here and there to keep me going. I knew I was being foolish, I ought to have shut the door immediately, but I was taken by surprise.'

'Don't feel guilty. She's trained in wheedling people.'

'Yes, but . . . It's no use, I do feel I handled it badly.'

I sought to clarify what Gillian Spry had tried to extract from her. 'Was there anything specific she wanted you to tell her?'

Another frown. 'Most of it spilled out – I mean details such as me being the daughter of the Foleys who lived here at the time and my inheriting the house last year. She seemed to be hoovering up everything she could get. Oh, there was one thing she kept coming back to, though. She pressed me to tell her where you live.'

I bit my lip and waited for the worst but she said: 'Fortunately, I had my wits about me by then and I refused to say. At least this gives you a little time to disappear, if you want to.'

Where, I wondered. Where could I possibly go that I wouldn't be found? Vanishing tricks are expensive and, besides, you always have to come back.

'It's all right,' I said, wishing she wasn't so perturbed. 'You did all you could. And don't forget, she's bound to

12

be checking with other people, too. Even if you hadn't told her anything, they will.'

June didn't look reassured. It crossed my mind she was withholding something from me.

'Is there more? I'd rather know if there is.'

She denied it. 'Nothing else. I'm simply cross with myself for blurting out things she'd no right to hear.'

I attempted a casual shrug. 'It sounds innocuous enough.'

'Yes, but . . . Oh, dear. I suppose what angers me most is the way these television people feel they have a divine right to push their noses in everywhere. I told Gillian Spry the family have put the dreadful business behind them and won't welcome any attempt to revive it.'

'Good. I'm glad you said that.'

'I'm afraid I was rather firm with her. I said it was unfair to rehash personal tragedies in the name of entertainment and the ratings war. And she stood there, Anna, looking kind and understanding, and I knew damn well I was wasting my breath.'

I commiserated with a murmur and set my empty glass on the spindly table near my chair. June glanced at her watch and began to rise. As I followed her to the kitchen I enjoyed the ironic thought that at least I wouldn't have to listen to over-dramatised stories about the grocer while we ate. The taboo had been breached. The time had arrived for us to dwell on murder.

We were already at variance and looking, as usual, from different angles. June was convinced our problem was a potential television programme.

As we entered the kitchen, her spaniel, the inaptly named Frisky, shifted from the warm patch in front of the cooker and slouched towards its basket. He's unpleasantly over-weight. June and her dog defy the convention that people resemble their pets. In their case, it appears that all the fat that ought to accrue to June is added to Frisky. Being lame, June can't exercise him and he's bored and over-eating. I watched fascinated to see how he'd squeeze into the basket.

She can't walk the dog but surely she could buy a bigger basket?

June was talking to the animal, addressing it as though it was a dim-witted child. I heard myself joining in. 'How about a romp in the park tomorrow, Frisky? Would you like that?'

'Oooh yes, aren't you lucky, Frisky?'

I promised June: 'I'll really do it this time. Last time rain stopped play, do you remember?'

'Yes, it was the day of the cloudburst, wasn't it? By the time I'd hunted for the lead, the whole town was awash.'

She nodded towards the back door. 'The lead's kept there now. Ever ready.'

I wondered when it was last used. Weeks ago? June didn't say but I'd heard the dog's claws clicking over the tiled floor, a clue that they hadn't been worn down by healthy walks.

Chat about the fat spaniel continued until we were seated at the kitchen table, although neither of us was genuinely engaged by it. We gave up the pretence once we were forking the first course, a vegetable terrine. I let June begin.

'Anna, should we, do you think, have a plan for coping with Gillian Spry and her crew?'

'A plan?'

'Because I made a mess of it on Tuesday . . .'

'Oh, you mustn't think that.'

'No, you're being very nice about it, dear, but I do think it. So, I thought we might decide what, if anything, either of us should say if she comes back. *When* she comes back. She gave me to understand she intends to.'

'I see. Well, I shall refuse to say anything at all. Except that I'm far too upset to discuss it, ever.'

June nodded. 'I expect that's best. Be resolute and she'll have to do without you. As for me . . .'

'Don't add anything fresh. What's said is said, but you needn't add to it.'

Again June said she thought that was best. She cleared the plates and brought a crock of rich lamb casserole to the table. I paid her more of the usual compliments and then, while we were helping ourselves, she asked, with a slight hesitation, what I actually felt about Rita's death.

'I've been wondering, Anna, is it something you think about often?'

'Hardly ever.' I wasn't the least inclined to tell her how I'd dragged down a shutter in my mind to keep it out, or about the three anniversaries that nudge me into reminiscence.

'It's not surprising, really,' she said. 'After all, it was such a long time ago.'

'Forty-five years.' My words came automatically, too pat. I begged she wouldn't notice.

She didn't. 'Heavens, as long as that?'

'I was only eight when she died.'

'An awful age to lose your mother. Worse to have her murdered, I should imagine.'

Rather than grow maudlin, I pointed out the comforting aspects, in the way people used to point them out to me. 'Luckily we were a big family. Grandparents, aunts and uncles, cousins . . . My father, of course. I had lots of people around me.'

'Well, all the same, I think you were very brave. A mother is special, losing one is the worst blow. And particularly for a girl to lose her mother . . .'

'Hmm.' My grunt was meant to convey agreement but not wholehearted agreement. I chewed on a mouthful of lamb for a few seconds, before adding: 'Plenty of children lose their mothers. I don't know that the method matters.'

It does, of course. It matters hugely and who knows better than I? But it doesn't do to delve into it too deeply, so I diverted June by asking how the news of Rita's death had reached her.

'You mentioned being on holiday at the time.'

She set down her knife and fork to tell the tale. 'I heard on the telephone. That was exciting in itself because it was the first call I ever received. We didn't have a telephone at home, not everybody did, although we'd been on the waiting-list for years. But the parents of the girl I was staying with ran their own business, haberdashery, and there was a telephone in the store-room behind the shop. I remember her mother calling upstairs that my father was on the phone.'

'Where was he ringing from?'

'The public call-box outside the Post Office. Well, I went downstairs feeling rather important. My first phone call! But as soon as he spoke I knew something was wrong because he didn't bother to ask if I was having a nice holiday. He said something like: "It's going to be in the news but I want you to hear it before that. Your Auntie Rita has been murdered." I had to ask him to repeat it, not believing I'd heard properly.'

'An amazing first phone call.'

'Yes, wasn't it? And then he said they'd decided they didn't want me to come home and I was to finish my holiday but, and this was the important thing, I wasn't to tell a soul about it.'

'But that must have been impossible.'

'Completely. For one thing, my friend's mother was standing at her counter three steps away and I knew she'd overheard. As soon as I hung up she was staring at me, waiting to be told. So I told her.'

Over second helpings of lamb, and over fresh fruit salad spiced with ginger, June relived the summer of forty-five years ago. But she'd been on the periphery of the family drama, confined there by protective parents who shielded her from the darkest moments. She wasn't interviewed by the police because she'd been away when the crime was committed. Everything she knew about the crime, the investigation and the trial was secondhand. Chunks of it were seriously inaccurate, too, but I didn't challenge her. I was interested to discover what she believed.

By the time we were drinking our coffee, her attitude to Gillian Spry had softened.

'I do see why Rita's case appeals to her. It has a number of period flourishes, and television does enjoy those, doesn't it?'

I said drily: 'My mother's murder as Fifties costume drama?'

16

'Oh, sorry, Anna, I'm sounding pitiless. No, I didn't mean it quite like that.'

But as she didn't elucidate I was left with a mental picture of a fashionable young actress, clad in a tight sweater, playing my mother.

Meanwhile, June was saying: 'You were too young to appreciate it, dear, but it was a case that attracted attention because of the type of people involved.'

I busied myself adding unwanted sugar to my coffee. What was she hoping I'd say? Was I supposed to acquiesce or to launch a defence of my mother and the type of people she knew? But I pulled myself up, realising I was being unnecessarily wary, because June had already handed me the answer.

'I was too young, as you said.'

And so I fell back on the line that I'd understood little and remembered less. It always worked.

'Sandy!' she exclaimed, as we were clearing the table a while later.

A hand clutched my heart. I swallowed hard before saying: 'What about Sandy?'

'What's become of her? Have you any idea?'

'None at all.'

'She must be in her fifties by now. So odd to think of her grown up. I wonder what she's like? She was such a spirited little creature, wasn't she?'

And for a moment there was Sandy in my head, a lively little thing although not quite as little as me. Sandy who was my great good friend, my inseparable companion of two summers. Sandy who'd vowed to be my friend for ever and ever.

June wiped crumbs from the wooden table with a damp cloth. 'Do you know, I hardly remember you without her. That can't be right, can it? But it's the way I remember the pair of you. Together. Sandy and Ann. You were plain Ann in those days. Sandy and Ann, always together.'

She rinsed out and wrung the cloth, then hung it on the

rail on the front of the cooker to dry. 'What was Sandy's family's name?'

'Minch. She was Sandra Minch.'

'Yes, of course. Minch.'

While I was stashing the last of the crockery in the dishwasher she added: 'Perhaps she turned herself into Sandra when she grew up, the way you turned from Ann into Anna?'

She'd made it a question and I couldn't think of a reply, but almost immediately she was reminiscing about her own childhood and my failure went unremarked.

'When I was about six I used to think the world would be perfect if my best friend Babs and I could live together in that tiny cottage on the far edge of the park.'

'The park-keeper's lodge?'

'Yes, that's it. We decided to run away from home and our beastly brothers and live there in girly bliss. The plan was to play all day in the park, you see, and go to the sweet-shop whenever we wanted. When we were properly hungry we'd go to the fish-and-chip shop. And we hadn't overlooked the need for coupons. We were going to steal away with our ration books. Oh, we had it all worked out.'

Through laughter I asked: 'And did this include working out what to do with the parky?' I pictured him clearly, a querulous one-eyed man with a spare cigarette tucked behind his right ear.

'That was the easiest bit. We were convinced he'd be getting his call-up papers any day and, once he'd sloped off to win the war, we'd move in.'

'But he was ancient! Weren't the great British parkies wounded soldiers from the *First* World War?'

'No one had told us. We were patiently waiting for him to make his move so we could make ours.'

'You didn't actually do anything, then?'

'No, except tell lies to Babs's parents who guessed we were up to something. And do you know, the lying was difficult because we'd been brought up to be truthful children. Unfortunately, her parents were barging in on our

18

secret and we felt forced to protect it. It was proper lying in the adult moral sense, I may say. A nasty conscious act, not childish fantasy. Oh, we hated it, Anna, you wouldn't believe how we agonised over it!'

I laughed. 'Did your guilty faces give you away?'

'We didn't think so. Anyway, we didn't run off, we abandoned the adventure and we grew up.' She paused for laughter before adding: 'It's extraordinary, isn't it, the way children's minds work? Their reasoning is so warped, even when they're intelligent which I think Babs and I probably were. No experience, that's what does it. You can't blame them, can you?'

'Childhood is the sleep of reason.'

Her frown proved she couldn't quite place the quote, and I immediately felt absurd dragging Rousseau into the conversation. Without enlightening her, I screwed up the paper napkins and lobbed them in the rubbish bin.

She said: 'I wonder how old you have to be before information settles down inside your head and becomes immutable truth, instead of swirling around subject to wild interpretation? I feel I ought to know, having lived through it, but somehow one doesn't measure one's own development. Do you see what I mean?'

I said she should try the question on a child, not another equally ignorant adult. Privately, what interested me more was her belief that truth is unchangeable. In my experience, it's worryingly subjective, a slippery thing, elusive. Perhaps I should have challenged her but, cautious where the conversation might end up, I didn't.

Instead, the bag in the bin being practically full, I volunteered to carry it outside to the dustbin. The chore is one June loathes because of the steep steps from the back door.

She gave me an appreciative glance and carried on with what she was doing, which was tipping what was left of the excellent lamb casserole into Frisky's bowl. The spaniel opened a lazy eye and quivered a nostril.

Outside by the dustbin, in the sharp evening air, I wondered where the rest of the weekend would lead us. June had sorted through her own rags of memory and soon, surely, she would demand I do likewise. *Quid pro quo. I'll tell you mine if you tell me yours.* Yet it wasn't a fair swap because June's were mere trifles, she knew next to nothing and what she did know she misinterpreted.

Another thought formed. How much does she truly know? There was that moment over sherry when I was certain she was holding back. I cast around for an explanation. Perhaps Gillian Spry had dropped a remark which didn't tally with making a television programme and June was suppressing it. Wilfully, to mislead me? No, but she might want to ponder the discrepancy and its significance before troubling me.

Abandoning the futile puzzle, I turned back to the house. And as I did so I felt within me the strange child on a bedroom window-sill, gazing out on mysteries. The moment was fleeting. She might once have been me but I cannot become her. Neither can I feel responsible for her, or for the way she thinks and the things she does. She is herself a mystery, locked in the past.

CHAPTER THREE

She dragged the stick over the wet sand, shaping the letters. SANDY MINCH. The C came out too small, harder to do than the flourish of the initial S or the straight lines of the other letters in her name.

Spotting the mistake, she fiddled with the c, trying to bring it up to size.

'Leave it,' Ann said. 'You'll only make it worse.'

Sandy grunted, concentrating on the ruined letter. She didn't want Ann's advice. She never did.

Ann tried another tack. 'It isn't worth it. The water will wash it away soon.'

Sandy flung down the stick and stamped all over the c. Wet sand flicked up and spattered her shoes, her sagging ankle-socks, her legs. She gave another grunt, a sort of growl, and spun round and flounced away. Ann stretched out a sandalled foot and smeared the y into oblivion. Then she went after Sandy.

Hearing her coming, Sandy broke into a run, glancing over her shoulder and yelling, not words but whooping encouragement to chase. They ran wildly, flowery cotton skirts and hand-knitted cardigans flying. Over the patch of sand they went and up the river bank, along the edge of the field for a short distance until Sandy veered back to the river and vanished into a clump of trees.

'Can't catch me.'

Ann, blundering just behind her, could. Sandy's red dress was a beacon in the dimness of the foliage. She'd stripped off her cardigan and was rubbing her sweaty forehead with it. Ann slumped against a tree beside her and clapped a hand to her side.

'I'd have caught you sooner if I hadn't got the stitch.'

Sandy feigned belief in the specious stitch. 'You've got to bend double for the stitch, not sprawl on a tree trunk.'

Ann bent double.

'Better?' Sandy asked, playing the game.

For answer, Ann sprang up and flung her arms about. 'What shall we do now?'

There was a momentary frown on Sandy's face, as if she was thinking: '*You always ask me, you never say what you want to do. Unless it's something stupid.*'

What she said was. 'We could see if they're back.'

'Wish we had a watch.'

'We did have one.'

Ann coloured. It was her fault they'd lost it. It had been her turn to wear it the day they'd gone to the pantomime and just before she was due to hand it over, she'd looked down at her wrist and realised it was missing. That made it her fault.

'It isn't my fault,' she'd wailed.

But Sandy had said: 'You were wearing it when it got lost.'

And that had made it Ann's fault.

Ann turned to look at the river, to prevent Sandy seeing her blushing. 'They might be back,' she said.

'All right. We'll go and see.'

But neither of them moved. Below them the water gurgled and swirled as the wash of a rowing-boat slapped against the bank. Spring sunshine lit the river but it was cool among the trees. Sandy pulled her cardigan on, getting the sleeves straight and the front buttoned up before she reached round and freed her trapped hair. She had reddish-brown hair which she was growing.

'I'll be able to sit on it by Christmas,' she used to say,

gloating over Ann whose hair was finer and whose mother kept it regularly trimmed to avoid split ends.

Ann knew she'd never be able to sit on her own hair but she didn't care. The idea of sitting on one's hair seemed silly to her, she didn't see why any girl should want to. But she didn't tell Sandy that, mainly because it was accepted she admired Sandy, who was older and generally thought to be cleverer. Sandy's cleverness might have been open to question, because she'd been held back a year at school, but it wasn't. People liked her. Grown-ups said what a nice nature she had and lamented that their own offspring weren't like her.

Sandy, plaiting the ends of her hair now, asked: 'What do you think they do?'

'Who?'

'You know who. Your mother and that man.'

'Dennis.'

'Dennis Mallard.'

'It's Aylard.'

'Dennis Mallard and your mother. He *looks* like a duck to me, short and fat and ugly, with pouting lips.' She stretched her neck and pouted, tucked her arms up to make wings and flapped and quacked. 'I'm going to call him Dennis Duck. Dennis Duck and Rita. What do you think they . . . ?'

Ann batted away a fly that was dancing about her face. 'They go to meetings. That's what she said. You heard her. Business meetings.'

'In a pub?'

'You can't call the Ship a pub. It says hotel. You saw the sign.'

'Lots of pubs are called hotels. It doesn't mean they aren't pubs.'

'But if it says hotel . . .' Ann didn't know how to go on but she was keen to keep this theme alive. It was better than hearing Sandy's theories about her mother and Dennis.

Sandy spoke over her. 'If you have a business meeting, you do it in an office. Not in a pub, not even in a hotel. It's obvious.'

'Dennis is in the hotel business, so that makes it all right to have meetings in a pub. A hotel, I mean.'

Sandy let the plait swing down and danced a couple of skipping steps. She began to sing, made-up words to an old tune. Ann didn't know whether it was supposed to mean anything. She couldn't join in because the words were spontaneous but she tried to hum the tune. Sometimes Sandy meant things and then she felt stupid not to have understood. Other times it was only singing.

'Your mother,' said Sandy, breaking off in the middle of a bar, 'is in love with Dennis Duck.'

'They can still have business meetings.'

'But she isn't in business. She's just your mother.'

'She works with him.' Ann bit her lip. She was remembering the rows, her mother determined and exultant, her father worn. The war had changed him into a timid man, an invalid. It was impossible for her to imagine what he'd been like before.

Sandy was probably right, she thought. A smiling liveliness came over her mother whenever Dennis was around, she was changed by her proximity to him.

'Supposing,' Sandy said, 'she runs away and lives with Dennis Duck in one of his hotels. You wouldn't like that.'

'I wouldn't mind.' For a moment Ann pictured smiles and lightheartedness. The prospect didn't seem too bad.

Then Sandy said: 'You'd miss her.'

'Miss her?'

'Well, she wouldn't want to take you, would she? And he wouldn't. They'd want to be together, on their own.'

Ann had the uncomfortable feeling Sandy was trotting out ideas overheard. Talk. There must be talk. Talk had been a threat held over her mother's head for ages. Now, perhaps, it was reality.

Casually, she asked Sandy: 'Where did you hear that?'

A shrug.

'Sandy, who says it?' She felt a surge of anger, at the talk and at the listening, but mainly at her mother. Not at Dennis, so much. Men couldn't help it, not when women

24

threw themselves at them. Ann herself had heard mutterings
to that effect.

Sandy said: 'Anyway, you'd *want* to stay and look after
him. Your father would need you if she went.'

A nasty, watery feeling flowed through Ann. She began
buttoning her cardigan although the cause came from deep
inside her. Some days she felt incomplete, afraid to grow
up, fearful of an unfriendly adult world.

'Perhaps,' said Sandy, 'your father can't do it any more,
because of the war.'

When Ann's face framed a question, she hurried on. 'You
know, Ann, what they do. Perhaps the war made him not
able to. Some men can't.'

Although Ann didn't understand exactly what they were
talking about she felt that was all right because neither did
Sandy, who was parroting other people's words.

Sandy waited but when Ann offered no reply she tried
another line. 'You'd be like Peggy Moffitt. Remember her?
Her mother ran away and she was made to live with her
granny, but there wasn't any money because her mother
took it with her.'

Ann stopped listening. She'd never met Peggy Moffitt,
the girl was a mere name; but it was painful anyway. There
were things about her own family she'd never told Sandy,
although they'd been close for years. She had no intention
of telling her now. It comforted her that she was good at
secrets. Not everybody was, but she was.

With an exaggerated sigh Sandy stomped through the
trees to the path. 'Come on, Ann. Let's see if the lovebirds
are ready.'

Ann trailed unhappily. She was supposing this and supposing that, but none of it was cheering. Sandy's speculation
had shaken a few ideas loose and they rattled around in her
mind, worrying her. She didn't know what to hope for, what
would be best. As things were, they were bad. Quite bad.
She realised they might have been worse and could grow
worse. It didn't matter that Sandy teased her with what
people were saying and what fate might be planning to

hand out. In a way, it was good to know. Interesting, at any rate.

Her friend lingered for her on the path, gave her hair an affectionate tweak. 'It'll be all right, Ann.'

'I know.'

Ann began to run, along the path beside the river, past the spot where SANDY MINCH was a scuffled mess, all the way down to the bridge. As the Ship came in sight, she slowed to walking pace.

She'd tried asking her mother about her work for Dennis, but questions were always brushed aside with a laugh. They weren't foolish questions. They were the ones other people were asking. A few people had slyly tried to winkle information out of Ann and been disappointed she had none to give.

Sandy caught up and looped her arm through Ann's, forcing a quicker pace although Ann was inclined to hang back. She didn't want to see the car in the car park behind the Ship, or to see her mother with Dennis. She wished she hadn't come. Sandy had been offered a choice but Ann not. The same as the other times, Ann was told she was to go with them and Sandy was invited. Mrs Minch, an easy-going chatterer with a clutch of younger children, had minded more about losing a few hours of Sandy's help than about how her eldest daughter might spend the day.

Sandy hadn't agreed straight off. 'It'll be boring. Nothing to do but hang about by the river.'

Ann said: 'And have lunch.' The lunches were usually the high point.

'I can get my own lunch at home, thank you very much.'

'Oh, do come, Sandy. *Please*. I'll die if I've got to wander about on my own all that time. You haven't got anything better to do.'

'Or worse,' Sandy said darkly, but she was on the point of capitulation.

Arms still linked, the girls came to the end of the path and entered the car park. Dennis's car wasn't there. It was obvious straightaway but Ann insisted on prowling around the parked vehicles to check. Sandy perched on the pub wall and tilted her face to the blue sky.

'You won't find it.'

Ann, pretending not to hear, gave a stern look at a big black Standard that stood where Dennis had earlier parked his rather more luxurious Humber.

With a chuckle, Sandy called over: 'I told you they would run off.'

'Shut up.'

'Temper, temper.'

'It isn't funny.'

'I know. Here we are, two poor little girls abandoned in a pub car park without the price of a lemonade between us . . .'

She broke off as Ann ran to her, on the verge of tears.

'Don't worry,' said Sandy, 'we can ask the pub to telephone your father and he'll have us fetched home. Probably he'll tell them to put us in a taxi. We'll be all right.'

Ann scrubbed away a tear with a balled handkerchief. 'No, it isn't all right. He didn't want me to come. Or her. There was a big row about it. I heard them shouting. But, of course, she did what she wanted to. She always does . . .' Her voice changed, became less hysterical. 'Oh, that's the sort of thing he says. But it's true. I mean, very often it's true. And now . . .'

Sandy slid down off the wall and put an arm around her. She was wearing the especially interested expression that came over her whenever she pushed Ann into a revelation. As she was starting to speak, the back door of the pub opened and a podgy man in a khaki army battle-dress jacket and low-slung tweed trousers appeared. He was on his way to a lavatory in the far corner of the yard but she headed him off.

'Is there a Mister Mallard in the pub? Dennis Mallard?'

Ann winced. 'No, Aylard,' she hissed.

Sandy agreed, it was Aylard, of course it was. 'He's having a business meeting in there.'

But the man had never heard of him and looked askance at the idea of a business meeting in his local. He carried on across the yard. Two minutes later, on his way back, he studied the loose tiles on the roof and successfully avoided the girls' eyes.

Sandy investigated, peering through windows as best she could given the thickness of the frosted glass. A couple of men came out and unlocked the Standard but they couldn't help her with the whereabouts of Dennis Aylard. A woman with a '*Mother*' brooch on her sweater and an apron round her waist shooed a black dog outside, and Sandy tried her, too.

She reported to Ann: 'She says there are only a few of her regulars in there and she hasn't seen any unfamiliar faces today.' She slid smoothly into a lie. 'I told her she couldn't miss him, he looks like a fat duck.'

Sandy did the flapping wings and the pouting again, but Ann ignored it. Sandy ran at her, quacking and kissing the air. Ann shoved her away.

Sandy said: 'What do you think it's like, kissing Dennis Duck's rubbery lips?'

But Ann refused to guess and the conversation lapsed.

Soon, while they were arguing about what might have happened, a *hoot-toot* attracted their attention and they saw Ann's mother waving to them from a car out in the road. It wasn't the big shiny Humber but Dennis was at the wheel.

The girls clambered onto the rear seat and prepared for the story. Sandy exhibited polite attention. Ann felt sulkier and looked stonily out of the window.

The tale they were told was that something had gone wrong with the engine of Dennis's car and this Wolseley had been borrowed from a business associate to get them home.

'Gosh,' said Sandy, catching Dennis's eye in the driver's rear view mirror. 'Was yours towed away?'

He hunched forward, hugging the wheel, as he drove.

From behind, he looked as though he was balancing a roll of hairy flesh on his stiffened shirt collar. It was horrible. She kept staring at it.

He answered her question about towing. 'It will be.'

Then he did a bit of throat clearing before running through a list of engine parts that might be to blame for the mishap. This was very dull and neither of the girls encouraged him to say anything further about it.

'Did it spoil your meeting?' Sandy wanted to know. She wished she could catch the front passenger's eye too and direct her questions better. As it happened, Ann's mother answered her, anyway.

'Well, yes, because we wasted such a lot of time calling a garage out.'

Dennis took one hand off the wheel, tweaked his gold cigarette case out of an inside pocket and passed it to Rita. She lit two cigarettes and handed one to him. Twin columns of smoke rose and the smell of tobacco filled the car. Sandy screwed up her face and, for Ann's benefit, mimed being sick.

By the time they were on home territory, Ann had barely spoken. She and her mother were dropped off first, then Dennis was to drive Sandy the final few hundred yards to her home.

'Coming up front with me, Sandy Minx?' Dennis asked before pulling away.

Sandy jumped out of the back door of the car and in through the front passenger one. Ann waved to her but she wasn't watching so Ann stalked up to the house.

'Wait,' her mother insisted, once they were in the porch. She tried to draw Ann to her but the child pulled away. 'Listen, Ann, before we go in . . .' Her voice was low, conspiratorial.

Ann flared up. 'You went away. You ran off with him. You weren't where you said you'd be. I didn't know what had happened.'

'Hush. Keep your voice down.'

'You didn't care about me, you went off with him.'

29

'You're being ridiculous.'

'No, I'm not. You told us you were going to a meeting in the Ship.

But Rita's words had been careful. 'Now wait a minute, Ann. I said we'd see you in the car park in a couple of hours. And we would have done if the car hadn't broken down.'

'It didn't break down at the Ship, did it? The pub lady said you hadn't been in there. You waited until we walked out of sight and then you went somewhere else.'

'Shhh. Keep your voice down. It was better for you to be by the river instead . . .'

'Instead of where? Why's it such a big secret?'

Rita didn't tell her. She got the key in the lock and pushed Ann ahead of her into the hall, as though she was afraid she might run off and broadcast the news to the whole town, or at least as though she was afraid she might run off.

Ann went upstairs to her room. She was hungry. One of the many inconveniences of the car breaking down was that the girls had been given no lunch. Whether Rita and Dennis had snatched a bite was among the many other things left unclear.

Lying on her bed, counting window-panes, Ann reflected that Sandy was right about the Ship being a pub. But what if the other things she'd said were equally true? It was often hard to know whether she was playful or serious.

One thing she was fond of saying was definitely wrong, though. Dennis Aylard wasn't ugly. He was handsome, even if his face was plump. Anyway, Sandy didn't mind him, whatever she said about him being fat and ugly. She liked him teasing her and calling her Sandy Minx.

The door creaked open and Ann's mother entered, bearing a sandwich on a plate. She offered a nervous smile, one that said sorry and begged forgiveness and urged her complicity and silence. Ann ignored the smile and accepted the sand-wich. But when she tried to eat it, her hunger vanished in a wave of nausea. She opened the window and threw it onto the flat roof below where the birds could feast on it. Mabel, next door's marauding black-and-white cat, got there first.

Two weeks later Ann stayed for a weekend at Sandy's house. Sandy was keen to take the bus out to Copperton Woods. There wasn't anything special to do there, and if any adults had known they were planning to go so far they would have been warned off, but they didn't mention it to anyone.

On the way Sandy showed Ann the smallholding where one of her uncles lived. The bus was travelling fast and Ann caught a flash of white buildings and rows of vegetables in fields.

'Once when I went there he killed a duck,' said Sandy. 'It was awful. I didn't know he was doing it and I went out into the yard and he was tearing and tearing at its neck, like he was trying to rip it off.'

Shuddering, Ann covered her ears. 'Oooh, no. I don't want to hear.'

Sandy grew matter-of-fact. 'It's what they have to do on farms, otherwise the ducks and chickens would never get dead and there'd be nothing to eat. I understood that really, but it was a surprise because I didn't realise he was doing it right then. And I ran out of the door and he was tearing and tearing, and . . .'

Ann turned away from her, screwing up her eyes in a vain hope of shutting out the sickening mental images. Luckily, they came to a bus stop and a family boarded and took Sandy's attention so the story stopped in the middle, while the tearing and tearing was going on.

They got off at the crossroads in the woods and said goodbye to the bus conductor. He'd been too nosy for Sandy's liking, wanting them to chat about why they were travelling alone and whether anyone would be meeting them when they got off. He called it alighting.

'My brother and his friends,' said Sandy who didn't have a suitable brother, only tiny ones.

Blushing, Ann had concentrated on looking out of the window at the crowding trees. When they got off, she went first and hurried down the nearest path away from the road. Sandy, laughing gaily, caught up with her.

31

'Nosy old bugger! What's it to him where we're going?'

Ann looked with misgivings at the acres of leafy emptiness. She wished she was home or at Sandy's home.

'Good thing he didn't ask me,' she said, 'because I don't know what we're going to do here.'

'We're taking a country walk.' Sticking her nose in the air and swinging her arms stiffly, Sandy strode away.

'Sandy, don't go too far.'

'We haven't begun yet.'

'I know but we might not find the way back.'

Her fear was pooh-poohed.

An hour later they were nervously wondering where the road was. They had paths a-plenty but the trees they chose as landmarks turned out to have replicas, there was no sound of traffic to guide them, and the afternoon was drawing in.

'This way.' Sandy took a decision.

Ann stood firm. 'You said that before. Twice.'

'All right. So I was wrong. It doesn't stop me trying again, does it?'

Biting her lip, Ann avoided saying the useless things that might result in her finding herself in the wood alone. She knew she could bear it if Sandy were with her, but not alone.

'All right?' Sandy waited for her answer.

'Yes.' She was pleased her voice didn't waver. It sounded much happier than she was.

Again Sandy's choice was the wrong one. She became cross with herself, and frightened too. It seemed so simple. You took a path and when you'd had enough of it you turned round and came back. But it wasn't like that. She'd missed something, they both had. They . . .

She held up her hand, bringing them to a halt. 'What was that?'

'Sorry, I didn't see anything.'

'No, I mean a sound.'

A few minutes later they drew closer to the sound. The sound of voices. The sound of people laughing and chattering, and clinking glasses and enjoying themselves.

32

'In the wood?' whispered Ann, deeply puzzled.

She got a withering look in return. 'We must be near the road.'

'Yes, but . . .'

'Hush.' Sandy cupped a hand to her ear, stressing the need to listen.

Ann looked around. She hadn't heard anything special, only the noise of people having a party in a house by the wood. Her instinct was to hurry up to them and ask directions to the bus stop. Sandy had other ideas.

They went softly towards the house. There were lights in the rooms and a group of people were on a terrace outside a drawing-room. It was a grand house. Ann wondered whether there might be servants they should approach instead of the house owners. It seemed rude to wander in from the woods into the middle of a party and start inquiring after buses.

By the hedge separating the wood from the garden, Sandy crouched down and gestured to Ann to do the same.

'No,' Ann objected, 'let's go and ask them about the bus.'

Sandy clutched at her and drew her down. 'We can't march in there.'

'I don't see why not.' Ann was casting about for a gate or a gap in the hedge but there was neither. 'If someone got lost and came to my house I'd be very willing to tell them where the buses ran.'

Sandy clapped a hand over her mouth to stifle giggles. 'It isn't a house, dopey. It's a club. Only members are allowed in.'

Faltering, Ann struggled to sound resolute. 'I don't care, I'm going in. I'll go on my own if you're too scared.'

'I'm not scared! But it's a club, it's private. They probably have dogs to keep people out.'

'That means burglars, not us.'

They watched for a while. Extra lights came on in the garden. Music started up and they recognised the quirky singing of Alma Cogan. Ann, who always noticed what people wore, saw that the women's dresses were beautiful and their hair was curled immaculately. But she didn't like the raucous laughter of several of the men. On the whole, she didn't like the people. It was impossible to imagine them reacting in a friendly manner if she burst through the hedge and begged directions to the bus stop. The people, rather than Sandy's reservations, deterred her.

She reverted to her idea of asking a servant. A second later she told Sandy she'd had enough, and the longer they waited and the darker it grew, the more difficult everything would become.

'I'm going to follow the hedge and hope it brings me nearer the house. If I find a kitchen I'll speak to the cook or somebody like that.'

Sandy muttered disapproval but didn't stop her and no sooner had Ann moved off than she heard her close behind. The hedge turned a right-angle and Ann crept beside it until she came to a wicket gate. She jiggled it open and slid through. By now she was at the side of the house.

A hand pulled her sleeve. 'Keep out of the light,' Sandy whispered.

Together they scuttled towards the house, choosing shadows rather than pools of lamplight. They came to a car park where virtually the first vehicle they noticed was Dennis Aylard's Humber.

A theatrical gasp escaped Sandy. 'Do you think your mother's here, too?'

Ann sought a loophole. 'It mightn't be his car now. After it broke down he said he was thinking of selling it.'

But a minute later Sandy spotted him in a room off the terrace. Then he and Ann's mother came outside and when people began to dance, they did too. He held her tight, his free hand stroking the silky fabric of her dress, the curving shape of her buttocks.

Ann turned away, pretending to miss Sandy's sarcastic remark about another business meeting. She ran recklessly across the car park and out into a lane.

Sandy kept pace, protesting: 'We didn't ask directions.'

'I don't care.'

Ann scurried up the lane, encouraged by the drone of traffic ahead. They reached the road and a bus slowed and picked them up.

She didn't know what to do. She didn't want to stay at Sandy's that night and be made to talk about it. Neither did she want to go home because it would be bad if her mother was there and bad if she wasn't. Everything was bad. Quite bad. It could still get worse.

'I've got a headache,' she said when they were at Sandy's house, and she went up to bed to be peaceful and alone.

Each time she shut her eyes, the dancers on the terrace danced beneath her eyelids. Repeatedly she heard their music in her skull. She thought she would never be able to listen to that music again, or see people dancing or pass by a wood or . . .

Then she became cross with herself, realising the only suprising thing about the fondling was that she'd witnessed it. The man had driven her mother to a party miles from the town and, by a remarkable coincidence, she had stumbled across them.

It was weeks before it occurred to her it was too much of a coincidence and Sandy had contrived it.

CHAPTER FOUR

Gillian Spry said her goodbyes and pushed the telephone away. Dismissing the call with a shake of the head she focused her thoughts on the young man lounging by the office window.

'Sorry, Richard. Where were we?'

He spoke without turning his gaze from the busy street below. 'Dalton. I was saying we ought to have more on him by now.'

'Oh. Yes.'

Her tone alerted him to her indifference and he looked at her over his glasses. 'You still don't agree he's important?'

She laughed. 'No, to be honest, your powers of persuasion haven't extended that far. He was only a technician. I'd rather we concentrated on the principals.'

'Hmm.'

Richard came away from the window and pulled up a chair, facing her across her desk. She thought he looked peaky, either over-tired or about to go down with a cold. He took off his glasses and absentmindedly jiggled them while he spoke.

'The thing is, Gill, Dalton could be the glue that sticks the rest together. If we were to discover he'd been corrupt, or just inefficient . . .'

'Negligent.'

'Yes, it would amount to negligence.'

'But don't you see, whatever he did he was only a technician. A bit player. A man whose work was overseen. He wasn't wholly responsible, not in any instance.'

He suffocated a sigh. He'd known in his heart she'd resist his idea. 'What you're saying is you really don't want me chasing after him.'

She was careful not to sound dogmatic, like big sister to his bright beginner, senior partner in a team where experience was of incalculable value. There was a fine line between steering an inquiry and blighting a colleague's enthusiasm. Richard hadn't worked at CJI with her for long but she thought she knew where, for him, that line ran.

'Richard, even if you catch him, he won't be enough. Proof of Dalton's wrongdoing would only confirm what we know: that investigations were flawed and cases bodged. We can't lay the blame at the door of a lowly lab technician.'

He capitulated with a sigh and stood up. 'You're right. When you put it like that, of course you're right.'

He was pacing to the window again when she said: 'There's a "but" you haven't said.'

The glance he gave her was rueful. 'I expect I meant "but we aren't getting anywhere with the others". The principals, as you call them. Pickford and Winterlea.'

'Oh come on, we haven't drawn a complete blank.'

He shrugged. She argued: 'No, we haven't. Look, let's run over it again.'

She clicked at the keyboard on her desk and text flickered on the computer screen. She understood why he fancied aiming for Dalton. Ultimately, it was because it was a course that offered quick results. An easy option. Richard, she'd noticed, was a young man who enjoyed a quick result. To her mind it was wiser to play the big fish, no matter that it took longer to land them.

Richard was rubbing at the window-pane with his fist and determinedly looking down at the pedestrians. She studied him for a moment. He was relaxed, no recalcitrance in his stance. When she first met him she wasn't convinced he would do. He was younger than his predecessor, a keen Scot who'd resigned to take on a high-powered job in Edinburgh. Her first choice for replacement had turned her down in favour of a role with the Crown Prosecution Service. CJI was where you made your name, not your money, and it didn't suit everyone.

Richard King sounded good on paper but her first impression was that he looked too young and bewildered. Brown eyes had blinked at her from behind wire-rimmed glasses and he had a habit of flicking a fall of dark hair out of his eyes before he spoke. The effect was schoolboyish. Old-fashioned schoolboyish, at that.

She'd revised her opinion once he began talking about a couple of her earlier cases. Richard displayed an acute understanding of the issues involved in CJI's work and an eagerness to contribute. Like her, he lacked the temperament for a nine-to-five existence and, as he was unmarried, nobody would be bullying him to cultivate one. Finally, Gillian had reminded herself that people frequently told her she looked younger than her late thirties, and it would be absurd to hold his youthful appearance against him. So she didn't.

Richard, gazing down into the street, said: 'Gill, we keep on going over it. And over it. And we're getting nowhere.'

'Rubbish. We've unearthed that stuff about Pickford and the case in Yorkshire . . .'

'Fascinating but it doesn't amount to anything.'

She wasn't convinced that was true but she let it pass. 'All right, then. Winterlea. You can't say the same about him.'

'No, I don't. That's shaping up. Marcus Winterlea's reputation is severely undermined by what we've learned so far, but it isn't enough and now we've stalled.'

Gillian found what she was looking for on the screen. 'Listen to this.'

He was impatient. 'I know it by heart.' He began to look vaguely around, wondering where his glasses had disappeared to.

'But . . .'

The telephone rang. With reluctance she lifted the receiver.

'CJI, Gillian Spry speaking.'

Richard guessed who was on the line: Stephen Kuyper, a one-time police officer and, for several years, CJI's part-time helper. Sometimes his information was helpful, sometimes it was worse than useless because it tied up time better spent in other ways. Richard, feeling jaundiced today, wasn't predisposed to believe this would prove one of the good times.

The call was lengthy but boring because Kuyper was doing the talking and Gillian was reduced to grunts and murmurs. By the end, Richard had located his glasses, made coffee and set a mug down on the desk in front of her.

He asked: 'Does he still address you as Miss Spry?'

'No, I cured him of that.' She sipped the coffee, marshalling her thoughts before encapsulating Kuyper's information.

'Richard, he's been to see Mrs Margrove.'

'The landlady who saw the fight in the Peckham case?'

'Yes. She's suggested where he might find two other people worth talking to. They weren't called to give evidence but she says they were on the spot.'

'Good.' He didn't sound delighted.

'There's no harm in checking them out. Anyway, I've agreed now.'

They wrangled a little about the cost-effectiveness of letting Stephen Kuyper roam freely. At least, Richard King chose that term. Gillian Spry refuted it. CJI was a charity, its budget had to be eked out and he saw no justification for it being eked into Kuyper's pocket. In Gillian's eyes the man was an asset and in Richard's a doubtful one. This was one argument he knew he was forever destined to lose.

She toyed with the computer again, scrolling through the file on Winterlea. Some words jogged her memory. 'Oh yes, it was Kuyper who noticed Winterlea was involved in the Rita Morden murder case.'

'I know, Gill. But we aren't going to re-investigate every

one of Marcus Winterlea's cases, are we? He enjoyed a long career, we could waste CJI's annual budget for several years poking around among paperwork and survivors and without achieving anything of value.'

Gillian gave him a mischievous look. 'Funnily enough, I have a feeling the Rita Morden case might provide us with what we're after.'

He snorted. 'If this is woman's intuition, I won't play.'

'Nothing so quaint. But the Morden case was the first one after Winterlea moved to the south coast. Everybody and everything would have been different, but if the pattern of events was the same it strongly suggests he was the person who influenced them.'

'The first since he moved? I didn't realise.'

She decided against retorting that the information was right there on the computer and he could have read it whenever he liked. So much for them going over and over the material.

Richard, following her line of thought, opted not to defend his laxity. He was feeling off-colour and under-powered. In truth, he was tiring of the investigation. He preferred swift results and on previous occasions had got them.

He chose to sound confused instead of lazy. 'This case is like staring into a bowl of spaghetti. Plenty of interesting stray ends, but no guessing where they lead and how any of the strands connect.'

She rewarded him with a smile, wondering whether he realised how frequently he used food analogies.

Up on her screen came the earliest case involving the two men. Marcus Winterlea was a pathologist, living in retirement in France. Ross Pickford had been a police officer. He died in the late Eighties after a lengthy and apparently comfortable retirement in the north of England. They met on the Dancing Doll case in the Forties. A man called Doone had been bludgeoned by his business partner, Rhea, who stood to gain the entire business and the patent on '*Biddy, the wonderful dancing doll*', as she was described on the packaging.

Biddy danced for the jury during the five-day trial at the Assize court. She watched Rhea sentenced to death. He was hanged three weeks later. No one said a good word for him and he was made out to be stupid, as well as violent, when it transpired that Biddy would have danced forever beyond his grasp. Doone had safeguarded his invention, making a will in favour of his estranged wife and son of whose existence Rhea was ignorant. Detective Sergeant Ross Pickford arrested Rhea. Dr Marcus Winterlea damned him with forensic evidence.

Half a century later, the number of people having second thoughts was considerable.

Richard came and looked over Gillian's shoulder. 'Show me what you've got on the Morden case.'

Together they scanned newspaper reports of the magistrates' court committal proceedings, the Assize court hearing, the unsuccessful appeal to the Home Secretary, reports of the hanging at Winchester prison, and features written about the case when it was long over.

'He hadn't a hope,' Richard said. 'Look at the language they were using. Black marketeer. Philanderer. Unscrupulous.'

'The one that's missing is spiv. Basically, that's what he was, in the jargon of the day.'

'But Rita Morden fell for him.'

She made a moue. 'Aylard had money to spend on her. Her husband was enfeebled by the war and she saw her life slipping away.'

'It slipped right enough. He killed her.'

'No sympathy for him and none for her, either. Do you see how she's reduced to being the faithless wife? No redeeming qualities anywhere. Actually, I think this case gives us a flavour of the Fifties. In the wake of war, the woman who becomes a giddy girl instead of caring for the wounded hero is particularly contemptible.'

But Richard was wondering about the husband. 'John Morden. Wasn't he under suspicion? The killer's usually the husband when wives go erring.'

Gillian said numerous people had said he was at the party

when Rita was killed. 'Besides, there were intimations that he was too weak – I mean irresolute rather than physically frail, but he might have been that, too. The case doesn't teach us much about him.'

'You can understand *her*, though, can't you? Years of drabness and deprivation, then along comes Mr Wrong with his car and his fast friends, and a new world opens up.'

'They kept up a pretence that she was working for him. As a personal assistant, though I shouldn't think they'd coined that term then.'

'At what stage,' he asked, 'did she discover the business was criminal?'

'Nobody says. I suppose it's possible she didn't.'

He jabbed a finger at the screen. 'Hold on. It says here she was killed because she found out the truth.'

'I know it says there but it's only an opinion, it isn't substantiated.'

When he showed surprise she added: 'Like several of the statements made in court, it wasn't backed with what you and I would regard as proof. A tigerish lawyer might have ripped the prosecution case apart. I've read the court record and that didn't happen.'

Putting on the quavering voice he used for pronouncements by dotty Mr Justice Sniffle who lurked inside him, he peered at her over his glasses. 'There are no hopeless cases, only hopeless barristers.'

She laughed. 'As your honour pleases.' Then: 'Mind you, I have a modicum of sympathy for his defence team. He insisted on giving evidence against their advice and he alienated the jury. The defence strategy was shot to pieces. They knew he couldn't stand up to cross-examination. He contradicted himself, argued with everyone including the judge, and finally lost his temper with his own counsel. The weakness of the prosecution case hardly mattered after that. His own performance hanged him.'

Mr Justice Sniffle chipped in again. 'There are few things more dangerous than an unruly client.'

'I dare say in *your* court they might survive but in reality they convict themselves.'

Richard was ready to move on to Winterlea's role. 'Leaving aside Aylard's own contribution, how strong was Winterlea's forensic evidence? Better than in the Dormer case? Or Johnson? Or the Dancing Doll?'

She said it was on a par with the majority of those they'd examined. 'The pathologist gives evidence which accords with what the prosecution hopes to hear and the defence can't get him to admit the slightest room for doubt or alternative interpretation.'

Richard completed it for her. 'And in five cases we know of he doctored his original notes to bring his findings into line with what the police required. What *Pickford* required, in three of those.'

'Exactly.' She tapped the screen. 'Here, in the Rita Morden affair, he was unusually specific about the time of death and the defence couldn't budge him. Neither could he be persuaded to agree there was a possibility that the car starting-handle wasn't the murder weapon. Honestly, Richard, the jury were being asked to regard as incriminating evidence the fact that Aylard's starting-handle had his own palm prints on it!'

He reverted to what he'd said earlier. 'If Aylard hadn't antagonised them, made himself appear a hot-tempered, arrogant, untrustworthy crook . . .'

She interrupted to say, at her driest: 'Greed and bad temper have never been against the law. Perhaps they should be, but they aren't.'

Richard remarked that the Aylard case sounded like cross-examination at its most reckless. 'No wonder no other system of justice uses it. I mean, the very idea that you attack a witness's personality as much as the evidence he gives . . .'

Gillian agreed. 'The system is extremely cynical. Unfortunately, that's virtually a professional secret. Lawyers know it but ordinary people don't.'

Flaws in the system offended her sense of justice but she

was doing the only thing she could about that, making a career of correcting the mistakes and righting the wrongs. It explained her dedication. Colleagues came and went but she would stick to her last. The work was mentally exacting, could be physically demanding, and it played havoc with her private life. The once-in-a-while reward of clearing an innocent name made it worthwhile.

Richard was saying: 'You know, I pity the poor sods called for jury service. There they are, doing their level best, and the whole thing is skewed. I often wonder whether it wouldn't be safer if they didn't see the defendants and contended with facts instead of faces.'

'At least they couldn't be swayed by appearances. Shifty eyes, hesitations, squirming . . . the apparent manifestations of dishonesty which, as we know, are actually signs of stress. And who, in the dock or on the witness stand, isn't subject to stress?'

He gave her a puckish grin. 'Marcus Winterlea?'

She swivelled her chair away from the screen. 'You're happy about me poking around in the Morden case, aren't you? I mean, if it's going to become a problem I'd rather we argued it through today.'

He reassured her. Then: 'It's a pity you couldn't get more out of the niece, though.'

'June Foley? Yes. An odd woman. Kept me on the doorstep but spouted all manner of details I hadn't dreamed of asking her for. Stories about being on holiday when her aunt was killed, and her parents being unable to bear living in the town afterwards and letting the house.'

'Perhaps she liked being asked about it, despite what she said to the contrary.'

'Maybe. I'll find out, I expect, when I go back. She was cagey about what had become of the rest of the family, especially Rita Morden's daughter, Ann – or Anna, as I gather she calls herself now. I thought I'd leave it until, say, Tuesday and trot over there again. She'll have had time to give the matter thought. Either I get the boot very decisively or she opens her heart.'

Changing her mind about a second drink, she carried her mug to the coffee machine and poured. 'Oh, by the way, June Foley assumed we make television programmes. I didn't disabuse her.'

'Funny how everyone does that.'

'Just goes to show what a grip television has on the public mind. Anyway, if it encourages them to talk, I don't care what ideas they run away with.'

The mistake always made her smile, partly because the glamour that attached to television certainly didn't apply to her own work.

He said: 'She *didn't* talk, though.'

Gillian pulled a face at him. 'She will, later. That was only my preliminary approach. When I swing into action she'll find me irresistible.'

'We all do, Gill, we all do.' Quickly, while she was casting round for something to throw at him, he added: 'Any idea where you'll find Anna?'

'No, but it shouldn't be too difficult. June gave away that she's alive and in England. I gained the impression they keep in touch.'

'And after your visit, June has almost certainly contacted her.'

'I would expect so. And there's another thing, Richard.'

He queried with a raising of the eyebrows.

She said: 'Tomorrow's the forty-fifth anniversary of the murder.'

He gave a derisive laugh. 'Oh no, you aren't going to tell me they hold a reunion at the scene of the crime.'

'Certainly not. But someone puts an *in memoriam* notice in the local paper every year. Now who do you think that could be?'

They grinned at each other.

She took a newspaper from her desk drawer and showed him. 'This is the midweek edition, the main one's published on Fridays. I'm assuming the notice will be in that as well. Reckon I can wheedle the information out of the advertising department?'

His face clouded. 'What makes you sure June Foley doesn't put it in?'

'Mainly her insistence that the family tragedy should be allowed to fade into history rather than be revived as public entertainment. Also, now her parents are dead, the number of candidates has shrunk to a short-list. I put Anna at the top of it.'

He nodded. 'Me, too. But don't be disappointed if she can't remember anything. She was terribly young when her mother was killed.'

'Eight, Richard. She was eight. You've never been an eight-year-old girl but I was. Believe me, there's a sporting chance she's the best witness who never saw the inside of a courtroom.'

CHAPTER FIVE

Early on the morning of the anniversary it rained. I woke to hear it beating against the window and lay there for a while listening and picturing the rain-sodden park across the road from June's house. It rained the day of the murder, too.

People forget that. They think of the summer dresses, the dash through the leafy garden and the laughter on the lawn. But later that day it rained. A wind rushed clouds from the west and, as evening deepened, there was a downpour that sent people scurrying for shelter and grumbling about April showers encroaching on March. There were two days to go to the new month, it seemed unfair. The police, too, were to bemoan the fact that everything was washed and wet, muddy and marred. It made their task harder.

Shying away from remembering the rest, I sat up and switched on a bedside lamp. The light was harsh, doing nothing to soften the unfriendly look of the room and its ill-matched furnishings. Again I had the feeling I was in a dreary hotel, a place where people passed through without leaving anything of themselves. There was no pleasure to be gained from it.

I got out of bed and went to the bay window. A lamp on the other side of the road lit a stretch of empty street and park. I tried to make out whether the sky was lightening but the sodium glow confused it and I went to the mahogany clock on the mantelpiece. How long was it, I wondered, since anyone lit a fire in this grate? A two-bar electric fire stood in it, the flex coiled at one side. I was startled to see the plug was the old sort, brown with round pins.

The clock had stopped at three-fifteen but whether it ran down that night or a previous one I didn't know as I hadn't looked at it before. Perhaps I was expected to wind it myself, with the dull brass key that lay beside it. Together, the antiquated electrics and the stopped clock gave me a peculiar sensation of slipping back through the years. It was a frightening moment because the era I feared I'd re-entered was the Fifties.

Jolting back to reality, I held my wrist-watch near the bedside lamp and discovered it was actually a few minutes short of seven. It didn't seem worth going back to bed but it was too early to take a shower, especially as I'd an idea June's bedroom was beneath the mezzanine bathroom.

I went to the window again. A miniature dog, sleek with rain, trotted along beside the park railings. Otherwise, nothing. I turned back into the room, worried that boredom was leaving me with only memories to occupy my mind, and on this, one of the three fateful days of my year, the worst thoughts could engulf me.

I'd already suffered one fright. In the moment before I was fully awake, my face was brushed by the fingers of a cold hand. It's a recurring dream but it seldom troubles me, I'm pleased to say. I call it Anna's spook. The weirdest part is that in my dream I don't see anything, there's simply a sensation on my skin; and yet I'm aware it's a hand drifting by me, unattached and terrifying. I can live without it for years but if I'm under exceptional stress, it's sure to turn up and make me feel worse. Whenever I can, I treat it as a warning signal that I'm in need of a rest.

On this occasion, though, there was no hope of respite. I wandered around the bedroom, feeling impotent and nervous about what else the day, which had started so badly, would bring.

Pacing, I was clasping and unclasping my hands, knowing agitation exacerbates worry but incapable of relaxing. I was

wishing I hadn't come, and June hadn't told me about Gillian
Spry or mentioned Sandy Minch. I was wishing none of it
had ever happened.

To be here, virtually at the scene, after forty-five years
was reckless. When I accepted the invitation for the last
weekend in March, I was relying on June's reticence about
discussing the murder. We had, I believed, a tacit agreement
that it was out of bounds. And now here I was, at the very
place and on the very day, and June had already raised the
subject over last night's supper. Gillian Spry's visit allowed
her no choice and, although June hadn't said as much, I was
in no doubt that visit had alerted her to the significance of
today's date.

I wanted to run away. Rather than struggle through
hours of torment under June's scrutiny, I was prepared
to flee. I grabbed my travel bag and reached for a dress
I'd hung up.

A door closed in another part of the house. Almost at
once water pipes on the landing began choking. I put the
dress back on the hook and shoved the bag aside with my
foot. Of course I couldn't run away. How on earth would
I ever explain such behaviour? And explanations would be
demanded because June wasn't merely a friend, she was
family and there are always family dues to be paid.

Instead of leaving the house, I headed for the bathroom,
longing for a stinging shower to awaken my wits. An
old-fashioned bathroom it had only a bath so I tossed in
bubbly balls and ran the water hot and deep, never mind that
it steamed so extravagantly in the cold room that I knew my
towel would be damp before I'd touched it.

For a while I floundered beneath the froth, closed my eyes,
and prayed the rain would let up. Walking the dog was the
only pleasing prospect because I could be legitimately on
my own for an hour.

As I dried and dressed, I dreamed up other ways of
filling the day. An old film we might watch on television?
Or perhaps June would be eager to go for a jaunt in my
car. A lame woman who rarely left her house must surely

welcome a change of scene. I began listing the reasonably local places she might like to see.

Downstairs I found her at the kitchen table, a pot of tea to hand and two packs of tablets. She gulped a dose as I was coming into the room and swilled the tablets down with tea. Pain made her look skeletal. We held a routine conversation about how well each of us had slept and whether the tea was fresh, which it was. But when I suggested an outing, she turned it down.

'It's the damp, Anna. I have trouble on days like this. Believe me, I'd love to but when it's wet and chilly I'm better off indoors in the warm.'

Tearing up my mental list of venues, I commiserated, adding that the weather did, though, appear to be clearing up.

She shook her head. 'Not for long. They said on the radio we're in for a day of heavy showers.' She laughed. 'Not that they need to tell *me*. I can feel it in my bones, as people used to say.'

I didn't try to coax her. Instead, I revived the idea of my walking the dog.

'And if there's any shopping you want fetched, I can bring that back,' I finished.

June said she didn't think there was but if I were to notice some nice crisp apples she would rather like a few. Seeing my eyes slide to the fruit bowl on the dresser she explained: 'The ones the greengrocer delivered are woolly. That's the trouble when you can't choose for yourself, you're at the mercy of tradesmen. They palm the rubbish off on you, knowing you daren't complain.'

After saying something non-committal, I changed the subject by lifting down the dog's lead from the back of the kitchen door and examining it. Frisky, watching from his cosy spot in front of the stove, evinced no enthusiasm whatsoever.

An hour later I led the dog through the park. There had been a mildly anxious couple of minutes as we crossed the road outside the house, because he didn't appreciate the need to hurry and the oncoming traffic didn't grasp that I couldn't get him to. After that episode, it seemed prudent to take to the park.

We weren't alone. A knot of boys were kicking a football around, using two trees as goalposts. Three men were giving their dogs a run. A young woman with two toddlers crammed into a push-chair was speeding along. Frisky and I were the only creatures slouching at a snail's pace.

'Take as long as you like,' I murmured to him. 'See if I care. The longer we're out here, the less I'm indoors.'

Thoughts of June hunched over her aches and pains caused me a pang of remorse, but I was relieved to be out and about on my own.

When we'd trundled across the park I discovered it wasn't only flowerbeds which had been removed. So had a gateway. The path still ran straight over the grass from the entrance Frisky and I used, but the gateway on the far side had been replaced by a wall.

Instead of coming out into Willow Road near the Methodist chapel, we now had to stroll along the edge of the park, past a diminutive Victorian mansion, the park-keeper's lodge that June and her friend had earmarked for theirs if they ran away from home. Beyond it was another gateway. This one led into Oak Road.

Given a choice, I would have avoided Oak Road, preferring to follow Willow Road to the main shopping street and then walk through the remnants of the mediaeval town. Doing that I could come full circle to the suburb where June lives. Finding myself in Oak Road was a complication because it was here the town had concentrated its effort at modern embellishment.

First off, I realised a modern housing development had been flung down on land abutting the park, and this was a self-contained affair that denied me a way through to Willow Road. I can't recall what used to stand there. A row of kiosk shops, I think.

Next I noticed that the Victorian police station had been replaced by a supermarket and car park. The old Gaumont cinema had also disappeared, which was no loss as it was unused for decades except by pigeons. Nearby was a new roundabout, clogged by traffic racing through a one-way system, but there was no indication how pedestrians might negotiate these hazards and deposit themselves and their dogs safely on the south side of Oak Road.

Frisky launched his own protest, by lying on the pavement and settling to sleep, while I was trying to fathom it out. Tweaking his lead, I teased him back to wakefulness.

'Come on, old boy. We aren't going to be defeated by this, are we?'

We abandoned all notions of crossing over and set off east along Oak Road. This is the route I dreaded. It leads straight into reminiscence. Ahead of me rose the dark stone of the church tower, nosing above old roofs and modern intrusions. Opposite it stretched the façade of the Royal Hotel, traditionally the town's oldest coaching inn. At least no one has seen fit to raze either of those two or turn the market-place that stands between them into a roundabout.

I was pleased to note the Royal had recently been painted and someone thinks it worthwhile to polish its brass, including the sign that invites *Please Ring for Ostler*. The ivy trickling over its walls is more abundant and the hotel sign continues to creak in the wind. In the cobbled coachyard, glimpsed through the arch, a number of cars were packed in tight.

But there was no reason for me to go into the building to check for survivals and changes. As I child I didn't once cross the doorstep. Children seldom entered licensed premises in those days, unless their parents ran the business, and even then the rules banning them from the bars tended to be observed.

Sandy's cousin, Peter Minch, grew up in the Royal. He was a pug-nosed boy with a sly glint in his eyes and, usually, a plaster or two covering up scrapes. I don't remember whether his parents owned the pub themselves or managed it for somebody else, and it makes no difference to the story except to demonstrate another gap in my knowledge.

Anyway, Peter it was who fed Sandy the gossip from the Royal. Given its status as the town's premier hotel, and its importance for businessmen and farmers on Wednesday market days, anything said in the Royal was destined to echo around the neighbourhood.

As I dragged Frisky passed the main entrance I checked the name of the licensee on the plate over the door. The name of Minch had long gone. And where was Peter himself now? He was about three years older than Sandy and after the murder he'd taken a special interest in me. For weeks I'd dodged round behind the hotel to avoid meeting him coming out of the front door.

Looking back, that seems foolish because he probably used a private entrance that kept him apart from drink and drinkers. Yet I remember clearly my discomfort whenever the Royal was mentioned or when I imagined there was any risk of my bumping into Peter.

Sandy began referring to him as Peter the Policeman, which she said she called him to his face. I don't necessarily believe that. The murder so impressed Peter that he declared he wanted to be a policeman when he grew up. The fact that he knew me a little, through Sandy, and had seen my mother and Dennis Aylard together in the Royal made him feel especially involved in the affair.

I suppose he was far from being the only one, but adults were cautious about what they said in front of me or other members of my family. Peter, brimming with curiosity, had no scruples. After he'd waylaid me with frightful questions, twice, I took to dodging.

From then on I relied on Sandy's word about what he was saying and doing. She relayed news from the Royal, as she'd done for months previously. Sandy, the conduit of Talk, of news good and bad. Sandy who promised to be my best friend for ever and ever, and lasted less than three summers.

Leading Frisky over the market square, between hotel and parish church and past the Post Office from where June's father had telephoned her the fatal news, I considered what

I might say to Sandy if she materialised in front of me right then. Dared I accuse her of being a deceiver or would I lack courage, as I always had when called on to face her down?

When I was eight and she was nine, I believed I needed her protection. But was it really so? Which of us had the greater need? And what does she think of it all now? How often does she remember? I would love answers but without the pain of posing questions. Besides, how could I be sure she was speaking the truth?

Aged eight, I trusted in her friendship for always. What happened appeared to bind us together, inseparable forever, and yet within a few weeks I was uprooted to live in a different part of the country and we never met again. She didn't reply to either of the letters I wrote. I thought at the time it was because they were dull letters, empty of anything interesting because I couldn't write about the important things. Over the years I've wondered whether she was punishing me for leaving her, albeit involuntarily. The promise had been mine, too, you see – friends for ever.

Frisky dawdled in the path of a milk float. A woman criticised: 'That animal ought to lose weight, you know.'

Disconcerted, I mumbled about exercising the dog for its invalid owner. This switched her attitude from scorn to sympathy but I felt annoyed with myself for claiming to be a do-gooder.

Twitching the lead, I bullied Frisky into an approximation of jogging.

At the church gate I relented. His reasons were mysterious but he expected us to go in there and I let him have his way. This allowed us to give up the fatuous jogging but I didn't fancy taking him round the churchyard, dogs and consecrated ground seeming an unhappy combination. Before I'd worked out which street the other gate would bring us into, Frisky was plodding with determination towards the graves. When he leans with all his force, he's impossible for me to stop.

Fighting down emotions urging flight, I let Frisky drag me

onward. There was no one else near the church, no one to see
if I were to grapple with him and force him to the narrow gate
in the corner, but if he resisted and a commotion of barking
and remonstration broke out, everyone in the market-place
would learn that Anna was visiting the grave. *Ann.* They
knew me as Ann Morden, not Anna Foley. If, after all
these years, there was anyone left in the town who knew
me at all.

That was a chance I preferred not to take on a day when
luck was against me. My route had been diverted, I kept
having frights, and now a usually lazy animal was rushing
me towards my mother's grave.

Frisky hurried past the last row of standing stones and
came to the bare green space which had been cleared.
He stopped and squatted. Moving as far away as the lead
allowed, I mimed admiring the church tower, the short spire
topping it and the weather-vane floating against the clouds.

'I was right. Dogs and churchyards don't go together.'

I cast a furtive glance for onlookers who might raise the
cry that I'd brought my dog to foul the graveyard where my
murdered mother lay. Frisky lumbered up to me and licked
my shoe.

My plan to return the way we'd come changed when a
man entered from the market-place. I carried on instead, over
the greensward where the bodies of centuries of townsfolk
lay unmarked so that it was easy for a tractor mower to trim
the grass. A meagre proportion of the stones had survived
the clearance and were ranged along the walls like prisoners
waiting to be shot.

*'How do they choose whose to keep and whose must
go?'*

Looking at the first few I tried to guess. The stones
weren't of particular charm or antiquity, there wasn't anything to distinguish them from the hundreds of others which
had, presumably, been dumped. Dumped where? What
happens to rejected stones? And to whom do they belong?
The Church or the families that paid to erect them?

For me the Church is personified by a high-handed vicar

I once met. Not here, much later when I moved to a village near Salisbury. The village was a mistake. Everyone wants to know you in a small place, in so far as they want to weigh you up and decide whether they can be bothered to know you properly. I didn't stay there long.

I haven't, you see, stayed anywhere long. Certainly not long enough to become rooted. My work in marketing encourages me to be a bird of passage. I've had a number of staff jobs with big companies but mostly I've been employed by agencies to look after their clients who can be anywhere and everywhere. I've run my own consultancy, too. That's where I am now, working for myself again.

Currently, I have half a dozen clients but in six months who knows? They come and go, yet two of them are solid bets for my future and one has crossed the border from business associate to friend. Once I had a client in France and spent part of the year there. One of my staff jobs obliged me to live in Amsterdam. There's always change, you see. That's what suits me. A new client, a new adventure and, before life gets stale, a change.

The same with houses and flats, the same with towns and friends. Two or three of my friends are of very long standing but, as for the rest, there'll be a new set of faces by the end of a five-year span. This isn't deliberate, it's a pattern which evolves because of the way I move about. Maybe, though, I'm putting that the wrong way round and what happens is I take flight whenever I feel the pull of emotional strings. I've admitted I come of a selfish family. We sacrifice people, too.

I don't think I've seriously regretted any of my house moves. What drove me out, drove me on, were the mild disappointments. I discovered early on that when you're buying a place to live you should pay closer attention to its drawbacks than its advantages. The good things go on being good but the bad ones come to seem worse. I learned to choose places that guaranteed me privacy and peace. My only major mistake was the village with the lofty vicar. To be fair, though, he didn't favour tidying away gravestones.

Frisky sat down. I looked over the patch of grass, struggling to remember where my mother was buried. All possible landmarks had gone, she could be anywhere. The realisation that she was nearby yet her location was being kept secret was unpleasant. Unfair. Inappropriate.

Presumably somebody knows who lies where when a graveyard is cleared. I guessed that if I entered the church and asked the vicar or a cleaner, the information would be provided. Unfortunately, I can't ask. I can't draw attention to myself or to her. I'll have to think of the churchyard at large as her resting-place, instead of one slender plot.

Curiously, I don't think she would be as disturbed by her unscheduled anonymity as I am. She ought not to be in the churchyard at all. Rita, I recall the family saying, fancied her ashes blowing in the wind from a mountain-top. But, well, given the circumstances there was no choice. The coroner gave permission for burial. That's what commonly happens with murder victims, in case the remains need to be re-examined.

I decided to walk the length of the grass and leave by the narrow gate in the far corner. Frisky, recovered after his rest, set off willingly but pulling to the right and making me swap the lead from one hand to the other. As we went, we examined the stones, me running an eye over inscriptions and Frisky sniffing them.

The grass was flattened where we walked, proving that people continued to visit such stones as were left. And, yes, against the wall some way ahead lay a bunch of yellow flowers, their colour fresh.

This cheered me, the idea that this simple gesture was both a protest at the change but also proof that people surmount change. I, favouring change in so many areas of my own life, am generally content to see others resisting it.

A woman came through the far gate and walked purposefully in my direction. She was fairly young, dressed in expensive casual clothes and with a scarf covering her hair. I didn't know her but worried she'd recognised me. Then I realised she wasn't approaching me but was on her way to the stone with the flowers. Close to it, she stopped and read.

Perhaps I ought to have steered Frisky away from the rudimentary path and cut across to the gate, but my curiosity was roused by the woman and the flowers. I kept straight on.

As I drew closer, I saw she wasn't in front of the flowers, after all. The one that interested her was two stones away. By pausing to admire the flowers, I would also be able to glimpse what she was reading.

The dog ambled up to the flowers and nuzzled them. Daffodils, inevitable in this season. I loathe them. When people are astonished by that I say I can't bear their brash colour or their deep earthy scent. What I don't say is that my mother was accompanied to the grave by wreaths, sheaves, banks of daffodils, an abundance that exceeded Wordsworth's fantasy.

Lifting my eyes from the flaring trumpets of gold, I took in the first line of words on the grey slab.

Rita Margaret Morden

Shock surged through me. My throat closed painfully and I clamped a hand over my mouth, as though to stifle a scream. But the only scream was trapped in my skull, reverberating in my memory.

Frisky, sensing the change in me, looked up. With extraordinary clarity I noticed the yellow dusting of pollen on his muzzle, the way his coat grew in curling patterns, and the great sad orbs of his eyes. I read on through the carved dates and the **RIP**. Nobody had grappled with a verse or picked one of the brief and banal quotations. Nobody had carved a flower or a curlicue. The stone was completely unadorned. Whatever she'd hoped for from life, she'd been left with nothing in death.

Having demanded so much, she was reduced to a name. I was overcome by the pathos and had to flick away an unwelcome tear. At least, I thought, it doesn't say *Here Lies* because that would be untrue. Many of the other stones did, although it was obvious the dedicatees didn't lie there, not *exactly* there.

With a gentle tug on the lead, I urged Frisky away from the daffodils and I crouched down by them. Moving them slightly, I looked for a card. June hadn't mentioned it but I supposed they were from her. She couldn't have brought them herself, of course, but it was an easy matter to arrange. The maligned greengrocer, perhaps? As there was no card, the greengrocer seemed a likelier bet than a florist.

Frisky licked my arm, leaving pollen on my sleeve. I straightened, recalling how keen he'd been to come into the graveyard and with what insistence he'd drawn me along by this wall. June couldn't walk him here but someone did. This piece of deduction was rather pleasing and made me smile.

Just then I felt the eyes of the woman on me and I busied myself with the dog's lead for a moment, preparing to leave. I meant to meet her gaze with a polite nod of acknowledgment but when I looked at her she was facing the stone again. I murmured a good morning as I passed behind her. She didn't respond.

The stone she was studying was an older one. Victorian, I should say, with a carved skull and lines of doggerel below the name of Frederick Smith. Before I could read the epitaph or the dates, I was gone.

Frisky was less confident about the route to the rear gate and clueless about the residential street beyond. Whoever usually brought him must take him back the same way.

We wound round to the market-place. There was a green-grocer's on the corner and I checked for crisp apples and to see whether the shop was the origin of the daffodils. There were two plastic buckets of them by the door but they were a different type, cream and orange. Or are they narcissi? I warned you I don't know about flowers. To me they are equally repellent. My mother's wreaths were of every variety, and ever since I've detested them in all their guises.

I bought a pound of apples and ate one as I went along.

They were all right but that was no certainty June would approve. If she didn't, I thought, I would take them home.

I went round to June's back door as instructed, to prevent the spaniel tramping mud right through the house. June was at the kitchen table, exactly as I'd left her except that instead of poring over the *Daily Telegraph* she was now on the local weekly tabloid.

She looked at me over her rimless half-glasses. 'What do you know about this, Anna?'

To read the item I had to lift up the paper and hold it in a good light, but I realised what was coming as soon as I focused on the funereal illustration at the head of the column. *In memoriam* Rita Margaret Morden was as concise as the gravestone in the churchyard: her name was followed by the date of her death. Whoever placed the advertisement hadn't bothered to mention *Sadly missed* or *Asleep in Jesus*, or any of the cloying remarks that enhanced the other items on the page.

Rita Morden was there, so why add a *Not forgotten* or a *Forever in our memory* when her presence in the column made the sentiment plain? Someone had remembered her life and death and had paid to prove it.

Shrugging, I set the paper down on the table. 'I'm mystified.'

June nudged her glasses up her nose a quarter-inch and peered at the print again. 'I didn't think you were behind it, but if it isn't you and it isn't me, who can it be?'

'She had friends.'

The words, the tactless words, escaped before I considered them. *She had friends*.

Oh, she had friends all right, friends who led her astray and betrayed her. Because of these friends her life was in ruins and then she died. The newspaper reporters had rubbed their hands with relish at Rita's friends. The lawyers, with only a modicum of restraint, had made the legal maximum of these friends. Dennis Aylard was chief among them and it had been proved to everyone's satisfaction that he killed her.

When anyone referred to the friends of Rita Morden, they weren't conjuring up the girls she'd known from schooldays, her neighbours or her colleagues from wartime work. Oh, no, they meant always and only the flashy crowd she fell in with during the final year of her life, a free-spending, party-giving set who refused to play by the rules of the humdrum Fifties. And maybe the emphasis wasn't entirely unfair because, as soon as she had the chance, those were the people she chose for her friends.

June took off her glasses and stared at me. 'But *those* friends, Anna . . . I mean, none of them would be sufficiently interested. They didn't show up at the funeral, you know.'

'No. No, I suppose they didn't. Look, I didn't really mean those people. I don't know what I meant. Except that I'm mystified. If you didn't . . .'

'Of course not. I prefer not to draw attention to it.'

'And if I didn't . . . ?'

But I had an inkling. Without allowing second thoughts, I plunged in. 'Tell me who walks the dog for you, June.'

'Why are you changing the subject?'

'I'm not.'

'Mr Tompkins from two doors down takes her out. Not often enough but occasionally. Now, what has that to do with this announcement in the paper?'

'Frisky led me to the gravestone. He's obviously been there before. And someone's placed flowers by the stone.'

'Flowers?'

'Daffodils. Did you ask anyone to do that?'

One of her combs began to slide as she shook her head. 'Definitely not.'

'Mr Tompkins?'

'But does he know about Rita? Or where the stone is?'

Immediately, we accepted it was inevitable he knew because he'd lived in the town most of his life. And anyone seeking the stone wouldn't hunt for long as so few remained.

'He hasn't mentioned the subject to me,' said June

thoughtfully, 'but I suppose what you suggest is entirely possible.'

'Will you ask him about it?'

She saw the humorous side of it. 'With care. I don't wish to make him feel a fool or a ghoul. The important thing is to retain his dog-walking services.'

Above the sound of Frisky noisily lapping water, she added: 'In fact, I've been plotting to encourage them.'

This Mr Tompkins, a bachelor whose own dog had expired and whose cat had a habit of sloping off for months on end, entertained us for a time. June regarded him as a useful neighbour and a congenial one who was always willing to help. Walking the dog was one of a number of services he provided.

I did register, of course, that the obliging Mr Tompkins had been a well-kept secret during June's regular moans about her vulnerability and isolation. Well, no matter, but I intended to bear him in mind when next she grumbled. Meanwhile, I made her promise to tell me whether he admitted visiting the gravestone and adorning it with flowers.

She tapped the paper with her glasses. 'Not this, though, surely. I can't imagine him paying to put a notice in the paper. It's in a different league, isn't it?'

I said yes, it was.

June said: 'I'll telephone the newspaper and ask who did it and I'll ask whether it happens every year. For all either of us knows, it could be an annual event.'

I said yes, it could. 'Will you identify yourself?'

'I'll have to, I think. They won't want to give anything away unless I own up to being a member of the family.'

Her decision made me nervous. 'June, be careful. You don't want the local rag taking an interest.'

But she'd thought of that. 'I won't admit to living locally. I'll pretend I'm ringing from London, that someone's told me there's a notice and I wish to trace whichever member of the family put it in.'

My face revealed my scepticism, making her add: 'It'll be

all right, Anna. I can handle it. I'll be gleaning information, not offering it.'

I tried to look convinced but I was remembering that she had, by her own admission, made a mess of the Gillian Spry encounter. Babbling, she'd said. Running on. Might she not do the same with an alert advertising sales-girl on the telephone or, worst of all, a reporter? How skilled was June at evasion and lies?

We wrangled about whether she ought to make the telephone call there and then. My view was that there weren't many people at a newspaper office on a Saturday, especially if publication day was Friday. June was of the opinion that precisely because Saturday was a quiet day she stood a better chance.

Rather than listen in, I went upstairs while she made her call. I stood by the bedroom window and gazed out over the park. People and pets criss-crossed the grass, harried by gusts of rain. I played guessing what they were thinking about. That afternoon's football? What to buy for Sunday lunch? Meanly, I allowed them only a brief range of options.

I was sure I was the only one whose head was bursting with unwanted memories. The burden of the past weighed down and, however I twisted and turned, I was powerless to alter anything. For much of my life I'd managed to ignore the past but now I sensed matters rushing towards a crisis. What had been hidden might soon be revealed. People were already actively trying to achieve that. There was nothing for me to do but hold onto my secrets, bury the truth deep within me. I must stick to the story that always protected me. It was as familiar as the truth.

But these thoughts brought me only scant comfort because the new seekers-after-truth weren't casual enquirers. They were professionals practised in sifting truths from the past. They wouldn't be easily deterred and they wouldn't be kind.

I'd become accustomed to kindness, you see. When I relive the cursory questioning in the wake of the murder, I notice the sympathy on the faces of the policemen and

the solicitous proximity of the young woman police con-
stable they referred to as Jenny. She held a dainty white
handkerchief in her hand and when a question was painful
I took the cue and reached for it. Burying my face, I saw
the embroidered *J* worked in satin stitch in one corner and
I breathed the tang of eau-de-cologne.

No one coerced me or insisted or urged. They were kind,
excessively kind. I said I didn't know, I didn't notice, I didn't
remember. And they nodded at each other wisely because
what I was saying coincided with what they expected and it
would have been wholly remarkable if I told them anything
different.

After they finished their tentative questioning, I heard
them talking, and one of the men saying: 'Poor kid. Thank
God she didn't see anything.'

'There's the car park business, though,' Jenny said.

But he told her: 'No, we can forget that. If she didn't know
anything about the scene in the garden, she can't know about
the car park, can she?'

'Well . . .'

'No, leave it. I'm not putting her through any more. She's
had enough.'

So I was never asked about the rest, only about the episode
in the garden. I suppose this appears disgracefully lax but I
was eight and I was in tears and they were being protective.
Perhaps it sounds absurd but what I remember best of the
days immediately after the murder was how kind everyone
was, and that the kinder they became the worse my tears
flowed.

My tears and my shock were absolutely genuine but I
seemed to be thrust into a surreal world where everything
was dramatic and intense. Alongside the super-sympathy
and extra-kindness, people exhibited a deeper-than-usual
regret. I don't know whether this always happens when a
young mother dies a violent and sudden death, or whether
it's a phenomenon reserved for murder victims. It isn't,
thank heaven, something even the unfortunate experience
more than once.

In my tear-streaked, bleary vision of the world I knew myself to be one of the leading actors in a dreadful drama. And yet I wasn't only at the heart of it but also standing aside and following the tale as it unfolded: watching my flurries of tears, seeing my hand reach for Jenny's handkerchief with the embroidered initial, knowing how each further manifestation of misery would result in greater sympathy and a more cursory questioning.

They didn't ask me, ever, about the business in the car park.

'*Yoo-hoo!*'

June was at the foot of the stairs, signalling the end of her telephone call.

I scuttled down. 'What news?'

She looked rueful. 'None. You were right, Anna. A quiet day and no one's free to check up for me.'

'But they didn't actually refuse you?'

'Oh no, I'm to try again on Monday. I'll let you know what comes of it.'

I saw her tossing up what to say next, then making her decision. 'Look, would you hate it if we went to The Avenue?'

'*What?*'

She was apologetic without backtracking. 'Yes, I know, I keep saying I don't like to dwell on it, not attract attention and so on but . . . Well, the subject is well and truly broached now and I have a yen to see the place.'

'I see.' I didn't, especially as she'd previously refused an outing on account of the weather. I wondered if her bones were now telling her we'd seen the last of the rain.

'If you're utterly against it then we won't, of course we won't. After all, I'm living in the town now, I can go any day. I really don't have to drag you over there.'

Feeling sorry for her, I caved in. 'It's all right, June. I'll take you.'

If I didn't she'd be hiring a taxi or begging a lift from a neighbour. That would attract attention, all right.

She looked content with her victory. 'After lunch?'

I agreed to that, too.

And that's how it came about that my cousin and I visited the scene of the crime on the anniversary of the murder. She needed to direct me because the changes to the town mean the route I had in mind is no longer feasible. I would have got snarled up in the complications of the one-way system.

The Avenue is on the west side of the town. It's a wide residential street with red-brick gabled villas built at the turn of the century on generous plots of land. On closer inspection it becomes obvious the houses are carved into flats. When my parents lived there the houses were sliced into pairs, vertically. We rented the right-hand half of number seventeen. We didn't own it but that was another norm in those days. For a few pounds a week you could afford a splendid address.

There's a detail that didn't surface at the trial. The impression was given that my father had bought the property. My feeling is he encouraged that belief, because the family also made the mistake of thinking he was the owner. This doesn't matter except that it raises a faint suspicion about him. The whole country came to know of my mother's foolish aspirations but it's possible my father liked posing, too.

I parked my car opposite the entrance. The wrought-iron gates are as I used to know them but part of the front garden has been cleared to create a gravelled drive where cars can turn. Apart from a few such symbols of modernity, number seventeen is as I knew it.

'Much the same,' I said.

June shifted in her seat. 'Fewer trees and extra burglar alarms.'

She was opening the door and I didn't like this. 'You aren't going in, surely?'

'Up to the gate, that's all.'

At the gate she dithered for a couple of seconds and then entered. I expected her to make for the front steps although she would have a problem mounting them, but instead she went down the side of the house. Immediately, I was out of the car and dashing after her.

'June, you *can't.*'

'Nonsense. I'm only going to look at the garden.'

'Supposing someone comes?'

'Then I'm interested in renting the ground-floor flat. You noticed the agent's sign in the window, I suppose?'

'There's no need for sarcasm.'

'Irony, dear. Sarcasm's crueller.'

I caught her arm but she shrugged me off. 'Don't be silly, Anna.'

We emerged from the side path into the garden. There were indications that the occupants of the various flats use separate areas. In our day the garden was undivided, but the picture is broadly as I remember it. On the right stands the old greenhouse and beyond that a shed. I was pleased to see everything well cared for and the greenhouse full of flourishing plants, in particular a vine. In my day the garden suffered from gothic neglect.

June stopped. 'Tell me where it happened.'

I felt a frisson of distaste, an unreasonable delicacy about showing off my knowledge. I pointed. 'About there. Where the greenhouse meets that tree.'

'The beech?'

'I expect so. I'm hopeless at trees.'

'They found her there, did they?'

I feared June was going to hobble up to the spot, tramp around superimposing her presence on it. I said: 'Yes, found her. But they decided she was killed at the end of the garden and moved.'

'Oh? Do you mean she moved herself?'

'No. Whoever did it moved her.'

'That man Aylard.'

'That's what they said.'

June shuddered, as though disgusted by the discovery of what she was doing. 'Well, I think I've seen enough.'

As we returned to the car, I offered the explanation I felt was due. 'When I was, oh, quite grown-up I decided it was ridiculous not knowing about the case so I read it up. The newspaper coverage, I mean, and a few references in books on real crimes. I was interested in the police inquiry and why the jury convicted.'

June said my curiosity was natural. 'One's always entitled to know the truth, and in this country we make great play of justice being seen to be done.'

I felt a flickering smile at her interpretation of my words. Her confidence that truth and justice went hand-in-hand was hardier than mine. But, then, she had the benefit of believing in unwavering, invariable truth; and, if you can do that, it becomes easier to believe in unflawed justice.

Rather than challenge head-on I took a sneakier route, mentioning a case from the same year that reverberates through the history of criminal justice: Christopher Craig shooting PC Miles on a warehouse roof in London, and Derek Bentley, a sub-normal nineteen-year-old who was in police custody during the murder, being hanged for it. Ten years older than me, June would remember the storms of protest that fuelled the campaign to end capital punishment.

But either she was pretending not to hear or she was genuinely preoccupied because we reached the car without a word.

We sat in it for a moment, silent. Then I said: 'What did you expect to see?'

She didn't say.

I said: 'Or feel. What did you expect to feel?'

'Nothing. I don't know. I had an urge to go to the spot. It struck me as peculiar I'd never done so.'

I objected. 'Not really. People prefer to keep well away from places with hideous associations.'

'Oh, come, Anna! You know that isn't true. Most people are drawn like moths to a lamp.'

'But *you* haven't been, until now.'

'And now I needn't come again. I've seen all there is.'

'Except for the car park.'

I don't know why I said that. There was no call to mention the car park and June wouldn't have thought of it.

She said: 'Oh yes, the car park. There was debate about a row in the car park, wasn't there?'

I started up the engine. 'We'll drive round there.'

The lane behind the great houses of The Avenue remains accessible. I pulled up at the rear of number seventeen. We were in a tree-shaded car park, tarmaced whereas it used to be rough land. Oddly, while they were ripping the town about no one succeeded in building houses behind The Avenue. I say 'succeeded' because I can't believe it didn't occur to anyone to try.

Getting it over as fast as I might, I outlined to June what was said to have happened.

'My mother came to meet Dennis Aylard whose car was parked here. They had a row because she'd learned that the business he was involving her in was illegal. She threatened she was going to the police to stop the scam.'

'Which was?'

'I don't know exactly. Smuggled cigarettes? A second-hand car racket? Something terribly Fifties, anyway.'

I was waving my arm about suggesting where they argued and how Rita ran into the garden where he caught up with her.

June said: 'I remember he struck her a mighty whack with a tyre lever.'

'Starting-handle, actually.'

'Well, if he chased her up the garden with that in his hand . . . not exactly spur of the moment, was it? Plenty of opportunity to change his mind before he reached the tree and the greenhouse.'

I reminded her the body was moved.

June said: 'He denied everything, though, didn't he?'

'Including being here that evening.'

'He must have been pretty cool to drive away after that and pretend it never happened.'

I opened the car door for her.

She hesitated before easing herself inside. 'But there again, I suppose people do whatever they have to. You don't discover what you're capable of until you need to do it.'

We drove most of the way across town before either of us spoke again. Then June said: 'My brother came, you know. He and his friend walked over here about a week after it happened. They couldn't resist seeing it. But me, well they asked me if I'd like to go and I said no. I was too shaken, you see. I'd liked Rita. She had spirit. She made me laugh.'

I gave her a sad little smile and thought how seldom anyone had a good word for my mother.

CHAPTER SIX

Gillian Spry reached into her purse and drew out a business card. She'd hoped a bright smile would have been enough but this wasn't her lucky day. First she'd been kept waiting and now she was being asked for proof of identity.

The woman who took the card from her was greying, heavy-jawed, hiding her thoughts behind pebble glasses. Gillian tried to catch her eye with a smile but the lenses made it impossible for her to tell whether she'd succeeded. Suddenly she thought of Richard King's, his brown irises so clear through his lenses that she wondered whether it was possible he affected glasses to make himself look older, more dependable.

For a long moment the woman read the card. Then she said: 'CJI? That's Criminal Justice Investigations, isn't it? You're a lawyer.'

'That's right.' Unusual, she wasn't being assured she made television programmes.

'You look into miscarriages of justice.'

'Yes, that kind of work.'

The woman looked up, probably at her although once again the thickness of the glasses made it uncertain. 'Would you wait here for a moment, please?' She sped away.

Gillian quelled a sigh. She tried to guess whether she had time to telephone home before the woman returned. Her lover was making one of his trips to London, there was a chance he'd arrived at the flat. But she wouldn't like that call overheard. Perhaps she would ring Richard King instead. The office line was engaged when she tried earlier.

No time. The woman came back and, raising a flap in the counter, invited her inside. 'Mr Pritchard will help you, Miss Spry.'

Mr Pritchard, an avuncular man of less than average height and less than average hair, was the editor and looked as though he had been for a good many years. Gillian knew she was in for a tussle. He wasn't going to *give* help, he was going to trade it. They introduced themselves, shook hands and she let him open the bargaining.

'I'm a great admirer of the work CJI does, Gillian. Of course, my impressions come purely from the television programmes other people base on your cases, and I don't doubt you've got fascinating stories about the differences between real life and what gets on the screen.'

He allowed a pause for her to laugh, which she obligingly did. Then he said: 'Why are you interested in the Rita Morden affair?'

She decided to focus on her enquiries rather than his. 'Nathan, I'd like to know who inserted the *In memoriam* notice in last Friday's paper. I assume it's not difficult to check.'

He nodded in the direction of the world beyond his office. 'Yvonne's doing it now.'

'Thank you.'

'I've also asked her to look back in the files and see whether this is the first time we've published the notice.'

Gillian gave an impish smile. 'It isn't. It's been appearing for at least five or six years. I can't say exactly how long because I only checked back over a few years. And there it was, the same wording each time.'

Nathan Pritchard frowned. 'Oh, dear. We ought to have spotted that. On the other hand, we don't know whatever it is that's aroused CJI's interest.'

She continued to shy from telling him. 'And you're

74

unlikely to have any staff who remember the case so the name wouldn't have alerted anyone.'

But he contradicted her. 'Ah, wait now. We don't have anyone who worked on the paper at the time of the murder case. No, that was forty-five years ago, as you know. But several of our reporters have written about it from time to time. It's one of those local stories that never entirely goes away, you see. For instance, when we write our weekly snippet of news from, say, thirty or forty years ago, the Rita Morden affair might well get an airing.'

She said she was surprised because it wasn't an especially intriguing case or a legally important one.

He justified the paper reviving it. 'We haven't been cursed with much murder and mayhem in this town and the case made quite a splash locally, you know. It comes up in other ways, apart from our dips into local history. There was the churchyard fuss, for one. When the new vicar proposed clearing out the gravestones there was a debate about whether Rita Morden's should be retained. In the end, it was.'

Pebble glasses peeped around the office door. He beckoned the woman in.

'What have you found for us, Yvonne?'

'Only this.' She put a sheet of notepaper into his out-stretched hand.

He ignored Gillian for a minute while he asked: 'This was all? You're sure there's nothing in any of the other files?'

'I've checked the likely ones.'

'OK, we'll leave it for now. Thanks, Yvonne.'

As she withdrew, he explained the contents of the paper to Gillian. 'The notice was delivered to the office overnight, accompanied by cash to cover the cost. The girl who dealt with it decided it was *bona fide* because she looked at last year's paper and saw it had appeared then.'

'Oh. I blithely assumed you'd be bound to have the name and address of a customer.'

'It's certainly odd for us not to but it isn't essential.'

He watched her buttoning her jacket, preparing to leave.

Then he said: 'My uncle was editor when Rita Morden was murdered. You haven't revealed what you're after but if it encompasses talking to an old man who remembers it well, I know just where to find one.'

Gillian smiled broadly. 'I'd love to talk to him. But as for revealing exactly what I'm up to, I wish I knew myself. The Rita Morden case is possibly connected with an enquiry we're making, but possibly not. The *In memoriam* notice and the flowers by her gravestone are tiny puzzles that might be of no consequence whatsoever but on the other hand . . .'

'*Flowers?*' It was comical how the surprise almost catapulted him out of his chair.

'If I were you, I'd rush a photographer over there while they're fresh.' She enjoyed this chance to tease in return.

A few minutes later, hurrying to her car which was parked recklessly in a restricted area near the market-place, Gillian began calculating how the trading had gone. It had been worth throwing in the flowers to see his astonishment, but the result depended on how useful the former editor proved to be.

She unlocked the car, whisked it into a legal parking space, and telephoned Richard King.

'I suspect there's more to it,' she said, rounding up her account of her endeavours since she'd last seen him. He needed to be brought up to date on her visit to the graveyard on Saturday and the newspaper office this Monday.

'There always *is* more to it,' Richard objected. In his view, she was like a dog with a bone, getting her teeth into something tasty and unwilling to give up while there was a morsel left.

'I know, I know. We have to remember to draw the line. So you keep telling me.'

'Are you going to see June Foley today?'

'I thought tomorrow.'

'I know you said Tuesday but as you're there . . .'

'I'd still prefer to let her stew until tomorrow.'

'The old man, then?'

'Well, he *was* the editor which probably means he was on

chatting terms with the local police. Yes, I think I'll winkle him out today.'

Afraid she was going to hang up, he said: 'Hold on. I want to tell you about Winterlea.'

She'd assumed Richard had spent the weekend nursing his cold and hadn't wanted to press him. 'Have you learned anything new?'

With a self-mocking laugh he admitted: 'It's actually what Stephen Kuyper picked up. Oh, yes, he's crept out of the woodwork again. He didn't bother to explain where he was hiding himself when we wanted to talk to him. Anyhow, he's found a pathologist, near retirement and probably not quotable, who had a row with Winterlea about the ethics of altering forensic evidence to please the police.'

'Promising. But how long ago was this?'

'Towards the end of Winterlea's career. The way Kuyper relates it, Winterlea's argument was along the lines of why break the habit of a lifetime.'

There was a long silence while she digested Stephen Kuyper's latest findings. This was one of the days when Richard daren't protest at her giving the former policeman a free rein, but she didn't crow. She was horrified by the extent of the damage Winterlea appeared to have done.

If only a fraction of their suspicions were correct, he'd built a career on providing evidence convenient to the prosecution. Sadly, juries were willing to put their trust in the experts, because their evidence was scientific and therefore not coloured by a wish to convict or to dodge justice. Or so it seemed. Yet how was the most sophisticated of juries to consider what it had never been told: that evidence spoken in court contradicted earlier notes and statements which failed to support the case against the defendant?

By such deceptions Winterlea had succeeded in having men wrongfully convicted, imprisoned and executed.

CHAPTER SEVEN

I'd been expecting them and here they were. It's months since I realised it was going to happen and a full two weeks since June's announcement that the woman from CJI had pestered her. That's a lot of waiting, of wondering and, despite my promises to myself, it's a lot of fretting, too.

There were times when I was tempted to telephone CJI and say: 'Look, I'm here, what is it you wish to know?' But I think I was right to resist doing so because it isn't what the average person would do.

So I did nothing, except telephone June once to ask what the local newspaper people told her about the *In memoriam* notice.

She said: 'It was strange, Anna. They claim they don't know who puts it in.'

I noticed the tense immediately. 'Puts?'

'Yes, it's happened several years running. I squeezed that much out of them.'

By them she meant a woman called Yvonne.

For a moment we considered whether Yvonne was telling the truth, the whole truth and nothing but the truth. Then June said: 'I'm not convinced but I don't see how I can budge them.'

'I'm sure you tried your best.'

'It seems obvious to me, Anna, they'd *have* to know who was behind anything they published.'

'I've no idea about their legal responsibilities but I'd expect them to need identification in case the cheque bounced.'

Then she recited a rigmarole about cash slipped through the office door at night.

I changed my view. 'Well, if that's their story I'm inclined to believe them. Why should they bother to make up such a tale when they could simply refuse to tell you what you want to know?'

She said she hadn't looked at it that way but now supposed I was right.

I preferred not to end the conversation there, with me apparently scoring a mark against her, so I joked about her having to renew her attempt next year, assuming the mystery advertiser performed the trick again.

June said: 'Then it'll be a combined attack. I gather I'm not the only one asking about it.'

She explained she'd been quizzed about who she was and why she was concerned about the advertisement. Just as planned, she gave her true identity but lied about living in London. Then Yvonne had mentioned another enquirer.

'I couldn't squeeze that name from her, either,' June said, 'in spite of saying it was bound to be family. She discouraged the idea but wouldn't help beyond that. Oh, I was given the impression it was another woman.'

'Gillian Spry, I expect.'

'That wretched television woman? Oh, I do hope you're wrong.'

But we didn't know for sure and I spent two weeks mulling it over before it was confirmed.

I became sure on the morning I opened my door and found Gillian Spry standing there. She'd come for me and she'd brought a bespectacled young man with flushed skin and a nasty cold. Compared to him, she looked strong and reliable. I noticed her dark trouser suit and, slung over it with the arms hanging empty, a fleecy-lined jacket. The effect was casual but definitely not sloppy. Now I think of it, that sums up the young woman herself.

80

She switched on a confident smile. 'I'm Gillian Spry from CJI and this is my colleague Richard King.'

They were flashing business cards at me while she spoke.

I knew her. I recognised her from the churchyard. She was the woman who stood a few yards away from my mother's gravestone and lingered over the stone words written in memory of Frederick Smith.

I had a split second to decide what to do about this.

Whenever I've imagined them coming, I've planned what to say. The old story, naturally, but apart from that I've decided what impression to create. You see, I always assumed it would be the crucial first impression. Instead, I was confronted by a woman who'd seen me before. By the gravestone, on the anniversary of the murder, she'd seen me.

Good heavens, we'd almost spoken. Well, in actual fact I had spoken but she'd averted her face and avoided replying. The scene was vivid in my memory. The troublesome Frisky, the bunch of hated daffodils, the stones leaning against the wall, and the scarved woman striding towards me and taking up position two stones away from the one dedicated to Rita Margaret Morden.

Although I was ignorant of it then, that was no chance encounter. Gillian Spry arranged it. Perhaps she followed me across town, watched me battling with the dog, perhaps trailed me back to June's house. Worse than anything, she might have spied on us when June and I visited The Avenue, scene of the crime.

Anxiety makes me flush. I felt myself growing as red as the feverish young Richard King with the handkerchief clapped to his nose.

I took the business card out of Gillian's hand. My voice sounded amazingly calm when I spoke. 'I've been expecting you. Won't you come in?'

With murmured thankyous, and grumbles about the keen wind whipping down the alleyway that leads to my house, they followed me into the sitting-room. Gillian went to the big arm-chair near the window. In my imagined rehearsals,

I'd seen myself sitting there. The room isn't spacious and whoever uses that chair has the best view of other people. It's where I read, with the light falling over my left shoulder and my face shaded.

It was too late to claim the chair was uncomfortable or to resort to any other means of getting Gillian out of it. She was a professional interviewer who chose the most advantageous position in a room. To try to shift her would be tantamount to admitting I was nervous.

Richard King sneezed. I decided he was one of those men who always needs a woman around, to warn him to put a scarf on before he goes out, to feed and cosset him.

I said, immediately filling the role myself: 'That's a rotten cold you have. Why don't I make us all a hot drink?'

He thanked me while snuffling into his handkerchief. Having come into the warm, his glasses kept steaming up. He looked altogether uncomfortable.

'Coffee? Tea?'

They opted for coffee, which suited me because it took longer to prepare. Having invited them to take off their coats and generally settled them, I went to the kitchen.

Tinkering with coffee pot and crockery calmed me considerably. When I returned with the tray, I was over the shock of recognising the woman and had forgiven her for taking my chair. Perhaps the panic would rise up again later but, for the present, I was succeeding in controlling my feelings. I'd slammed down that shutter in my mind.

I was grateful to Richard King for having such a wretched cold. The sneezing and sniffing could hardly be ignored and created the occasional distraction whenever I needed one. When he sipped the coffee, his glasses steamed up again and he had to take them off and rest them on the arm of the chair. They slipped to the floor once and that was another timely diversion.

The idea came to me, shortly after we began talking, that one or other of my visitors had a concealed camera. It's the sort of thing you see regularly in programmes based on real-life investigations, isn't it? You know, those grey and wobbly recordings which are rarely upright but are all the more effective for being patently unrehearsed. Whatever is said in the rest of the programme, by people whose performances are recorded with the benefit of make-up artists plus lighting cameramen and directors, it's those snatches of raw life that have the impact.

Several of CJI's investigations have been adapted into television documentaries. If Gillian and Richard brought a camera into my house, I don't blame them. I admire the work they do and have no qualms about their methods. I am, unsurprisingly given my background, an avid viewer of programmes based on true crimes.

Crimewatch and its imitators, with their re-enactments and catalogues of crimes, don't interest me particularly, except for wondering how they might have treated the Rita Morden affair. No, I prefer the deeper studies of cases, where there's a commitment to discovering the underlying reasons for these disasters, and how the survivors live with the results.

We've suffered, as you know, the worst of crimes: children killing children on Merseyside; the horrors of 25 Cromwell Street . . . And at the same time as we're floundering for explanations and ways of healing our society, it's become routine for programme-makers to convince us of miscarriages of justice. Not only the number cases – the Guildford Four, the Birmingham Six and the Bridgewater Four – but a never-ending line of them wending their way from prison cell to television screen and newspaper headline.

Whenever there's a newspaper article about one or other of CJI's investigations, I read it with care. That's how I knew they were closing in. That's why I was confident they would come for me.

We sipped our coffee and talked. I kept considering the possibility of a hidden camera and guessing where it might be. On television they tell you it's in a bag. Richard King carried a black nylon bag similar in scope to a brief case, but he'd put it down on the far side of his chair and out of my sight. He dived into it several times and emerged clutching fresh paper tissues. I eliminated him as a potential cameraman.

Gillian had a medium-sized shoulder bag which she set on the floor beside her chair. I supposed it was credible it contained a camera and I made a conscious effort not to let my eye be drawn to it. However, a few minutes after we started talking she accidentally touched the bag with her foot and it toppled over. She noticed this but left it lying where it fell and thus convinced me there was no camera inside.

Elsewhere? Mentally I searched the room. But, oh, what a waste of time this was. Modern equipment is so tiny. For all I knew, it was concealed behind the woollen scarf over her shoulders or in one of the packs of tissues never far from his hand. I abandoned this nonsense and concentrated on our conversation.

I call it a conversation because that's the way they hoped it would appear. In reality it was an interview. They were there to wring information out of me. Their skill lay in letting our exchanges flow like a friendly discussion. Topics were picked up and side-stepped, revived and half-answered, then quietly abandoned in favour of more fruitful lines of enquiry. I was as free to pose questions as they were.

Early on I asked: 'How did you find me?'

Gillian said: 'We spoke to your cousin recently. Perhaps she told you.'

June had vowed not to point them my way and I was confident she hadn't. I didn't like this hint to the contrary and raised a sceptical eyebrow.

This forced a change of direction from Gillian. 'But we actually traced you by our normal methods.'

I suppose she thought she was conjuring up images of a dedicated team of investigators trawling through the computerised records of the Inland Revenue, the Ministry of This and That, or the National Health Service, and noting my changes of surname. But we're all on so many official records that it's impressive only when one of us *can't* be traced.

No doubt CJI has excellent contacts and every computer system spews out information for them. But nevertheless I was inclined to believe their means of tracing me were the oldest and simplest: someone told them where I was. That, I decided, we could discuss later if necessary.

Meanwhile, I tackled the question hanging between us since I'd opened my door and come face to face with Gillian.

'Did you know who I was when you saw me in the churchyard?'

'Not for certain.'

'But you thought it might be me?'

'Might, yes. There seemed to be a resemblance but . . .' She shrugged.

So then I knew she hadn't seen me before that and she hadn't seen a photograph of me as an adult. My face is one of those that hasn't altered much over the years. That's not my vanity speaking again. I don't mean I'm especially youthful, only that my appearance was determined in my teens and, as I haven't grown fat or thin, the face I show the world today is the same one.

I decided to stop asking questions and let her have her turn. With an apology for allowing my curiosity to get in the way of her work, I encouraged her to begin in earnest.

She said: 'The reason we're here, Anna, is that we're looking into cases involving a pathologist called Marcus Winterlea. Your mother's death was one of them.'

'I recognise his name. I don't mean from my mother's case, I was far too young to know about that. But I'm sure I read his name a while ago in an article about your work.'

She nodded. 'There have been a number of articles and also television coverage. Well, anyway, his name crops up in a number of cases we're considering as possible miscarriages of justice.'

'But surely . . .' I coaxed her to play her hand.

She said: 'No, we aren't here to tell you we think Dennis Aylard was wrongfully convicted. It's just that doubts have been raised about Winterlea's conduct.'

I waited.

Richard King took his handkerchief away from his face long enough to say: 'There's a pattern to his behaviour, you see, and it occurs in the Morden case, too. That's why we'd like your help. And if you can't help, maybe you can suggest other people we should contact.'

Gillian appeared eager to cut him off but she said nothing. In fact, she reined herself in, sitting still until he finished.

Keeping my eyes on him, not her, I said: 'I'm afraid you're right, I can't. It was an awfully long time ago and I was very young. Only eight.'

He said: 'Yes, we're sorry to dredge it up. And, of course, we understand you wouldn't know the first thing about Winterlea and his evidence.'

'I doubt I so much as heard his name.'

Gillian had been waiting too long. From the corner of my eye I saw her grow restive. It was only another second before she intervened, seizing our attention.

'It's important,' she said, 'that we clarify a number of points. It could make the difference between CJI building a solid case against Winterlea or the whole thing fizzling out. We don't want to quiz you about him, rather about aspects of the murder which puzzle us. I think you'll agree, you could easily have been aware of them even though you were only eight.'

Having taken back the initiative, Gillian kept it. She began by asking me whether I had any recollection of the evening when the murder was committed.

'Very little,' I said. 'I know there was a party in the house next door. By that I mean the other half of our house. Number seventeen was divided into two semi-detached houses.'

She didn't require a resumé of the housing shortage of the Fifties and dragged me back on track. 'When you say you "know" there was a party, are you saying you remember it?'

'Yes. I remember the preparations for it and I remember there being a lot of people and music. Jazz. My father hated jazz and he complained it was too loud. After that they played Ruby Murray.'

She teased out details and I was content to give them. I explained about the weather, an essential factor.

'For about a week it had been exceptionally hot for Spring and that's why the party was held in the garden. The women were wearing summer dresses and everyone was talking about the weather, the way you do when it's out of the ordinary. Our butter had gone rancid, although it was wrapped in several sheets of newspaper and kept in the corner of our coldest room. Neighbours had begged milk from us because theirs was on the turn. And my mother was hankering after a refrigerator.'

Gillian smiled. 'Isn't it odd to think most kitchens didn't have them until well after the war?'

I returned to the story. 'Well, because the party was to be outside I watched the preparations. My bedroom, you see, overlooked the part of the lawn where they erected the trestle tables. And when I went downstairs I could see that our neighbour had wheeled his console radiogram right up to an open window.'

Soon I was feeling pleased with myself. In spite of my shock at recognising Gillian and the unsettling business of her choosing my chair, things were now moving along smoothly in the direction I'd always imagined. My story – the party, my retreat to my bedroom, the fire-works and the sudden downpour – was scanty indeed and it was interrupted by regular apologies for failures of memory.

Richard King nodded sympathetically as, over and over again, my recollections stopped short of the very things they wished I'd noticed. When I said that oh, dear, it was *so* frustrating not to remember such and such, Richard offered the comforting thought that we protect ourselves by forgetting whatever is too painful.

Gillian said: 'Anna, I'd like to take you back to that moment in the garden before the fireworks, if you will.'

'I was scared of them. That's why I went indoors.'

'Yes, I see. What I'm wondering is, did you notice your mother then? I mean, did you find her to say goodnight and explain you were going to bed?'

Frowning, I tussled with it, eventually saying: 'I don't think so.'

'But you said a few minutes ago she was in the garden with everybody when you last saw her. Was that immediately before you went indoors or earlier?'

'I don't know.'

'Might it have been earlier?'

I understood where she was leading. My mother was supposed to have gone into the car park beyond the garden to meet Dennis Aylard.

I stuck to my vagueness about where and when I'd last seen her. In the garden, yes. Time and exact spot unknown. That's the story I'd always told and it would suffice for CJI, too.

'Forgive me,' I said, 'but I don't see how this helps you with Marcus Winterlea.'

She didn't mind explaining. 'Winterlea had a habit of reshaping his opinions to fit in with what the police wanted him to say. The issue here is whether the police version of events was accurate.'

Richard broke in. 'Anna, Gillian means there wasn't evidence of your mother being in the car park that evening. None of the people interviewed suggested she went out there.'

'And neither have I.'

A good thing I hadn't wavered, tempted by their persistent probing and willing to reward them with a hazy memory or two. Once again I was vindicated in sticking to the story that kept me clear of trouble.

None of it matters, you see. My mother is long dead. Her lover is long dead. As far as injustice to them is concerned, there's no sense in poking around in the past. What's done is done. But if Marcus Winterlea, living in retirement in France, were guilty of helping imprison people who ought to be freed, then let CJI concentrate on their cases. Prisoners stand to benefit from the belated truth but there's no helping the dead.

I let Gillian and Richard assume I was concentrating on remembering snippets helpful to their cause, then said: 'I'm sorry, I don't see there's anything I can add to what I've already told you.'

I stood up, offering fresh coffee.

While I was making it I wondered again about a hidden camera. And then it occurred to me that a tape-recorder would do equally well for their purposes. They were interviewing a quiet middle-aged woman whose mother had been killed while she was a child, not confronting a guilty party. What on earth would be gained by clandestine filming? On the other hand, neither of them were taking detailed notes and a record of our conversation would be exactly what they needed.

I pictured them playing through their tape. Tapes? Were they changing the tape now while I watched a reluctant kettle boil? I pictured them in their office listening to the tape, to my dodging and denying. How often would they play it through before one of them noticed me switching my attention to Richard's sufferings rather than give a simple answer to an apparently simple question?

Taking the fresh coffee to them, I gave them a chance to deny it. 'I'm surprised you didn't ask to record our chat.'

Gillian gave that easy laugh of hers. 'Oh, we have pretty good memories, Richard and I.'

The words were unfortunate. I knew she hadn't meant to be sarcastic but I bounced back with: 'Unlike mine, you mean.'

She was nicely wrong-footed for a moment. It was silly of me really, to take pleasure from her discomfort, but totally irresistible.

When they'd quizzed and questioned, probed and puzzled for another hour, it became obvious the interview was running down. They were hungry, I supposed. Perhaps they'd go for lunch and return invigorated, ready for another bout.

My telephone rang, providing the interruption I required.

A friend was on the line, confirming our plans to attend a concert at the weekend. Kate's always brief on the telephone and I had no need to make excuses and hurry her.

When I turned back to them, hoping the break had given Gillian and Richard a chance to confer about leaving, Gillian said: 'Do you know where Sandy Minch is?'

The question came like a slap. I rested my hand on the back of a chair to steady myself.

'No,' I heard myself say, in the unruffled tone that was so familiar and yet so surprising. 'I haven't seen her since, well, since a few weeks after it happened.'

I decided to remain standing, as a clue that I'd given them as long as I was prepared to. When neither of them produced a follow-up question, I felt a need to say more.

'We were going to be friends for ever. You know how little girls say that sort of thing. We said it but then we lost touch.'

'You went away,' suggested Gillian, who'd gathered this from her first conversation with June. On her second visit she'd learned absolutely nothing because June hadn't talked to her, being utterly resolved and refusing to open the door.

'Yes,' I said. 'And then my family left town, in dribs and drabs over the next few years. Because of the murder they were famous and they hated it.'

But the word wasn't famous. The correct word was notorious. I'd heard it flung about in arguments.

'*Because of that damned woman we can't walk down the street any longer without people whispering. She's made us notorious.*'

'*All right, all right. We'll go.*'

'*Go where?*'

'*Anywhere.*'

And eventually they'd all gone, here, there and anywhere.

I was first, though, first of the Morden evacuees, the one that led the tribe into exile. Except that it was a diaspora, not merely exile. Once there'd been a tribe of us living in a country town but after the sordid case of Rita Margaret Morden we scattered to the four winds. It's a fallacy that trouble binds people together. It's equally good at tearing them apart.

Gillian Spry tried again: 'Do you have any idea what's become of Sandy?'

In reply she got a firm shake of the head. 'And I don't see how she could help you where I can't.'

'She was at the party, though, wasn't she?'

I screwed up my eyes as if this took concentration. 'I think she was at my house earlier in the day but I'm not sure about her being at the party.'

'You said at the time . . .'

I laughed. 'Oh, dear, you do sound inquisitorial.'

She was quick with her apology. 'Sorry, Anna, I wasn't trying to trip you up over something you said forty-five years ago, I'm hoping to jog your memory.'

'I'm a great disappointment,' I said.

Any reply she might have made went unheard as Richard endured a fit of sneezing. I told him he ought to take himself home and go to bed with aspirin. My hints were dropping so thick and fast they could no longer be ignored. Gillian picked up her shoulder bag. Richard took another handful of tissues from his case and stuffed them into his pocket. A minute later I was closing the front door behind them.

I resisted curtain-twitching as they walked down the alley into the teeth of the wind, but in my mind's eye I followed them every inch of the way. They weren't what I'd expected. I hadn't imagined vagueness or blundering and certainly not the vulnerability of a streaming cold. I didn't dislike them but I resented them. You know how I've tried to consign the story to the past. Those two were forcing me to see that it wouldn't be over as long as I lived.

CHAPTER EIGHT

Sandy Minch sat on the kitchen table and swung her legs. Left, right, left, right, left, right . . . Her new white ankle-socks were flashes of brightness in the dingy room. Ann's father didn't own the half of 17 The Avenue in which the family lived and refused to spend anything on redecoration.

A whitened ceiling would have been nice. Fresh linoleum would have made it safer underfoot and a couple of cans of paint would have transformed the pre-war browns of walls and woodwork. As it was, the only fresh-looking things in the kitchen were Sandy's socks. Left, right, left, right, left, right . . .

Sandy tilted her head back, to see how close she was to sitting on her hair. Not close. By Christmas, maybe. She straightened and watched her socks.

Ann was breathing on a window-pane and using the steamy patch as a canvas for a girl's face haloed by curls. She wished Sandy would go away. She wanted to be on her own, had wanted to for days, but Sandy was determined to be loyal and kept coming round. They were in the kitchen because the boiler kept it warm.

The curls ran down in watery ringlets and spoiled the face. Ann rubbed her fist over it and wiped her damp hand down her polka-dotted rayon skirt. She wished Sandy would go.

They hadn't spoken for several minutes. There were

things they couldn't say. They couldn't say them because it was hard to find words that weren't accusing and because even the right ones would give reality to the nightmare. When no one mentioned it, as Ann was discovering, it was possible to pretend everything was normal.

At the corner of her eye, Sandy's cotton socks marched through the air, failing to keep time with the tick of the wall-clock with the yellowed enamel face blobbed with rust. Ann jerked her head away, troubled more by the clock than the socks.

The clock was a reminder of the rows and disaster, and because it was a clock it couldn't be ignored. You *had* to look at a clock, it made you; especially one that clanked away the seconds in an empty room and erupted into discordant celebration of each hour.

'That damned clock!' Rita had shouted. 'Why do we have to live with a thing like that? It belongs in the dustbin.'

Ann's father's reply was typically mild. 'It was my mother's, you know that.'

Rita groaned and flounced out of the room muttering that his mother probably *found* it in a dustbin. She'd argued frequently for a coat of emulsion on the ceiling and walls, a lick of paint on the woodwork, and a floor covering she wouldn't be forever tripping over because it was worn into holes.

When he proved implacably mean, she turned her anger against the decaying clock until it came to epitomise everything that was secondhand in her home and unsatisfactory in her life. Knowing that, he ignored her complaints, all of them.

Ann put her hands to her ears, shutting out the bad-tempered exchanges of remembered rows. Sandy, who never missed anything, said: 'What are you doing that for?'

'Nothing.' Ann spun round in a hopping dance. 'Nothing, nothing, nothing.'

Sandy had to keep her legs steady to let Ann float by. Her rhythm broken she dropped down from the table. She looked at the clock.

'Didn't your policeman say . . .'

Ann fetched up against the door to the hall and stopped spinning. 'He's not my policeman. I don't have a policeman.'

'Ha, ha. I mean the fat one with the funny red hair.' When she didn't like anyone she always called them fat.

Ann didn't respond.

Sandy said: 'My mother says he's squiffy.'

'What's squiffy?'

'Drunk. A bit drunk.'

'No he isn't. He's . . . he's all right.'

Sandy began: 'There you are, you . . .'

But the front door banged and Ann's father called. 'Ann?'

The girls froze. Sandy gesticulated at Ann, and Ann managed to call out.

'In the kitchen, Dad.' She hurried into the hall.

Her father was standing just inside the front door, looking like a stranger who'd burst in and didn't know where to go. He watched his daughter rushing to meet him but made no move towards her and no attempt to speak.

'Dad?' Ann was next to him now, pulling on his jacket sleeve.

Without looking down at her, he gave her the news.

'They've charged Dennis Aylard with murder.'

Ann's body weakened. She buried her face in her father's jacket and felt stinging tears.

Two or three days ago Sandy had warned her they might accuse her father of the murder. Ann had been too terrified to admit it was possible. Today, though, when he hadn't come home from the police station by the time he'd said, she'd suspected the worst imaginable mistake was being made.

His jacket was coarse, made from a thorn-proof tweed best worn in winter, except in his case. Since the war he was frail and shivery. People said he'd been different before but she hadn't been there to know. She drew her face away from the scratchy wool and looked up at him.

She noticed he wasn't putting his arm around her or his hand on her head, or offering her any comfort. In fact, he seemed unaware of her presence. He gazed, distracted and unseeing, in the vague direction of the stairs.

Ann gave a gentle tug on his sleeve, a firmer one when he ignored it. She felt him pulling his arm away from her. She relinquished his jacket sleeve and went back to the kitchen.

Immediately, Sandy said: 'I heard what he said. They're going to hang Dennis Mallard for it.'

'No!'

'Oh, I forgot: *Aylard*,' said Sandy, who knew this wasn't what Ann meant. 'All right, they've charged him and next they'll put him on trial, and after *that* they'll hang him.'

Like her cousin Peter Minch of the Red Lion, and like everyone else fascinated by murder, she was an expert on procedure.

Suddenly Sandy was convulsed with mirth. 'Dennis Duck's going to get his neck wrung!'

She stuck her neck out, flapped her arms and quacked.

Ann clapped her hands to her ears again. 'No, no, no . . . They *can't*.' She was seeing his fleshy neck, the way his starched collars gouged into it. She screamed.

Sandy's hilarity vanished abruptly. She was unnerved by Ann's display of anguish. Above the rising pitch of Ann's wailing she said, with ferocity: 'Shut up, Ann. I don't know what good you think you're doing.' It wasn't a child's voice that came out of her mouth.

Ann's reply was a blubbering, spluttering, outburst. 'No. They mustn't. It's wrong. No, no, no, no, no . . .'

Sandy thumped her.

The blow stunned Ann into silence.

Bossy, Sandy said: 'I'm not sorry, Ann. You're supposed to hit someone who's hysterical. Think how it looks, you screaming and cracking up because you're mother's fancy man is charged with killing her.'

Slumped on a chair at the table, Ann tried to calm her sobs. She was confused by Sandy's attitude. One minute Sandy was triumphant, taunting her with Aylard being hanged; and the next she was full of contempt for Ann.

Then it dawned on Ann that Sandy was scared. Lots of people became cross when they were scared. Sandy was scared the crying and shouting would attract attention; scared Ann was being weak; scared about lots of things and with one clear exception: she wasn't scared Dennis Aylard might be hanged.

Summoning her strength, Ann told Sandy to go home. 'I want to be with my father,' she said. 'I can't talk to you any more today.'

Sandy squinted up at the clock and said she ought to go home anyway but she'd call round in the morning to see Ann was all right.

'What about school?' asked Ann, forgetting next day was Saturday. She hadn't been to school for two weeks, not since her mother's death.

They fixed the time for Sandy to come on Saturday morning. She pulled up her socks, two quick flashes of white in the dimming room, and sauntered to the back door.

'Don't worry about Dennis Mallard,' she said, obviously convinced Ann would. 'The jury won't find him guilty.'

Ann nodded dumbly. Exhausted, she had nothing to say.

Sandy turned the knob and pushed the door open, accidentally letting in Mabel, next door's black-and-white cat. 'Don't worry,' she repeated, and went home to her gossipy mother and the lesser Minches.

Ann made a pot of tea and carried a cup around the house in search of her father. He wasn't in the sitting-room. He wasn't in the hall. He wasn't in the bedroom. She stared at the bathroom door. From the other side of it she heard sounds of retching.

She took the tea down to the sitting-room and left it on a table by his armchair. The room was chilly so she lit the gas fire. Then she went into the kitchen, hoisted herself up onto a cupboard, opened the glass cover on the face of the clock and twisted the hands until she was satisfied it would never mark another second or make another sound.

CHAPTER NINE

For the first time in more than forty years I'm desperate to speak to Sandy Minch.

I want to alert her that CJI, in the form of Gillian Spry and Richard King, is on her trail. I need to spill out everything about the *In memoriam* notice, the flowers in the churchyard and June's fruitless telephone calls to the newspaper. And I'd like to hear what she's done with her life during the decades since being friends forever became never speaking again.

'*I'll have to trace her myself before they do*,' I thought, as Gillian Spry and Richard King walked away from my house. It was daunting because they are professionals but apparently hadn't found her.

They'd scarcely reached the end of the alley before I was laying plans. These were, to be honest, rather feeble. For instance, I began by skimming through my local telephone book, seeking out Minches. There were four. One I ruled out straightaway because it was a fish restaurant, an arbitrary decision because how am I to know whether anyone in her family went into the business?

June's local directory would have been more useful, because if the name was recorded in the area where Sandy once lived, there was a higher chance of it belonging to a relative. Unfortunately, until I visited June again I couldn't browse through her directory; or so I thought, not knowing any another way of consulting it.

I set mine back on the shelf. Minch was a reasonably common name and I was afraid of ringing up useless strangers. Sandy herself was unlikely to answer my call because she was probably married and using another name.

Trying to be clear-headed, which wasn't easy since the CJI visit made me jumpy, I listed simple means of checking. Apart from the telephone directory, there were electoral rolls. To find out her current name, I could look in the register of marriages in London.

Knowing the date and place of her birth gave me a considerable advantage. Encouraged by the thought, I telephoned the Family Records Centre and sought information about opening hours. I saw no reason not to begin my search the following day.

Once I'd given myself a task to perform I felt less helpless and began day-dreaming about what would happen after I'd discovered who she'd become. If I were lucky, her husband would have a distinctive name, easy to trace.

The longer I pondered, the more it puzzled me that Gillian Spry claimed not to have tracked down Sandy Minch. Here was I, a complete beginner, mapping out a route to Sandy and they were saying . . . Or were they?

My alarm at being asked about her had thrown me completely off guard and left me unsure of the precise words. Gillian uses words with care. I'd spotted this when she hinted at June revealing my address and when she ducked my question about her method of finding me.

I poured a glass of wine, nestled in my chair by the window, closed my eyes and tried to relive the end of the interview, the startling moment when Sandy entered the conversation.

'*Do you know where Sandy Minch is?*' Gillian had asked.

What had gone before? Ah, my friend Kate's telephone call about the concert. There'd been a natural break and the question came after it. The sequence was Gillian's question; my deceptively calm reply; her comment about my moving away; my description of my family leaving the

100

town; and then, while memories were flooding in, Gillian's second sally.

'*Do you have any idea what's become of Sandy?*'

Next the challenge, Gillian suggesting: '*She was at the party, though, wasn't she?*'

During our talk I felt I was coping well, offering half-memory and doubt, but picking over it later I was less sure. If she'd taped me, she would notice how I cut her off by teasing her the moment she pressed.

'*Oh dear, you do sound inquisitorial.*'

Replying, she'd given herself away. '*Sorry, I wasn't trying to trip you up over something you said forty-five years ago.*'

Never mind her claim to be investigating the activities of the pathologist, she'd been studying what I'd said to the police. Yes, the sooner I alerted Sandy, the better.

Next morning I caught a train to London, took the Underground to Farringdon, and joined the busy band of searchers, at the Family Records Centre in Myddleton Street, Clerkenwell. Because I'd read about it I was prepared for the frantic activity as people pluck books from shelves, frisk them, thrust them back in place and snatch up others. At first sight, it looks like a wild day in a lending library, everyone speeded up but not finding books they like sufficiently to carry home and read.

One can spot the professional researchers, those with a confident hand outstretched to the right spot on a shelf. They, and the practised amateurs delving into family histories, were in the majority but I wasn't alone in being a slow-witted blunderer. The place caters for us with a patient man at an information desk to direct us where we seek to go.

I was there a couple of hours. The first few minutes were sluggish and uncertain but then I gained confidence in the system and wasn't despondent when the book I wanted was a mere gap on the shelf. I took up position nearby and awaited its return.

While I waited I wondered whether to look up my own entries. It's curious to think of our lives encapsulated in those ranks of dull volumes, tragedy and achievement distilled in rows of names and dates. My life must appear as banal as anyone's: date and place of birth, date of marriage, ditto the birth of my child and the date of my divorce.

You need a leap of the imagination to turn those unadorned declarations into family life. In my case, the briefness of my time-span with Rob hints at a turbulent marriage, a rapid collapse of the dream which one July seemed so promising. Imagination may fill the void but only I know the reason: the damning past that created an impossible wife. Yet it was my decision to leave, as it had been mine to marry.

I'd wanted to try marriage, wanted it very much, wanted children and a normal family life, wanted to be normal. Wanted, in other words, exactly what life always denies me. None of what went wrong between us was Rob's fault. He was confused then and he's probably confused now. I didn't tell him about the frightful events that shaped me. The worst he knew was that my mother died when I was small. Because he came from Australia her name meant nothing to him, but as I was using the surname Foley instead of Morden, few people would have made the connection.

The dates in my life throw up a discrepancy to tickle the imagination of a percipient researcher. Mikey, my son, was born months before the divorce. Given the length of time it took for a divorce to take effect in those days, it's possible to guess he was born after we'd parted but before the split was official. Rob doesn't know about Mikey. He's one of the secrets I keep from him. That sounds heartless, I know, but I was afraid of him using the baby as a hook to hold onto me and I valued his freedom as highly as mine. Knowing of the child, he mightn't have made a new life with a new woman, which is what he hastily did.

Unless he consults the records in Clerkenwell, he'll possibly never find out about Mikey. If he does, there's a chance he won't do the calculations that suggest I was a few weeks pregnant when I left him. Don't misunderstand me, I didn't know about Mikey then. My plan to keep quiet came later when I realised that, having given up my husband, I was carrying his child. Any reservations about the unkindness of that decision dissolved because of what happened later. The hurt and the disappointments are mine alone. Rob lives on in bliss.

Maybe what I'm describing is a splendid example of Foley selfishness, of my family's propensity to sacrifice people. Maybe. I'm simply telling you what I did and, in so far as I understand it, why. When I was resolving what to do, I honestly believed I was acting in the best interests of all three of us: Rob, Mikey and me. If I'd acted differently, the results could have proved worse, for Rob and Mikey if not for me. For Rob's sake, I pray he doesn't go and nose around in the records.

You know, these records offer a distorted portrait of our national life now that couples marry less readily. To get a fuller picture we need a supplementary register of those destined to live together and procreate outside marriage, don't we?

Well, before I'd decided whether to see myself reduced to a name and a handful of dates, a man raced up with the book containing the Minches and pushed it onto the shelf. My hand shot out as assuredly as any I'd admired since my arrival. After that, all the information I hoped for that morning came easily to hand.

By the time I left, I knew Sandra Minch married a man called Eliot Brown when she was twenty-four years old. She was living in Sherborne in Dorset then. He was described on the marriage certificate as a teacher. Other documents recorded the births of three children, twin boys and, eight years later, a girl. I saw no references to divorce or death.

For one brief and reckless moment, I was prepared to look up Dennis Aylard, to see in print the legally chosen date of his death. Then I came to my senses and hurried out into the fresh air, feeling guilty and stupid for entertaining the idea of seeking such a frisson. I don't understand why I considered it, unless I fancied gloating over my special knowledge of the story behind the words and figures.

My minor triumph in learning about Sandy made me

ridiculously elated. Feeling I'd earned a treat, I caught a taxi to the Oxo Tower on the south bank of the river. At the top, there are panoramic views from a restaurant and a brasserie. Kate took me there for drinks on the terrace after a concert last year.

I realise I haven't told you about Kate, although her name keeps popping up. Well, she's a steady sort of woman, personal assistant to the head of a large company, and she's the same age as me but a contrast. She favours camel coats and cultured pearls, and she wears a scarf with the designer's initials splashed over it instead of a proper design. I'm afraid I'm secretly contemptuous of that English Traditional style, which is what happens when a woman declares herself middle-class and middle-aged. It makes Kate look older than she is and dowdy.

Kate's convinced it means she blends in wherever she goes, but unless we're mingling with the up-to-town-for-the-exhibition crowd at the Royal Academy, it's rarely true. That evening on the terrace her very reticence stood out among the dashing lycra outfits and blazing jewel colours.

During my solitary lunchtime visit, though, the clientèle was focused on its affairs and Kate's camel cashmere wouldn't have merited a second glance. Actors were lunching with their agents. Brittle young women with jobs in public relations were toying with their clients. Skinny women from television production companies were limiting themselves to meals comprising starters. At least two businessmen were in thrall to their secretaries.

I asked for a table in fifteen minutes and took a glass of wine onto the terrace where I became enraptured by the view. It was a glittering April day. When you're out and about on your own you need something to absorb your attention. A river is perfect.

Kate insists it's folly to suppose wonderful scenery is open country, as most people think. A townie through and through, she has a top ten of Great Views and they are, without exception, cityscapes.

She nominates St Mark's Square in Venice; the Charles

Bridge in Prague; a street, the name of which I can't pronounce, in Amsterdam; the roofscape of Florence; Valletta, roseate in dawnlight across the water from Sliema; and practically any aspect of Hong Kong. I can't recall the others and, anyway, her list is fluid.

She's keen to show me those I haven't seen, and to convert me to cityscapes, but our tour must wait a few years. To do it properly we need plenty of time. Although I have work I can juggle, she's tied to office hours and will be until she retires.

I sipped my wine and watched boats moving up river against the tide. Midday and mid-week, two-thirds of the traffic was tourist cruisers and the rest empty yellow rubbish containers returning from dumping the city's waste on landfill sites. Orange and yellow buses were crossing Waterloo bridge and upsetting tourists who, like me, prefer to see red. The complicated outline of the Post Office tower was sharp against the sky to my left, and the dome of St Paul's unmistakable to the right.

On the walkway below the tower a toddler, who kept running to peer at the water, was wrenched away by its mother and smacked around the head. Its wailing became a descant to the thrum of cars and buses on the Embankment across the water and the grinding of boat engines. My heart went out to the child, punished for the small ambition of looking at the river.

When my table was ready, in spite of being hungry, I was sorry to go inside. Without a river to watch I was thrust back into the predicament of the lonely diner. Look vaguely up the room and you'll be assumed to be staring at people. But where can you let your eyes fall without seeming to be weighing up your fellow diners and finding them wanting?

It's a big restaurant, a light and airy place in restful blues with a wall of glass, a louvred ceiling and an arrangement of steel struts that creates the impression you're sitting in a tent against the sky. I had to walk a long way down the crowded, noisy room for the disappointment of a table without a view out. The waiter helped with the chair, there was fussing with my napkin and the menu, and then I took stock.

Sweethearts at the adjoining table, which was very close, were whispering. My heart sank. Apparently they'd already convinced themselves I was eavesdropping, and how could I refute it when I was sitting silently and appearing to listen? Well, at least they were on their pudding and would be gone before I was. To soothe them, I put my notebook on the table and read my new information about Sandy Minch.

Picturing Sandy as a mother of three and the wife of a teacher took an effort. The facts were unexceptional, it was just that I knew Sandy and . . . No, *I had known her*, which wasn't the same thing. She'd been sharper than me, quicker, sure of herself and absolutely clear what I should do and how I should do it. She'd watched over me and, as I'd gradually come to realise in the aftermath of the calamity, she had watched me.

Sandy was an astute observer but she hadn't been able to resist meddling. Manipulating, if you like. Exploring what she could do and make others do. Yes, I realise I'm not accusing her of anything other than the typical behaviour of a nine-year-old girl. It's an age for testing your power in this world and, if she'd had a brother or sister closer to her own age, there would have been a natural companion in her experiments. The pity of it was she picked me.

Realisation of our true relationship seeped in slowly down the years. I would have been indignant if you'd said it to me when I was young but I was an unintelligent child. If nothing else, the way I latched onto Sandy, with her extra year and her speed of mind, indicates it. I didn't trust myself to be the doer and the thinker because, at a deep level, I knew I wasn't capable of it. My own cleverness lay in linking myself to her. My guiding star. My eternal friend.

I was sitting in the brasserie, eating sea-trout with samphire and thinking along those lines, when a terrifying thing happened. Suddenly I was blinded to everything but the certainty that a man sitting by the window was my father.

My view of him had been obstructed until another man

left his table. The movement caught my eye and I found myself face to face with my father.

I gasped, causing the whisperers beside me to turn their heads my way. Apart from that, I was oblivious of everything except my father.

Fish fell from my fork and splashed untidily on the plate. The whisperers huddled closer and resumed their murmuring, ignoring me the way people do when they find themselves trapped with an oddball.

For a second I was stunned. Just to see him again . . . the sheer coincidence of us both being there . . . the extraordinary chance of us finding each other . . .

My brain was teeming with snatches of thought, incomplete ideas in helter-skelter confusion. '*A miracle . . . No, someone told him I'd be here . . . Should I go to him . . . ? Who is he with . . . ? Speak to him now . . . ? No, better wait . . . Who are those people . . . ? Waylay him on his way out or go to him now?*'

My fork clattered onto the plate. I was standing, clutching my napkin. The whisperers leaned away from me, like trees swaying in the wind. Sweat trickled from my hairline and I raised the napkin to dab it. The linen flapped like a flag of truce.

'*It can't be him,*' a contradictory voice in my head was arguing. '*It isn't possible. Not after so many years. It isn't . . .*'

My eyes hadn't shifted from his face, not once since he came into view, but he was unaware of me. His own eyes were on his companions, taking in one face and then the other. He was listening, smiling, then making a joke at which they laughed. His mind was entirely on them.

I took a step forward, forgetting the table until my thigh slammed up against it so hard that my wine glass crashed onto the plate. A number of people nearby glanced across but there was such a clamour in the room, no one else noticed. My father carried on giving his friends his full attention and sparing nothing for me.

Then where there'd been incredulous joy at finding him,

I sensed change. A cold hollowness was spreading rapidly through me, leaving no space for pleasure or happiness.

When the waitress appeared, full of professional concern, I discovered the disturbed table and my ogling neighbours, and I heard myself saying, in that relaxed tone that rises to occasions while I myself cannot: 'I'm so sorry. I had a bit of a shock but I'm fine now. Really, I'm fine.'

'Is there anything you'd like me to fetch you?'

'No, thank you.'

'If you're sure . . . Then let me replace your wine.'

When she brought it, I rallied sufficiently to order a pudding. The man I'd stupidly believed to be my father continued to sit by the window but the other one had returned and blocked my view nicely. I had no wish to see him again.

I can't tell you what it was about the stranger that suddenly convinced me it wasn't my father. My sense of recognition had overwhelmed my intellect and it was only afterwards, as I spooned up plum tart with mascarpone cream, that I appreciated that any resemblance was to my father as he'd been nearly half a century ago. I think it was the shape of the head and the way the man held himself that put me in mind of him. Also, I'd primed my imagination by reminiscing about the events of that long-ago spring.

Those events trouble me in dreams, but I do know they're merely dreams and I've trained myself to ignore them. There are two that recur. In one a hand brushes my face and in the other my mother is mocking me. The scene in the brasserie was the first time I've been fooled into seeing a person who wasn't there. It made me question my ability to carry through the scheme to trace Sandy. I began to worry about suffering delusions and panic.

Quite honestly, I don't know what I'd be risking in looking for her. I survive by slamming down that shutter: on one side of it the horror of my mother's murder, and on the other the rest of my life. I cope with the three anniversaries – the murder, the hanging and Sandy's birthday – but perhaps they're all I'm equipped to cope with.

They do say that, as you get older, sad events return to haunt you. You hear of elderly women driven to despair and neurosis by guilt over teenage pregnancies which ended in adoption or abortion. Ancient tragedies can engulf. Sitting there over my plum tart and my espresso, I was fearful that mine might.

You've noticed what I'm doing, haven't you? You've spotted my habit of sliding away from the subject. The subject here isn't really whether I'll crack up if I talk to my childhood friend. No, what I should be explaining is why encountering my father was so traumatic.

I'll try. However, sliding away is a device that comes naturally. It's my prime survival technique. I've been doing it, more or less consciously, ever since . . . But no, not now. If your listening is to be of any help, you must hear it all.

Very well. My father. I'll talk about him. I've already mentioned he was frail after the war. Back in those days, any infirmity could be blamed on the war and who could argue with that? People definitely said John Morden had been changed by it and I grew up believing it to be so. Either he'd been shot or blown up or had his nerves shaken to pieces. Nobody told me which.

This lack of information didn't trouble me. There were countless things I was 'too young to know about', if the adults I badgered were to be believed. I filed my father's wartime experience away with those. Living in a situation, you're inclined to accept it and not show the degree of curiosity you might if the story was unfolding elsewhere.

If you can bear an example, I recall showing naked interest in the fate of the deaf mute who lived at the top end of The Avenue. From hanging around outside the primary school while we were chanting our tables, he graduated to arson and 'had to be put away'. I used to study his brothers walking to school tainted with shame, and I squandered hours wondering what it was like in their house now he'd gone. Did they sit around fretting or were they glad to see the back of him? Did they visit him, wherever he was? And if you got yourself put away, how long was it for? Once, the greengrocer's son was sent to prison and yet he seemed to be back in the shop in a flash, much to the annoyance of the people he'd robbed.

Inevitably, it was Sandy the outsider who challenged the opinion that my father was numbered among the war wounded.

'He doesn't get a pension,' she said.

'I don't know whether he does.'

'I'm telling you. He doesn't. My auntie works for the Assistance and she said he doesn't.'

I shrugged, trying to be casual, but I was suspicious about where this was heading. Often what she said was inconsequential but occasionally she would be building up to revelations. She was an extremely useful source of information, telling me things I wouldn't have learned otherwise. Not everything she passed on was accurate but that's the chance you take when you listen to gossip.

Sandy wasn't deterred by being wrong, neither was she apologetic. Being a successful gossip requires a particular turn of mind, don't you think? The Minches were a family of gossips. Information gravitated towards them and it was their pleasure and their duty to disseminate it. With Sandy alert in the town, and her cousin Peter eavesdropping in his parents' pub, I was well-served with news. On reflection, I don't think she ever told me anything good.

Her bad news about my father's lack of pension undermined his status as wounded war hero. Well, to the extent that I began to take a critical interest.

As Sandy remarked: 'We can see what's wrong with the old parky. He has a scar on his face and only one eye.'

'Shrapnel,' I said, proudly identifying the cause.

She capped me with: 'Yes, the Somme.' Then: 'And everyone knows Mr Todd went into the army with two legs and came out with one.'

The one-legged chip-shop owner was one of the town's characters, singled out not only by disability but by a penchant for wearing his medals pinned to his overall while frying.

Sandy came to her point. 'But your father, nobody can make out what's supposed to be wrong with him. And he isn't paid a pension for it. It can't be anything to do with being in the army.'

I tried asking my mother. She said I was far too young to be bothering about such things. She laughed at me, then shooed me out of her way because she was eager to look in her wardrobe and decide what to wear that evening. When I asked, I was told she was going to a business meeting.

For a minute or two I lounged in the bedroom doorway, watching her nicotined fingers whisk clothes out and hold them up against herself in the mirror, before thrusting them back where they came from. There was a floaty dress in what she'd taught me was dusty pink. She looked like a blancmange in it so I was glad when it was rejected. Next was a blue crepe affair with a faint pattern of butterflies. That looked attractive but while she was holding it against her I saw her mirrored face pucker. She sniffed the fabric and flung the dress down, muttering about the cost of dry cleaning. All I could smell was the acrid combination of stale scent and tobacco smoke that clung to the contents of the wardrobe.

She opted for her black dress, brushed at a rime of make-up inside the neckline, and hung it up on the wardrobe door.

'Are you still there?' she asked, pretending to rediscover me.

I didn't say anything. I stretched as tall as I could against the door-frame, as if I was posing to have my height measured. She used to do that when I was little. I wonder whether the marks have survived? She scratched them into the panelling of the hall at our house in The Avenue. But it was only one of her fads. The highest mark was lower than three feet from the floor.

When she went into the bathroom, I took down the black dress and held it against myself. I looked grotesque, a young girl emerging from the folds of a sophisticated grosgrain dress. I wanted to rip it apart, force her to stay home instead of going off to her business meeting.

But if I wrecked this dress there were Dusty Pink and Butterfly Blue. There was no use damaging it.

Instead, I dragged the dress on over my own, straining to fasten the catch at the back. Then I snatched up the gleaming trinkets from her jewel case and I pinned on brooches, piled on necklaces, and shoved bangles and bracelets up my arms in jingling, clanking profusion. I clipped on a pair of earrings that dangled like chandeliers. I took her powder and changed the colour of my face. And, finally, I used her lipstick and painted full red bows over my own meagre little-girl lips, until they were the luscious lips of a mature woman, a woman dressed up and seeking pleasure.

When the bathroom door opened, I was performing for the mirror, a gross creature whose excesses revealed the finery for the tawdry rubbish it was in reality. I saw her in the mirror and began to turn but she was too quick for me.

Fingers locked in my hair. She yanked me away from the mirror, spun me around, slapped me across the face. Frantic to get away, I was tearing at the bracelets and bangles, casting them away from me, onto the bed, the dressing-table, the floor, anywhere they landed. She wrenched the earrings off. She got me out of the dress. I heard myself whimpering with fright but there was no screaming or shouting, only the savagery of her intense anger.

When my decorations were stripped away, and I was left with only the glaring red lips, she hit me hard across the mouth with the back of her hand. The next thing I remember was lying on the dark-brown landing and hearing her turn the key in the lock on her bedroom door.

You want me to say that I cried, wept into my pillow while she went out and had a good time. Another child might have. On another day *I* might have. But I was dry-eyed, impressed by both my fury and hers. Occasionally, a shocking and astonishing event is followed by perception, an interlude of clear understanding. That's what happened to me on the landing that afternoon.

I knew I'd touched a nerve in her, by dabbling in those matters I was too young to know about. Her violent stripping away of my adornments seemed a remarkable overreaction to the antics of an irritating daughter. Never mind that I lacked the vocabulary or the experience to explain it to myself that day, I later came to believe she'd been attacking an aspect of herself which my performance highlighted.

While I'd come out of the encounter the loser, with tufts of hair ripped out, face bruised and lips swelling, I'd also gained a peculiar sense of power. By such simple means as toying with a lipstick I could send an adult into frenzy.

In the bathroom I rubbed at my face, smearing the lipstick and then soaping and rinsing, soaping and rinsing, for ages until my skin was clear of powder and every trace of red had vanished. Checking in the mirror on the bathroom cabinet, I imitated the scowl that disfigured her usually pretty face while she lambasted me. I mimicked her words, the only ones uttered during the attack.

'I'll kill you, you little bitch.'

I waited a day during which nothing was said about the scene. My father failed to register my red patches and swollen lips. My mother went in and out of the house in her normal way. I waited a second day and felt the dissatisfaction of anti-climax. It didn't seem right for such drama to be overlooked.

Even Sandy didn't know of it. I made up my mind not to tell her and passed off my bruises by inventing a falling downstairs. Perhaps she believed me. If I'd told her the truth, she would have been fascinated and told Peter Minch, and then it would have been tacked onto the news filtering out of the Red Lion.

Another reason I kept it to myself was that I wanted to savour the secret. When you share a secret, it changes. Other people's interpretations and comments alter it. Their degree of interest affects the way you value it. Therefore I kept quiet.

By the third day my attitude was altering, anyway. I was less concerned with anti-climax and increasingly curious about my newly-acquired power. Another gesture was called for, to put it to the test.

When my mother went to a meeting with Dennis Aylard I took the same red lipstick and I wrote on the mirror in her bedroom: 'I'll kill you, you bitch.'

My father was in the kitchen, sitting in the warm spot by the boiler, listening to the Home Service and smoking a Gold Flake, which is what he did most evenings. I wandered about the garden for a while but then it began to rain and I went inside and tried to read a book. I'd learned to concentrate despite the chatter of the wireless in the same room but I couldn't take to the characters. They led happy-go-lucky lives with lots of money for parties and holidays, a car and a servant. We didn't know anyone like that, unless you count Dennis Aylard.

Now and then I thought about the lipstick threat upstairs but I wasn't tempted to wipe it off. I made my father a cup of tea and asked him to tell me about the army and how he'd been hurt. I didn't get as far as asking him about a pension.

He said he hated talking about the war. 'You know that, Ann. It's over and there's no use talking about it.'

I coaxed, trying to come at the subject from different directions, but he tutted and told me to hush. He turned up the volume of the wireless and sank into his habitual moody silence.

After I'd washed up the dirty dishes and put them away, I watched him. He was miles away, as they say. He was barely aware of me and it was painful to see.

That's what I've been striving to tell you about him. He evaded me. He rejected me. There was never a confrontation between us, as there frequently was between him and my mother or, on occasions, between my mother and me. I can't describe for you a drama that demonstrates his casting me off. It was the tiny day-by-day rejections that were so hard to bear. Even when there were only the two of us, I was of no interest to him.

CHAPTER TEN

They were on the roof of the shed. It was a flat roof easily reached by climbing along a branch of the tree. Foliage and the flank wall of the house kept them out of sight from anyone in the house or garden.

'I wish she was dead,' said Ann, in a sullen tone that begged to be challenged.

'You don't really.' Sandy sounded superior, as though her friends were always saying this and she was the sensible counsellor adept at dissuading them.

Ann said flatly: 'You're wrong. Sometimes I do.'

'When she has her business meetings, you mean?'

'They're not business meetings. They're affair meetings.'

Sandy erupted in laughter. 'They're *what?*'

'Shhh. Don't let the whole world know we're up here.'

'Sorry, but what you said . . . It sounds really strange.'

'You know what I mean. You ought to. You're the one who told me about it.'

Normally, it would have hurt her to admit as much but this afternoon nothing mattered.

Sandy looked smug but didn't agree. She changed the subject slightly. 'Anyway, she's gone away with Dennis Duck now.' She made pouty lips and kissy noises.

'Don't say she's gone.'

'You saw her. Running down the garden with a suitcase. We both saw her.'

Ann hadn't seen the case herself. 'She might come back.'

'Might. That's a big word. It's nearly as big as if. If's a *very* big word. That's what my mother says.'

Mrs Minch was a woman who kept up a stream of banal speech. She was kindly, always surrounded by friends and children, including children who were friends of her own children. She managed the muddle without noticing how much of a muddle it was, and she kept talking.

Ann thought Mrs Minch was nice. Lately, she'd taken to wishing she could inveigle herself into the Minch brood, indulging a fantastic idea of swapping her family for Sandy's and living happily ever after. Not that Sandy liked living there: she grumbled about having to look after her little brothers and sisters, and sloped off to Ann's house to avoid it.

Sandy was fond of saying she didn't like *any* grown-ups, that they were stupid. But Ann knew she didn't always mean what she said. Sandy didn't mind Dennis Aylard, for example, although she had silly names for him and said unkind things. Ann noticed Sandy enjoyed his teasing, when he said they were naughty little misses and Sandy Minx was the naughtiest. He would pretend to smack her bottom and make her scoot out of the way. He didn't have a nickname for Ann.

Ann scuffled about until she was kneeling close to the edge of the roof. She stared in the direction her mother had gone.

Mimicking a bossy grown-up, Sandy said: 'Don't fall off.'

Ann replied with an irritated wriggle of the shoulders.

Sandy said: 'I think it was a brown case. Has she got a brown case?'

'My father has one.' She pictured the case, cardboard visible where the shiny skin was scuffed.

'Oh, well, she must have taken his, in that case.'

The accident of the wording amused her. '*In that case.* Did you hear that?'

116

Ann grunted a yes. It wasn't funny. Nothing was, not when your mother was in the act of running away.

Sandy said: 'I wonder what she put in it?'

'In what?'

'In the case, dopey. We're talking about the case. If you were going to run off with him, what would you put in your case?'

Ann didn't want to play this game. She manoeuvred until she was sitting on the edge of the roof with her legs dangling. There was mud on her knees and the tree had snagged threads in her green skirt, but she didn't care.

Sandy carried on, saying: 'Jewellery and evening dresses, I think.'

'Don't forget red lipstick.'

Luckily, Ann wasn't called on to explain the suggestion because Sandy had a list of her own. 'Silk stockings. High heels. A cigarette-holder.'

'My mother doesn't like cigarette-holders.'

'Oh.' Sarcastically she tacked on: 'And a shorthand notebook and a pencil or two in case she has any business meetings.'

Ann distracted her. 'In case. You said in case.'

Having made much of it the first time, Sandy found it necessary to giggle again at the phrase. She pirouetted across the roof, perilously near the edge, and then flung a leg over the branch of the tree.

'Are you going?' Ann's question was out before she considered it.

'I might be.'

'That's a big word.'

Sandy pulled a face at her. 'There won't be anything interesting here now. She's gone. Dennis Mallard's car's gone.'

'How do you know? We didn't hear it drive away.'

'It's obvious. They won't be sitting in the car park when they can be off having an affair meeting.'

Ann wished she too had seen the suitcase in her mother's hand, seen Aylard's car on the patch of land behind the gardens, heard them driving away. Sandy was aware of everything and yet Ann missed it by looking in the wrong direction, just not quick enough.

Astride the branch, Sandy said: 'She *might* die. People get killed in cars, and he's a fast driver. Remember how we skidded coming back the last time?'

Since that day weeks ago, Ann's orders to join them on their jaunts, and Sandy's invitations to do so, had stopped. But the skid wasn't entirely his fault, Ann thought.

She corrected Sandy. 'That farmer drove his tractor out without stopping. You heard what they said.'

'Dennis Duck was still going too fast.' Sandy ran a hand over the rough bark, challenging it to sink splinters into her flesh. 'Anyway, now she's run off and you probably won't see her again.'

Ann bit her lip, averting her face.

'Never mind,' Sandy said. 'I expect she'll send you a postcard. And money. He's awfully rich, everybody says. Fat and rich. He'll feel sorry for you and he'll tell her to send you some money. To sort of say sorry.'

Tartly, Ann remarked that she didn't want his money. Sandy began guessing how much money might arrive and whether it would be cash in a parcel through the post or whether he would prefer postal orders. By the time she finished elaborating it was hard to believe the money existed only in her imagination.

'Anyway,' said Sandy, off at a tangent, 'she isn't your real mother, is she?'

Ann scowled. 'What do you mean?'

'Don't be dim. I told you before.'

Ann remembered then. She'd set it aside, not precisely forgetting but deliberately blinkering herself. Sandy had announced months ago that people were saying Rita Morden wasn't a mother. Ann had overheard conversations reinforcing the idea, comments such as 'She's her father's daughter, not Rita's.'

Now, reviving the subject, Sandy said: 'As she's gone, your real mother could come back. If she wants to. If *you* want her to.'

'My real mother?'

Sandy grew frustrated by Ann's slowness. 'Obviously, if Rita isn't your mother then another woman is. You're bound to have one, aren't you? Rita's only your step-mother. Your real mother is someone else.'

'Who?'

A mighty shrug. Sandy said: '*I* don't know. Whoever your father was married to before.'

'He wasn't married before. He wasn't.'

Sandy peeped at her through slitted eyes. 'I expect they think you're too young to be told.'

Ann shook her head. 'No, he wasn't married to any-one else.'

'Well, then, perhaps he wasn't actually married to . . . to whatever her name is.'

Ann was poised to parry whatever was coming.

Sandy said: 'People don't have to be married to make babies.' And when Ann remained quiet she added archly: 'Especially men.'

Ann's head spun. She was splicing together snippets of adult conversations that seemed to justify Sandy's claims, and yet she was far from convinced. If her father had been at home she would have flown into the house and demanded the truth of it, but he was out buying a new valve for the wireless.

Meanwhile, Sandy kept on at her, not giving her a chance to think. She was trotting out the names of various people, some film stars and others local folk, whose parentage was in doubt or else all too obvious. It wasn't encouraging. It wasn't a list Ann had any wish to join.

She slapped her hands over her ears. 'You're making it up. I don't believe you.'

But all the same, the idea that it might be true was exciting.

CHAPTER ELEVEN

Richard King was wearing a new pair of glasses. Biggish frames, dark brown plastic.

'What do you think?'

'They make you look like an owl,' Gillian Spry said, not unkindly. And when his face fell: 'A cuddly owl.'

'Oh. I was hoping for gravitas.'

'Sorry. Definitely cuddly owl.'

She knew which one. The toy belonged to her niece and was, unimaginatively, named Owlie. Yes, the optician had turned Richard into Owlie. The glasses didn't make him look mature and wise, they made him look wide-eyed and vague.

Richard, peering at his reflection in the office window, was still on the lookout for the serious-minded young man he'd faced in the mirror at the optician's. He failed. Between the high-street shop and the office a hundred yards away something weird had occurred. He'd been transformed into a cuddly owl.

He said: 'I don't suppose they'd take them back.'

She was reading the Winterlea dossier and didn't break off as she answered. 'I shouldn't think so. It isn't as though there's actually anything wrong with them.'

'Doesn't turning the customer into a figure of fun count?'

'You're a lawyer, you work it out.'

He removed the offending glasses and put them on his

desk. There was just about space for them amidst the piles of papers, the unopened post and miscellaneous detritus.

Gillian suspected his flat was a mess, too. She was right but would never find out because he'd promised himself not to allow her over his threshold. One glimpse into her tidy riverside loft had convinced him it would be a terrible mistake.

She was evolving the theory that each time he was dumped by a girlfriend he lapsed into sloth, only to be rescued from the sulks by a new love. She hoped the next girl would arrive before long. If she were to believe Richard's carefully placed hints, his life was an unbroken chain of amorous adventures. She didn't believe that but tactfully pretended to.

'Let's hear it, then,' he said, reverting to the conversation interrupted when he'd slipped out to collect his glasses. He rubbed the bridge of his nose where the unfamiliar pair had left a red patch.

'Right.'

She swung her chair away from the computer and pulled towards her a notepad covered with her firm, confident handwriting. Before she began she clicked a switch on the telephone to prevent them being interrupted by calls.

'It comes down to this,' she said. 'In nine cases we know of, Marcus Winterlea's evidence in court differed from his original findings and was effectively tailored to suit the prosecution. In those nine cases his evidence was crucial in securing a conviction.'

He broke in to say: 'Most of them date back to the Fifties and Sixties, right?'

'Six do but the Dancing Doll case was in 1947, Middlemarch was 1972 and Restoril was 1975. Anyway, our nine cases show that over a period of around thirty years, which is to say most of his career, he obligingly twisted his evidence to help convict people against whom there wasn't other forensic evidence.'

'So up until December 1964, when the death penalty was abolished, he was getting them hanged.'

'Yes, but don't overlook the significance of the 1957 Homicide Act classifying murders as capital or non-capital offences. After that came in it was harder to get yourself hanged.'

'Or have Mr Winterlea arrange it for you.'

She flipped over a page. 'Rhea was hanged for killing Doone in the Dancing Doll case. The family didn't accept the verdict and five years ago they produced evidence to substantiate his claim that he'd been in Scotland. Apparently, the police hadn't interviewed the alibi witness.'

She worked her way through the list. In a deathbed confession, a petty criminal admitted a murder for which Restoril had been hanged. In posthumous memoirs a member of a notorious London gang described how he'd shot a man through the head and let Bacton, a member of a rival gang, be executed for it. In several cases families battled to track down people who confirmed alibis or else offered telling tidbits of information that cast a different light on a case. Two resourceful men, whose death sentences were commuted to life imprisonment, were devoting their years of freedom to clearing their names.

Gillian cited examples. 'Sometimes all Winterlea did was alter the estimated time of death to make it fit in with other timings. Helmdon, for instance, didn't dispute he broke into the factory and stole the nylons, but he insisted he was there around 8.30 and saw nobody. The murdered caretaker was originally said by Winterlea to have died between 10.00 and midnight. Ross Pickford, who was a detective inspector on that case, discovered that Helmdon was busily selling nylons in the Green Man pub in Hackney at 10.00. So, lo, Winterlea's opinion becomes that the caretaker was killed between 8.00 and 10.00. Helmdon was hanged.'

Richard picked up his glasses and began to twirl them as he spoke. That's how he broke the previous pair, playing with them until one day the arm snapped off and they flew across the room. Jumping up to retrieve them, he'd stepped on them.

He said: 'Well, the case against Winterlea stacks up very

neatly. Nine instances that we know of. And Ross Pickford was involved in, what, three of them?'

'Yes, three. But don't forget the two men didn't always work in the same region.'

'I know. And now you're going to say the first thing Winterlea did after he moved was fix the Rita Morden case.'

Richard hadn't come round to sharing her enthusiasm for the case. He felt the Winterlea dossier was already strong and nothing but repetition would be gained by adding Rita Morden. He even caught himself wishing Stephen Kuyper would resurface again from the mysterious depths into which he sank between telephone calls, and provide conclusive information that would get them off the Rita Morden case.

Gillian riffled a few pages until she reached her notes on the Rita Morden affair. 'I'm cautious about this one. Winterlea's original notes are difficult to read but when he gave evidence he said she died between 9.30 and 10.00, which is unusually specific. However, there's nothing to say he didn't think so all along or that it isn't true.'

'You're bothered by that starting-handle, though.'

'Yes, he was adamant it was the murder weapon, and the prosecution wanted to hear that because the handle belonged to Aylard and his fingerprints were on it.'

'Palm prints, too.'

'Yes. But from what one can decipher of the notes Winterlea made during his examination of the body, he's describing subdural haemorrhage caused by fractured bone driven into soft tissue. In other words, he decides she was whacked pretty hard on the head, four blows. The words "rough wooden implement" are fairly clear and also "splinters of wood" which it seems he noticed in her hair and wounds.'

Richard was wearing an expression of utter distaste. He always disliked hearing details of the damage.

Ignoring his revulsion, Gillian pressed on. 'By the time he's in court he's convinced it was one blow from an iron bar, almost certainly a car starting-handle. And when the defence ask about splinters of wood he says they probably got there while the body was lying undiscovered beneath trees.'

Richard, getting to grips with the unpalatable business, elaborated. 'Multiple blows send blood flying all over the place but you might strike once without being messy. They didn't find blood on Aylard, did they?'

'Not a speck. You see how Winterlea's change of opinion serves the prosecution? If he'd gone onto the witness stand and talked about four blows from a weapon made of rough wood, the defence would have been delighted. The defendant had no blood on his clothes or in his car, neither did he have a bloodstained wooden implement. Instead, the court was told about only one of the blows, that it was "almost certainly" caused by an iron starting-handle, and that Aylard owned one. Well, as a car owner he would, wouldn't he?'

Gillian dropped the pad on her desk and prowled to the window. 'I'm cautious, as I said, Richard, but if this wasn't another deliberately mismanaged case then it was a genuinely bungled one. There's that story I heard from the retired editor, remember. He was pally with police officers and claims he had misgivings about the way the inquiry homed in on Aylard.'

There was a pause while she watched a woman with a push-chair crossing the road and a cyclist weaving around them. She wished she were on the New York flight with Geoff. His days in London were too short, her trips to the States rarer. It was no way to run a love affair. Well, at least she'd driven him to the airport this morning, seen him to the barrier, spent every last second with him. Now she felt empty. When you felt like that there was only one thing to do. Work. It was a huge effort to arouse interest in the wretched Winterlea business, or anything else.

Richard broke into her thoughts. 'Tell me about Aylard's background.'

Gillian plucked the answers from her memory. 'He made his money on the black market. Smuggled cigarettes were a big item. When he met Rita Morden he had an estranged wife and child, plus a string of former mistresses. The police were interested in him because his name recurred during their inquiries into some major robberies. I don't mean he went out clad in a balaclava and carrying a sawn-off shotgun, but he was suspected of being behind the raids.'

He spotted a flaw. 'Not a Mister Big. He doesn't sound right for that.'

'Oh no, they thought he was involved with a network of criminals. In fact, although they kept looking into his activities and hauled him in for questioning after one robbery, they were never able to link him with any of the big crimes. He wasn't charged with anything, until the day he was charged with murdering Rita Morden.'

'So the old editor had private information about the police taking a previous interest in Aylard?'

'Yes, Mr Pritchard and two detective inspectors drank in the same club in the town. He knew they'd had Aylard in their sights for years. But, as he said, ripping off Customs and Excise by smuggling, or hiring a couple of thugs to break into a warehouse, isn't the same as bashing your girlfriend over the head in her own back garden.'

'Because one's business and the other's personal?'

Gillian came to a halt by the window and watched the umbrellas gliding below. 'I think that was broadly his idea. Mind you, the prosecution argued that Aylard and Rita rowed because she realised his business was illegal. She'd been used several times as a front. Mr Pritchard says the police were disappointed not to find a witness to the row, especially as it was supposed to have taken place in or close to the garden where a party was being held.'

Richard risked a joke. 'Perhaps they were rocking and rolling too loud to hear.'

'I think that's what's called an anachronism,' she said sweetly. 'Rock was later. Bill Haley and the Comets shot across our skies in 1955.'

He pretended to be chastened. 'I never was any good at history.'

126

'Anyway, back to Mr Pritchard, if you don't mind. My talk with him revealed a discrepancy between what was stated at the trial about events that evening, and what people previously told the staff of their friendly local paper.'

'Witnesses changing their minds?'

'No,' she said, 'it was a matter of witnesses not being called to give evidence. Another fine example of British justice in action: the prosecution selected witnesses whose evidence supported the case against Aylard and ignored the rest. If they'd admitted the existence of the others, doubts would have arisen over Aylard's whereabouts that evening.'

'Presumably he couldn't produce an alibi.'

Aylard, she told him, mentioned alibi witnesses but the police were unable to trace them. 'One of Mr Pritchard's reporters interviewed a neighbour who left the party at 9.30 for fifteen minutes to check on her daughter who was left at home alone. As her house was in the street behind The Avenue, she went through the gardens which meant crossing the patch of land in between, the spare plot they call the car park. She was certain Aylard's car wasn't there then.'

'And who last saw Rita?'

'Well, not necessarily Mr Jermyn who went onto the witness stand. He described seeing her in the garden at about nine but Mr Pritchard's senior reporter interviewed a guest who was convinced he spoke to her in the side entrance to her house half an hour later. He said he was arriving late, she was coming out of a side-door and they said hello.'

Richard wanted to know whether the man knew Rita and was sure it was her.

'No, he hadn't met her before.'

He stifled a yawn. They were getting bogged down, the emphasis sliding from Winterlea to Aylard. He was wary of Gillian's tendency to re-investigate every case that came to their attention. In his blacker moments he suspected she would like to work her way through the entire criminal history of England, starting with the arrow in the eyeball in 1066 and taking it from there. Well, she wouldn't succeed in dragging him along. He knew how to dig his toes in.

Putting on his glasses, he peered at the calendar poking out of his clutter on his desk. As wavering Mr Justice Sniffle he read the day's slogan. 'Injustice anywhere is a threat to justice everywhere.'

Gillian laughed. 'As your honour pleases, but Martin Luther King said it first.'

She stopped umbrella-watching and went back to her desk, aware that Richard was restive and possibly with good reason. 'I didn't intend to get engrossed in the Morden case, you know, but so many aspects make me distinctly uncomfortable. The police home in on a man they've wanted to nail for ages. The pathologist adjusts his evidence to please them. And the press have a field-day because there's a nasty little spiv in the dock and they've got a lively tale of fast living.'

'Don't forget the two girls who could easily have discovered the body. The daughter and her friend. The local paper enjoyed Tragic Ann, didn't it, in the days before the arrest?'

'And *she* was muddled, too. First she says she saw her mother at one time, later she changes it. First she says Sandy was at the party but later she says no, she'd been to Sandy's house.'

He jibbed at that. 'No, Gill, I won't let you read any significance into a little girl getting into a muddle when her mother's just been murdered. She must have been in a terrible state, and the doctor might have given her something that half knocked her out. You really can't . . .'

She flung up her hands in surrender. 'OK, OK. You're right. I'll shut up about it and concentrate on our friend Winterlea.'

So they did.

CHAPTER TWELVE

Even while the words were tripping off my tongue I knew it was foolish. 'I'm a journalist.'

And then, naturally, I faced questions and fired back lies. Lies, I hate them. If you aren't careful you find yourself mired in dishonesty and it's completely impossible to back out. On occasions, a simple lie is effective but only if you're capable of sticking to it come what may. Saying I was a journalist was the other sort of lie, the kind that leads to others.

Luckily, I had the wit to say I was a freelance rather than on the staff of a newspaper or magazine, let alone working in television. Television would have been fatal. You know how people treat it as a branch of show business. I would never have escaped if I'd mentioned television. No, I'd still be standing there making up answers to queries about what Trevor MacDonald is like in the office.

'I'm a journalist,' I said, and the two women in the council offices of the pampered little West-country town launched their assault. They didn't wait for replies.

'Who do you work for?' This from the elder of the pair, a matronly thirty thanks to an ill-fitting suit that made her belly stick out.

'Do you know Lindy Loughborough? She writes about gardening. I met her once.' The younger woman had the unhealthy pallor of the compulsive dieter. Perhaps she was impressed by Ms Loughborough's musings on low-calorie lettuce.

Her colleague's contacts weren't confined to the editorial floors. 'My cousin's daughter's boyfriend's aunt sells advertising space for the *Mirror*. Adrianna Boulton. I wonder whether you know her?'

'Oh, you're a freelance. Er . . . well, I suppose you know people on all the papers?'

Eventually I broke in, by looking at my watch and pleading: 'Sorry, I'm in rather a hurry. I wonder whether you would mind looking it up for me?'

They rootled around and returned with a fresh line of enquiry.

'What do you think of the way the press are covering the story of the missing child in Newtown?'

'Or the way they harassed that poor man in the Forest of Dean?'

I stuck out a hand towards the piece of paper the elder of the two had put on the counter. She didn't relinquish it immediately. I read it upside down.

Sandra Brown, 2 Uffington Road.

Before she accepted there was no excuse to prolong our conversation, I had to make a show of comparing my watch with the clock on the wall beside her. Then she pushed the paper towards me. I took it.

'Thanks so much. You've been really helpful.'

As I was leaving, the younger one said: 'Oh, er . . . don't papers pay when you help them?'

The begging surprised me but I laughed it off. 'I'm not a paper, only a humble freelance.' Before they could argue, I shot through the door into the rainy street.

I walked a hundred yards down the High Street, wondering whether it was possible they were right. Of course I'd heard of cheque-book journalism but I never dreamed it extended to tips for every question answered, every favour rendered. Surely not, but I decided there and then to abandon my disguise as a reporter.

At the corner of the street I entered a hotel which

had a notice-board outside proclaiming morning coffee. The building was pleasantly old-fashioned but modernised inside to a comfortable standard: chintz arm-chairs and thick carpet, touches of chinoiserie, tasteful prints hanging against flowery wallpaper. Kate in her English Traditional would fit in perfectly.

That, at any rate, is what the lounge you walk into from the street is like. But you can't judge the state of the bedrooms from the degree of luxury displayed in the foyer, can you?

Morning coffee was being served in that lounge. Two tables were occupied. A couple of women, sixtyish with country accents, were trilling about the inspired selection of soft furnishings in a shop which seemed to be called Dimity. I decided it was likelier to be the name of the shop than its owner.

One woman, who held her grey hair off her face with a black velvet Alice band, said: 'She's absolutely marvellous and, of course, one likes to support local shops whenever one can.'

Her friend with the Liberty peacock scarf agreed. 'Oh, definitely.'

At the other table a shrunken white-haired man with a tremor struggled to read the *Daily Telegraph*.

After I'd ordered coffee, I asked the receptionist for a copy of the town plan. Taking me for a tourist, she swung the page round to face me and pointed out the castle ruins and the church.

'Are we in the main shopping street?' I asked.

Before telling me, she had to loop her long loose hair behind her ears. Then she leaned over the plan and trailed a finger along the street with the hotel in it and then down one that left it at a tangent.

'Most of the shops are in this area,' she was saying. 'You'll find the market here, but not much will be going on today. Market day's Saturday. Up here you'll find mostly antique shops.'

My coffee arrived while I was thanking her. I ran my eye briefly over the plan, then inspected the reverse. Framed by advertisements for a variety of businesses, was a gazetteer of street names. Working from the end, I quickly spotted Uffington Road.

There was a telephone in the hallway leading off the lounge but no directories. I rang Directory Enquiries and offered up the surname Brown and 2 Uffington Road. A minute later I was writing down a telephone number.

And then I realised I had no intention of ringing it. Absolutely no inclination whatsoever.

My legs felt watery as I went back to my cooling coffee. I berated myself with questions such as 'Why did I come here?' and 'Why did I start this absurd chase?' I didn't have anything to say to Sandy, not seriously. There wasn't really any advantage in alerting her to the CJI interest. Now I came to think of it, there was a compelling reason *not* to. If I spoke to her, I would risk her revealing the fact to Gillian Spry.

After weeks of imaginary conversations, in which I warned Sandy, I grasped that my reasoning was adrift. Unless her personality had changed radically, she wouldn't care what I thought. Any approach from me would amaze her and it was inconceivable she would keep it to herself. She might actually contact CJI rather than wait for them to trace her.

Oh, yes. I could imagine her doing that.

Drama, you see, was always irresistible to her. What was true, she exaggerated. What was non-existent, she invented. Ordinary things were too dull for her, and Sandy unfailingly worked a spell that evolved them into something exciting.

I felt hot, unable to breathe regularly, shaken by my narrow escape. At every stage while I was hunting her down, I'd been notching up tiny triumphs, but they were nothing of the sort. They were steps on the way to disaster. I'd drawn back but not until I was teetering on the brink.

Supposing I'd dialled her number? Within seconds I could have spoken to Sandy, heard her voice and given my name, perhaps been unable to prevent myself saying I was in her home town, so close to her it would be crazy not to meet. Without appreciating it, I would have taken the fatal step.

Sweat dampened my forehead and I surreptitiously used a handkerchief, but no one was taking any notice. The *Daily Telegraph* trembled in the old man's hands. The women's fluting voices had stopped discussing Dimity and moved on to Cara, who was marvellous. I dropped the street plan into my bag and raised my cup to my lips, able at last to swallow. The coffee was cold. I drank it anyway.

Gillian Spry marched through the door as I was marshalling my bag and car keys and rising to leave.

'Anna!' Her voice was a touch too loud in the quietness of the room.

The Cara and Dimity women gave us their unashamed attention. The *Daily Telegraph* was lowered. Behind the reception desk a long-haired young woman was poised to be helpful.

'Good heavens,' I said, 'fancy seeing you here.'

It's depressing the way we reach for these hackneyed expressions when we're caught by surprise, and I'm as bad as anyone. At least Gillian was being ironic when she replied: 'Small world.'

Before I knew it she'd ordered two cups of coffee and was sitting opposite me.

She said, in a coy manner unsuited to her: 'I suppose we're on the same errand.'

I gathered my wits. 'You first.'

'Desperately seeking Sandy.'

'No,' I said, shaking my head. 'I'm not seeking her.'

The lie was slight, a matter of chronology. I hurried on with: 'Have you found her? Here? I imagined her swallowed up in one of the bigger cities.'

Gillian smiled but it was a smile I failed to interpret. 'She lives here, Anna. She's married to a company director but separated. She has two or three children, grown-up now, of course.'

As casually as I could manage, I put the crucial question. 'Have you spoken to her?'

'Not yet.'

I don't know how I sat there, pretending to be grateful

for the cup of coffee she'd bought me while it was obvious it was a device to stop me rushing away. I was anxious about what she might say to me and how well I would stand up to it. Soon, though, I decided she wouldn't drop bombshells while we were under such flagrant observation.

Gillian said: 'Would you like to meet her? I could suggest it to her.'

With an effort I resisted shouting an immediate 'No.' Everything was topsy-turvy again and I didn't know what to do for the best. I stalled.

'We could talk about that another day,' I said. 'After you've seen her yourself, I mean.'

'Very well.' She occupied herself by stirring sugar into her coffee and drinking.

Perhaps she was deliberately letting me make the next move. I can't say because I didn't know her well enough to guess. After a pause I said: 'Actually, I thought you *would* have spoken to her by now.'

Another lie. What I truly believed was that if Gillian had spoken to Sandy, she would have come winging back to me. She hadn't. We'd had no contact for weeks.

Ironic again, she offered a mock apology. 'Sorry to be so slack. But we're frantically busy and Sandy is peripheral. As you know, our enquiry centres on the pathologist.'

'Of course.'

There was a hiatus. She appeared to be waiting for me and I was at a loss to understand what she expected from me.

At last it occurred to me to ask about my mother's case and whether it was likely to feature in CJI's report on Winterlea. When she and Richard King were at my house, that hadn't been clear.

I framed the question in such a way it didn't involve words like murder that might heighten our neighbours' interest.

Gillian replied without hesitation. 'There *are* aspects of his work on the case that continue to arouse suspicion. I'm afraid I can't say anything more definite than that.'

I was rueful. 'I suppose it was too much to hope there was nothing in it for you. Well, I dare say I take a selfish view, but it will be a shame if a forty-five-year-old tragedy is opened up again for public scrutiny.'

Underlying anxiety made me sound uncharacteristically pompous. I wish I was able to use irony with the ease that Gillian does. If you have that knack you can say anything and get away with it. Still, I shouldn't complain because I'm able to sound calm under pressure and that's a greater asset.

There was a little to-ing and fro-ing around us as the old man left cash on his table and began an unsteady progress to the door. A tubby young waiter dashed up to offer him an arm, and it became apparent this was a regular service. Having deposited the man on the pavement, the waiter came back inside and a general discussion broke out.

The receptionist began it with a sigh and a shake of the head that set her long brown hair swinging. 'Poor Mr Smith.'

'So sad,' said the woman with the velvet hair-band.

Her companion diagnosed. 'Parkinson's.'

The robust little waiter reported. 'He's like a feather. There's no weight to him.'

Hair-band said: 'He used to be captain of the bowls club, you know, a marvellous man, but now . . .'

Everyone observed a minute's silence for what had already been lost of Mr Smith.

Then Gillian said to me: 'I'm glad I've run into you, Anna. It gives me a chance to quiz you. If you don't mind, that is.'

She'd made it impossible for me to do other than agree. 'Go ahead.'

There was no deflecting her. Without a sneezing Richard King or the equivalent, she could grill me as fiercely as she liked. I had to put up with it lest my reluctance made her suspicious about my reasons.

She focused on the confusion about the time my mother was last seen alive and by whom. She wasn't happy with the evidence Marcus Winterlea gave about the time of death. For a while we talked about that, with Gillian reminding me of details I'd long forgotten about the trial and telling me others I'd never known. Then she slipped in a question and I trotted out my usual story about not remembering.

After ten minutes of this we moved on to an area I did know about and I could tell she was convinced I did. My vague replies grew increasingly unsatisfactory. Something further was required. I could do one of two things: tell her part of the truth or justify my refusal to answer.

We parried a while longer and then I made my decision. Batting away her latest attempt, I said, in what I trusted was a relaxed fashion: 'Memory's a funny thing, isn't it? We can't select what we retain. Often it's the material we want to hang onto that vanishes and at other times we throw out whatever is too painful to keep.'

'Oh, yes, but when you concentrate on remembering, you can recover memories you thought lost. I frequently talk to people who say they can't remember but later, perhaps weeks later, it comes back to them. Our conversation sets them thinking and eventually the memory is triggered.'

I looked penitent. 'I'm a great disappointment to you.'

I guessed I'd said that to her before and in much the same way, half ashamed and half frustrated. As I've told you, my method of dealing with questions has become a habit. I tell the tale that keeps me free from trouble, and in the telling it grows increasingly real. To me, at least.

To Gillian? She'd heard me twice now and I sensed she was picking up the rigid way my mind works. But wait. If she'd taped me at my house, then she'd heard me over and over and had analysed how I glide away from matters I don't want to face. It was no good, it was necessary for me to offer her a decent explanation.

'Look,' I said, in the tone of one offering a confidence. 'I don't like to harp on this but I did have a rotten time after the murder. You know about the family leaving the town but do you realise how fragmented we became? Having been at the heart of quite a large family I was suddenly . . . well, to all intents and purposes, alone.'

She was looking sympathetic, as I'd intended.

I went on. 'The upheaval was tremendous and I didn't cope with it well. People say children are resilient but usually they say it because they pray it's true. In my case, it wasn't. I was shattered.'

By now she was murmuring pity.

I said: 'I've come to believe the reason I don't have memories of that awful business is that I fought against them. You might think that was the wrong thing to do but I was only eight, don't forget, and nobody was giving me professional advice. Nowadays you only have to sneeze and you're surrounded by counsellors. But the idea when I was young was that I should put it out of my head. Plenty of people told me that. So I did and it stayed out.'

My declaration made Gillian uncomfortable. In reply, she recited a few platitudes but made no effort to question me further. I began fiddling with my bag, a prelude to going to the cloakroom. She misinterpreted, thinking I was leaving and said she would pay for my earlier coffee, too. She was unusually flustered. I could tell she thought she'd made a mess of the interview but there was no harm in letting her think that.

Then she said: 'Anna, before you go there's something else.'

'Oh?'

'It's Meryl Aylard. She's asking to meet you.'

I frowned. 'I've never heard of her.'

'Dennis Aylard's daughter.'

I hated Gillian Spry at that moment. Hated her for pursuing me, hated her for doubting me, and hated her especially for bearing this message to me.

Gillian, studying my conflicting emotions, said: 'You knew he had children, didn't you?'

Shaking my head I denied it. Another lie, a stupid one because that sort of information had been in the newspapers. A life that leads to a famous murder trial in an Assize Court is a life recorded in detail by the press.

I hedged. 'Well, I don't know whether I used to know. I didn't know now. I haven't been thinking about it.'

I shut up before I rambled, June-like, and let out too much.

'Anyway,' I said, 'I'm appalled at the idea of having to meet her.'

Gillian put out a placatory hand. 'Oh, Anna, no. You mustn't think you *have* to. You don't have to do anything. Meryl asked me whether I thought you'd be prepared to and all I could say was I'd ask.'

'You haven't told her where I live?'

'Good lord, no! We're strict about confidentiality. You really mustn't worry we'd let that sort of information escape.'

I accepted that with a nod. 'But you obviously told her you'd talked to me because otherwise she wouldn't have made the request.'

'No, it wasn't like that. She approached CJI because her family heard we were looking into a number of cases involving Marcus Winterlea. They're convinced Dennis Aylard was innocent and were hoping our researches were proving it for them.'

I opened my mouth to object but there was nothing worthwhile I could say. I let her carry on.

'Anna, she telephoned me three weeks ago to say the family are launching a campaign to clear his name.'

'I see. You're saying you provided her with evidence.' I couldn't keep the accusation out of my voice.

'No, I'm not. I've been truthful with you, believe me. There *are* those curious aspects that you and I have been going over, but we don't have evidence.'

I forced out the difficult question. 'And Aylard's daughter, Meryl, what exactly does she have?'

Gillian considered how to answer. Then: 'I regard what she told me as private. You'll understand that, of course. But if you asked my opinion about her progress I'd say she was a long way from proving innocence. If her campaign achieves anything, it will be to draw the case to public attention.

Therefore, if our investigation into Winterlea results in a review of several of his cases, the Rita Morden affair would almost certainly be included.'

I swallowed hard. 'Please, tell me what she said about me.'

Gillian made a helpless gesture. 'The murder was forty-five years ago. Who's left, apart from those who were young then? She knows from newspaper files that Rita Morden had an eight-year-old daughter and that you were at the house the evening she was killed. So she said to me: "If you come across her during your enquiries, please ask her to talk to me."'

I gave a sigh, almost a groan. 'My answer has to be no. I haven't anything to tell her. Well, you discovered that for yourself. I'm a completely useless witness, whatever she's trying to prove. Tell her that, would you?'

'If that's what you want.'

Shifting the focus I asked about Meryl Aylard. 'How old was she when . . .' It was too dreadful to say and I left it unsaid.

'When her father was hanged? Eleven.' She left me with the thought for a full thirty seconds before adding: 'Meryl is the child of his marriage. There are also illegitimate ones from other liaisons.'

She was putting pressure on me, in a subtle enough way but I was aware what she was up to.

I said: 'Sorry, I can't help. Don't let her fancy that if she approaches me direct she can talk me round. I have nothing whatsoever to tell her. Make that clear, please, Gillian.'

This time when I picked up my bag I was determined about leaving.

Gillian stayed behind to pay. I walked back up the street in the direction of the car park. The rain had stopped but wind was rippling puddles where gutter drains were blocked. Crossing the road by the church, I discovered I was more disturbed than I'd realised and was stamping along. A knot of elderly folk outside the church hall tucked themselves against a wall as I strode towards them, my manner making it plain I was in no mood to yield to anyone.

As so often, I was displaying one set of emotions and concealing another. My anger wasn't against the world at large, principally it was against myself for becoming entangled with Gillian Spry. I ought to have invented an appointment and not settled down to chat over the coffee cups. I didn't believe we'd met by chance. Easier by far to imagine her following me, guessing I would go looking for Sandy.

Despite her pledge about having always been honest with me, I distrusted her. She'd been underhand. Oh, I didn't doubt she had professional reasons, but that didn't mean I had to be gullible enough to accept her claim to be open and truthful.

I began to worry about what had actually taken place between the woman from CJI and Dennis Aylard's daughter. I suspected Gillian's version was incomplete. Wasn't it more likely she'd *offered* to enlist my assistance for the family's campaign?

Reaching my car, I sat in it for a while running over in my mind what this development signified and what, if anything, I ought to do about it. Answers eluded me.

I took the town plan from my bag and worked out the route from the car park to Uffington Road. There was no apparent danger in driving along it to see what kind of a place it was, but I decided against stopping. If Sandy popped out of her front door and discovered me it would be disastrous, and it would be equally bad if Gillian Spry saw me.

The road out of the town is called Castle Road. It runs downhill and leads roughly north. Uffington Road is a continuation of it. This was ideal because if Gillian was trailing me there would be no proof I was snooping. From the plan, I conjured up a mental picture of Uffington Road: a main road with a ribbon of semi-detached houses, possibly along only one side, a road typical of the outskirts of practically any English town. Most of the houses would date from the nineteen-thirties but there would be recent infill, maybe also a modest block of flats.

When I drove down it I was surprised. Uffington Road runs through open country with a handful of enormous houses standing in mixed woodland and well-distanced from the road. As I trundled by, I caught names on gateposts at the ends of curving drives. Deepdene. Wardour Lodge. Stoddens. Nothing as dull as a street number.

I carried on, wondering which of these mansions Sandy called home. And I was irritated that I was so lacking in imagination I'd assumed her to live in an ordinary house in an ordinary street. Uffington Road was the local Millionaire's Row.

Yet what have you gathered about Sandy Minch? I hope I've shown she has a quick mind, likes to be in control and turns situations to her advantage. If so, you can see how dim I was to assume she'd settled for anything run-of-the-mill.

As much as anything else, it was my inadequacy over this that convinced me I must ignore any temptation to see or speak to her. No knocking on her door. No tapping out her telephone number. Sandy's world is far removed from mine and it's best for both of us if it remains that way.

For a year or two our lives had been intertwined, and with a girlish intensity, but those children have long been strangers to me. Their thoughts and deeds belong to creatures with whom I have no point of contact. The past can't be re-entered and, sadder still, it can't be altered.

I drove on, worrying that Meryl Aylard might pursue Sandy. Then memories jostled in and I could think of nothing but the day of the hanging.

CHAPTER THIRTEEN

They hanged him one November morning, on a foggy, dull day that looked like the end of everything.

Ann woke during the night, roused by the coldness of the china hot-water bottle pressing against her leg and by the suspicion of a hand touching her face. Drowsily, she wriggled away from the bottle but it slid after her.

She didn't trust this bottle. One night it had dribbled and left her a damp patch to lie on. She complained the rubber ring was perished but was told no, it was her own fault for not screwing it up tightly enough.

She was burrowing beneath the bedclothes to retrieve it when realisation struck. At once she was wide awake and fighting her way back to the air, the bottle abandoned.

Bolt upright, trembling, she heard herself muttering: 'It's today. This is the day they're going to do it!'

For a second she feared she was going to scream. She clapped a hand over her mouth and stared horrified into the darkness.

The words became a silent chant. *Today. They're hanging him today.*

The room was icy. She sat there in her thin nightdress letting the temperature punish her body. Gradually, the urge to shout the words aloud, scream her anguish, faded and she felt able to take her hand from her mouth.

Inside her head the chant continued. *'They're hanging him today.'*

Ann was crouching, hands clasped so hard her nails scraped her skin. Her eyes gazed on gruesome, imagined scenes.

'Stop it.' It was the softest of whispers, a desperate order to herself not to stoke up her terror.

But it instantly took on a separate meaning: *'Stop the hanging. Stop the hanging. Stop the hanging.'*

The words were a slogan, paraded on placards in newspaper pictures, but Ann could think of only one hanging, the imminent one, Dennis Aylard's hanging.

'It's today. They're hanging him today.'

She got out of bed, moving as slowly as if the iciness of the room had stiffened her limbs. With outstretched hands she felt her way towards the door. The light switch was by the door. It was an awkward room, an unfamiliar journey.

Misjudging the length of the bed, she blundered into it and stubbed her toe. She ignored the pain and the discomfort of walking over cold linoleum, and continued to the door. She was bent on knowing the time. There was a clock on a cupboard. With a flick of the light switch, she could find out the time.

Ann reached the door and felt the wall to the right of it. Her searching fingers stroked the brown bakelite casing, then the round-headed switch.

As she was poised to press it down, a thought occurred to her and she hesitated.

'If I put a light on, they'll know I'm awake. They'll know I know.'

She stepped back from the switch and made her way to the window. Luckily, there was very little furniture so she didn't crash into anything. In daytime she disliked the room because it was ugly and almost empty. Once upon a time someone had hung tea-coloured wallpaper with a brown ferny print, and it hung there still. The furnishings didn't include a rug, which was mean because outside every door in the passage were peg-and-stuff slip mats, home-made from ruined lisle stockings.

Walking into the room for the first time, she'd been repelled by a musty, dusty, unused smell, a junk-room odour. In a while she stopped noticing that although the dismal look of the place continued to dismay her.

It was a typical spare-room in a house where people didn't bother about making a pleasant guest-room. One of the family actually referred to it, in her presence, as the box-room.

'We've put Ann in the box-room.'

'Oh, that'll be plenty big enough for her.'

She'd ceased to care. The room was just somewhere to sleep until she moved on, or rather until they had enough of her and moved her on.

When she reached the window she fumbled for the curtains and yanked one back a few inches. The rings were rusted and resisted sliding along the pole. Dragging the curtains open or closing them was always a job.

Standing by the window she felt even colder. With one hand she clutched her nightdress against her body while she leaned forward to peer through the glass. Frost filmed the inside of the pane. She rubbed a clear circle and pressed her face close to it.

The village was obliterated by the night. At its heart stood a Norman church and on its tower was a clock. In daylight the village, the church and its clock were clear. The only nice thing about the room was the view from its window.

Ann turned back into the room disappointed. It was the blackest of nights. No stars, no moon, no village, no church. All had been swept away. Only the room around her existed, and her evidence of that was merely her sense of touch.

She wondered again about switching on the light, trying to decide whether one quick flash would be enough to alert anyone. As she seldom woke during the night, let alone moved around, she had no idea whether the people in the neighbouring rooms were light sleepers and would come running to her.

Unkind questions suggested themselves. *'If they came, what would they say? Something like "Don't worry, it's only a nightmare"?'*

For a brief, bitter, moment she was tempted to rouse them to find out what on earth they could say to a nine-year-old girl who realised the man convicted of killing her mother was to hang in a few hours. Instead, she felt her way to the clock and carried it across to the light switch, still uncertain how risky it would be to flash a light.

She hovered, hand on switch, the ticking clock held at the correct angle for a swift glimpse, but she lacked the courage to do it. Seconds passed and she was stuck there, scared, all her anxieties centring on the outcome of clicking the switch.

And then it happened. An initial grating, rather like throat-clearing, was followed by the measured strokes of the church clock. Five. It was five o'clock on the morning Dennis Aylard was to be hanged for the murder of Rita Morden.

Ann put down the alarm clock and climbed onto the bed.

'In three hours they're going to hang him.'

She sat, scrunched up with her chin on her knees, her eyes shut. A tear escaped through her lashes. She tried praying but she had no prayers left. They hadn't worked, how could they? *'Please let it not be true. Please let her be all right. Please don't let them decide he did it. Please . . . please . . . please . . .'*

Now there was only one plea left. *'Please don't let them hang him.'*

And that one was no use, either.

She didn't believe in a last-minute dash through the streets to the prison with a reprieve, although she understood this happened on occasions in the past. She wondered whether Dennis Aylard was putting any faith in a rescue, whether he was also lying awake and counting down the hours.

In the months since his arrest he was gradually trans-formed from an ambitious provincial businessman into a monster. They did it in the press and they did it in conversation. He became a ruthless killer, a greedy evil man who let nothing, not even his passion for his mistress, stand between him and his determination to get richer quicker. Their words changed him until he was no longer the man Ann knew, any more than the Rita Morden of the courtroom was her mother.

She chewed her lip, thinking of him in his cell next to the gallows. Aylard, who loved his big cars and his parties and splashing his money around, had nothing and soon would become nothing. She rubbed her fists into her eyes and wondered whether he was crying, too.

He would be a fool to expect a reprieve. People said that on the day he was sentenced, and again when he appealed to the Home Secretary to commute the sentence to one of life imprisonment, and she heard it repeated yesterday when they thought she was out of earshot.

'If he thinks he's going to dodge the rope, he's got another think coming.'

'His solicitor reckons he's going to fight for a reprieve right up to the last minute.'

'Waste of time. Aylard's as guilty as hell.'

She was picturing him in his cell, a few steps from the spot where they would kill him in the official way at the appointed hour. There would be two prison officers guarding him to prevent him committing suicide; and if he'd been ill or had a bad cold his execution would have been delayed until he was fit. She'd learned a shocking number of things about hanging.

One thing people said was that being executed was the worst way to die because you knew exactly when and how it would be. And if . . .

Ann caught her breath. A faint grinding disturbed the night. The church clock struck five-thirty.

A tremor ran through her thin body. Half-past five in the morning. He would hang at eight. The church clock would strike five more times until he was dead. She knew she was compelled to listen and to count.

Once her trembling subsided, she thought how odd it was she hadn't considered the church clock while worrying about the time. Until several weeks ago it hadn't been working but since then its interruptions were much remarked upon. Her tramp over the chilly linoleum had been completely unnecessary, the penalty for forgetting.

She wondered how efficient she could become at forgetting. People kept telling her she must try to forget rather than brood on what couldn't be changed.

'You're young,' they said. 'You'll get over it. Time is a great healer. You'll see.'

They sounded wise but she was wiser. She knew by instinct that certain kinds of hurt can't heal because they cut you to the soul.

Ann slid down into the bed and rediscovered the cold bottle. She trapped it between her feet and tried to draw up her knees to bring it within hands' reach, but the tightly tucked sheets restricted her movement. She wriggled further down and got a hand to it, then set it gently on the floor beside the bed. She thought, sourly, that they'd made the bed as narrow as a coffin.

'Tomorrow,' she thought, 'I'll make it myself. And I won't jam it against the wall and I won't make it so tight.'

But tomorrow was today, and today was the day they were hanging Aylard. A hollowness opened up inside her chest as she remembered it all over again.

'Forget,' they said to her. 'You must learn to forget.'

But what she'd learned was that after every brief forgetting came a fresh remembrance. She squeezed her eyes tight, afraid of what she knew.

The clock struck six.

Her mind filled with pictures of Dennis Aylard with her mother: in his car, in a pub by the river, in the garden at The Avenue, at a party, in the Red Lion. If it was evening her mother was wearing the dusty pink chiffon dress, or the blue crepe silk one patterned with butterflies, often the elegant black grosgrain dress, but otherwise one of a clutch that Ann didn't know how to describe.

Depending where they were going, she wore a fur stole, one of her silk wraps or an evening coat trimmed with satin. For daytime she had a variety of dresses and suits to choose from, with jewellery, shoes and handbags to go with them. Several of the outfits were mentioned in court.

In the particular scene that lodged in Ann's mind just then, Rita was wearing a sharply-waisted turquoise suit in shantung silk with a big brooch on the lapel. The ornament was a twist of gold encircling a cluster of stones, mainly red, blue and green. The effect was cheap and flashy.

'Hey, you look fabulous,' Dennis Aylard called from his car as she hurried towards him.

Rita cast an anxious glance over her shoulder. She didn't see Ann watching from an upstairs window but Ann didn't matter. The ground-floor windows were the ones Rita checked.

She entered the car and resisted, momentarily, before letting Aylard pull her across to him for a kiss. Freeing herself, she urged him to drive away, not sit there at the entrance to her drive where anyone in the house might notice them. Ann saw her gestures and interpreted correctly.

That was the last occasion she watched their rendezvous outside the house. Since that day, Rita took to slipping out the back way while the Humber waited for her on the patch of rough land beyond the garden. Occasionally Ann heard her mother whispering into the telephone in the hall, usually while her father was engrossed in a wireless programme in the kitchen.

The house shared a telephone line with a house across the road. Party line was a good name for it, Ann thought, because almost all the calls that came were for her mother and they whisked her off to parties in her dusty pink, butterfly blue or smart black, in her fur stole, silk wraps or satin-trimmed coat.

'Socialising is an essential part of business,' Rita explained to Ann.

While she was out, Ann used to poke around in her mother's wardrobe and dressing-table to see what was new.

There was usually something. A pair of French shoes with a matching handbag. A dress or a blouse. A bottle of perfume. Jewellery. A hat, even.

Ann decked herself in the latest acquisitions and minced up and down in front of the mirror, holding herself like the mannequins she saw in magazines. She was a cover girl, she was a film star, for half an hour at a time she was a princess dressed for a ball.

Then she would hang up the garments, scrub off the make-up and sit in her room, hunched by the window, wondering what love was like and how she would know it when it came her way. Dennis Aylard loved her mother. Every wink of jewellery, every stitch of clothing and every inch of high-heels proved it. He loved her and he couldn't stop himself buying her things. Things to make her prettier and posher. Things to help her fit into his glamorous life. And now she'd acquired the things what was there to stop her fitting in entirely, leaving The Avenue for good and joining him in his rich new world? As far as Ann could see, nothing at all.

For months she had watched the moment drawing nearer, felt it in her bones. Sandy Minch had, too, and pointed out the bits Ann missed, which was both a friendly act and a nuisance because then Ann couldn't tell herself she was overdoing it. If Sandy sensed it too, it was indisputably true.

She took Sandy to her mother's room one rainy evening, after Rita had dressed in a grey flannel suit of severe cut and announced a business meeting. She said it was connected with the purchase of potential building land on the edge of town.

Ann's father, who was watching the television set Rita had insisted on paying for the previous Saturday, grunted and walked over to adjust the picture.

'Don't be late, Rita,' he said, without looking away from the screen.

He twiddled with a knob but it was the wrong one and sent horizontal bars, falling, falling, falling down the screen.

The front door closed behind Rita like gunshot. Because he didn't own the house, Ann's father refused to fix the door so that it closed quietly without the need to slam. Ann and Sandy stood in the sitting-room and stared at the screen. Falling, falling, falling until he went round the back of the set, touched another knob and, gradually, the picture steadied.

They watched him counting his paces as he returned to his chair. You weren't meant to sit closer than twelve feet because if you did it damaged your eyes. He decided he'd infringed the twelve-feet limit, and jiggled his chair back a few inches, until it bumped the sideboard. Sandy smirked at Ann and tipped her head towards the door. They went out of the room without a sound.

Upstairs, Ann shared her dressing-up session for the first and last time.

'We ought to be photographed,' said Sandy, preening in the turquoise suit. She had fastened an ornate diamond bracelet watch around her wrist but it was too big and flopped like a loose bangle.

Ann shuddered. 'No, it's a secret.'

'Anyway, we don't have a camera.'

Ann hoped she wouldn't remember the Ilford box her mother had used to snap them in the garden the previous summer. They'd posed, smiling into the sun, for ages until Rita was ready to press the shutter. When the photograph was developed, she chided Ann for wearing a sickly grin. Sandy, who'd eventually given up smiling, was caught with a distinctly knowing look but Rita said how much nicer she appeared.

After a while Sandy thought she heard someone coming into the house so she gave a squeal, kicked off a pair of strappy high heels and began tearing at the suit.

'Hush,' Ann said, and tiptoed onto the landing. Normally, when her mother went out she was gone for hours.

But from below she heard Rita's voice. A thrill of fear darted through Ann. She made 'hurry up' signs at Sandy.

Out of the jacket, Sandy was whipping off the skirt and

thrusting it into the cupboard. In her flurry the big brash brooch came unpinned and caught on one of the hanging garments. She forced the shantung suit into the space, grabbed her own clothes from the bed and fled across the landing to Ann's room. She was still wearing the watch.

Ann was trapped in a brown dress with a mink collar. The zip wouldn't shift. She shoved shoes and bags into the cupboard, whisked up her own pinafore dress and pelted after Sandy.

Sandy burst out laughing. 'Oh, if it isn't a cover girl.'

'Shh. Help me with this zip. Quick.'

They eased two inches of it undone but that was all. Sandy rolled around on Ann's bed in paroxysms of laughter, largely feigned. Annoyed, Ann pulled on her dressing-gown to conceal the dress. Sandy declared this even funnier.

'Shut up,' Ann said, intense. 'And take that watch off.'

The bedroom door opened. No knock or calling out, Rita just walked in as she usually did.

'Sandy?' she said. 'I didn't think you'd still be here.'

Immediately an adult appeared Sandy was always sensible. 'Gosh. I'd forgotten the time.' She had her hand in her pocket, standing casually, concealing the watch.

'You mentioned your mother was expecting you by seven. It's a quarter past.'

Sandy thanked her for the reminder, said goodbye to Ann and was gone. Ann wondered about the watch.

'Well,' Rita began, looking hard at Ann. 'How long has this nonsense been going on?'

Ann was mute. She clutched the dressing-gown around her, unsure what Rita meant. To Ann, so many things were nonsensical.

Rita shot out a hand and wrenched the dressing-gown open. Mink and brown wool spilled out.

Ann flinched, remembering the blows the last time she was caught dressing up in Rita's things. Rita snarled at her to take it off.

'I can't,' Ann admitted. 'The zip's stuck.'

Rita spun her round and tweaked at the zip but it resisted.

She gave a mocking laugh. 'Well, that's *your* problem. You wanted to wear it and it looks as though you're going to have to.'

She went to her bedroom, leaving Ann encased in the hideous brown dress. For an hour Ann squirmed and struggled, alternately trying to undo the zip or to escape from the garment without undoing it. Neither worked.

The effort made her arms sore. She felt generally tired. Worry in itself was tiring, she noticed, and these days she was perpetually worried. Worried Rita would leave, worried Rita would have another row with her father, worried from one moment to the next how Rita would treat her.

Just then she had one of those small revelations, a leap of understanding. She realised she was capable of coping with anything that happened. It dawned on her she knew this because she saw other people doing it. Disasters befell them, their prospects looked hopeless, and yet they managed and their lives went on. All at once, Ann grasped that she could do so, too, and that it was uncertainty that caused all the worry. Once an event had taken place or a situation arisen, people became strong and able to go ahead.

Her theory excited her. She put it into practice straightaway. Knocking on the door of her parents' bedroom, she called out to Rita.

'I can't undo this zip.'

Rita shouted back: 'Hard luck.'

'Mummy, you'll have to undo it.'

Rita was sarcastic. 'Oh, yes? And why should I want to do that?'

'Because if you don't I'm going to ask Daddy to do it.'

There was no answer for a moment and Ann added: 'It's up to you. I'm going to count to ten and then I'm going downstairs.'

A pause, then: 'One.'

Another pause then: 'Two.'

When she reached six there was movement in the room. She heard: 'Blackmailing little bitch.' Then the door was opened and Rita seized her, jerked her round, and tugged at the zip. Ann glimpsed the fancy watch on her mother's arm and was glad Sandy had returned it to the dressing-table on her way out of the house.

Ann decided to keep counting. The zip yielded as she said eight. Ann dropped the dress to her ankles, stepped out of it and marched to her room. She was shaky but she was pleased with what she'd achieved. The blackmailing slur didn't bother her because it seemed inappropriate. All she'd done was take the uncertainty out of a very doubtful situation.

In a way, she thought, it was a shame Rita capitulated because now she would never know what would have happened if she'd asked her father to free her from the French model bought by her mother's lover.

Instead, she went softly downstairs and joined him watching an Interlude, the one showing the potter shaping clay, letting it flow from one form to another with a casual grace, yet subject to his subtle control. Ann and her father sat side by side, entranced.

Too soon the moulded clay was replaced by a continuity announcer in a dinner-jacket. He'd hardly begun speaking before the picture went wrong again and horizontal bars began falling, falling, falling . . .

The church clock struck six-thirty. Ann's thoughts flew to the present, to the cold bedroom in the blanked-out village; and to that bleakest of rooms where Dennis Aylard was spending his final hours before prison officers rushed to pinion his arms and speed him to the gallows in the adjoining cell. Once he was there, he would have only fifteen seconds to live, the time it took the executioner to put the cap on him, adjust the noose to ensure the knot was beneath the angle of the left jaw, and pull the lever. The executioner, Mr Pierrepoint, prided himself on being humane and efficient, so that the downward plunge severed the spinal cord and death was instantaneous.

Sometimes it alarmed Ann that she knew so many of the appalling details of hanging, but it had proved impossible not to learn them. People discussed the subject, people wrote about it in the newspapers, people mentioned it on the wireless. Ever since the day of Aylard's arrest, she'd been sucking in information with every breath.

The fate awaiting him was hideous but she couldn't wrench her thoughts away from it. Waves of nausea washed through her, spasms of pain shot through her clenched hands, but her mind stayed fixed on the noose, the drop, the broken neck.

She'd heard that hanged men were buried in the prisons where they died, buried in lime to destroy their bodies quickly, disposed of without ceremony. There would be no flower-decked hearse, no weeping relations, no show of regret at the death of Dennis Aylard. Yet she wept for him. Piteously, she wept, because it was too late for prayer or for hope.

The noose.

The fall.

The snapping of the cord of life.

Ann covered her face with the sheet. Tears dampened it. Her throat ached with suppressed sobbing but in her head she was wailing that what they were doing was wrong, all of it wrong.

Some while later, worn out, she briefly drifted near to sleep but her mother appeared in the beginnings of a dream and Ann fought to keep awake. Rita was wearing the jacket of the turquoise suit which Sandy once tried on. It was ripped and she was accusing Ann of slashing it with the pin of the glittering brooch.

'Look,' Rita was saying, waggling a flap of torn silk in Ann's face. Rita was laughing horribly.

Ann sat up, struggling to calm her agitated breath. She seldom dreamed about her mother but whenever she did Rita taunted her with minor misdeeds. This dream was as silly as its predecessors. For one thing, it was Sandy who tore the jacket when she'd jammed it into the wardrobe while the savage pin of the brooch was unfastened. For another, Rita had been in an apoplectic fury when she'd discovered the damage.

The turquoise suit was mentioned at the trial. The court reports in the evening paper were detailed, often with long excerpts from the day's hearing. Ann read a couple of days' evidence before her aunt noticed and decreed the paper wasn't to be brought into the house. While she was reading, Ann invented sonorous intonation for the lawyers and a deeper seriousness for the judge who occasionally intervened.

'And did you,' the prosecution barrister had asked Dennis Aylard, 'make a present to Rita Morden of a jacket and skirt made of turquoise shantung silk?'

'I did.'

'Would you look at the photograph, please? Does that photograph show Rita Morden wearing those garments?'

'Yes.'

Then the judge asked Aylard to speak up and he was made to repeat his answer. This happened several times during his cross-examination.

As far as Ann could follow it, there was an allegation that Aylard didn't pay for the suit. Apparently, this was connected with one of his business ventures which the prosecution invited the jury to regard as scams or confidence tricks. Without understanding the intricacies, she learned that Aylard was supposed to have set up an expensive clothes shop to launder the profits of shady business deals; and the presents he showered on his girlfriends were, in effect, stolen.

Clearer, and far more disturbing to her, was the revelation of other girlfriends apart from her mother. Ann tried not to think about that but the information had been planted in her mind and every so often it flowered into conscious thought. And when that happened she worried that Rita hadn't been on the point of running away with him. Possibly, Rita herself had been keener on that idea than he was, and hadn't known about her rivals.

The aunts, the uncles, the older cousins and family friends muttered about the additional girlfriends. Ann noticed their prurient interest in this, although it was merely one among many black marks recorded against Aylard. She noticed, especially, that the girlfriends led to a revival of head-shaking over 'Poor Rita'. That hadn't happened for a while, and certainly not when the courtroom argument was about Rita's feckless ways and neglect of her wounded-hero husband.

On some days Ann had felt like talking to her aunt at the farmhouse about the case, asking her own questions and squeezing answers. But her only couple of attempts collapsed when Auntie Meg clung to the family rule that Ann wasn't to be burdened with any of it, that she was to forget the murder and put it all behind her.

On other days Ann was glad the family took that line because, if they hadn't, they would have been the ones with the questions and she would have been pestered for answers. All in all, it seemed best for her to say nothing.

She crept down in the bed again and lay there, eyes closed, thinking about her roving life. She'd been at the farmhouse with Meg, Meg's husband Freddie, and their children Lucy and Jimmy, for nearly two months, which was as long as she'd stayed anywhere. Time to move on, she thought. Time to find another aunt with a spare room in another part of the country.

Ann called her minders aunts but some weren't true relations and the title was a courtesy. Two, on her father's side, were actually his cousins. She cast around in her mind for people who might take her in future. It would get harder, she thought, for people to shunt her about the country as she ran out of aunts, cousins and willing family friends.

It didn't cross her mind that she might go back to The Avenue. Of course she thought about the house often but it no longer had the pull of home. Even her father didn't live there any more.

There was another reason. They'd changed her name, the aunts and uncles. Morden wouldn't do because she might be picked out as the daughter of the notorious victim. They made her a Foley, bestowing on her the maiden name of her dead mother. They didn't consult her, they did these things 'for her own good' and 'for the best'. Ann couldn't bring herself to tell them she loathed that name.

In a little while a now-familiar sound disturbed her. The church clock stuttered and then struck seven. Exhausted and sickened with sadness, she stared in the direction of the window and waited for day to break.

But the darkness held. November. Winter had come early and there was no pleasure to be had from the shortening days. Every morning for a week frost had spangled window-panes and danced along hedgerows. Spiteful winds detected gaps and infiltrated houses. This house, her aunt's house, was always cold anyway.

It was the sort of house where you put on your cardigan when you went indoors. For all its draughts, the building had a clamminess. Everything you touched felt damp. On Ann's previous visits, short ones lasting a few hours, she'd marked the difference between the airy orchard outside the farmhouse and the dank within.

Her mother said, after one dutiful visit: 'Thank God they keep that stove going. The kitchen's the only place that's warm.'

Her father said. 'It's the old way. Everybody used to live like that.'

And her mother retorted. 'Yes, but hardly anybody does now. They're too mean to spend the money on modernisation, that's their problem.'

Then they had another of their arguments about money: the way to get it and the way to spend it, and their own depressing shortage of it. That visit was when Ann was six, a year before her mother began going out to business meetings with Dennis Aylard and bringing home money, dresses and jewellery.

The old farmhouse was virtually the last place Ann would have chosen to live but the aunts were passing her around like a parcel in a game. Since the murder she'd lived with four of them. They were temporary billets, until the problem of what to do about Ann was resolved, but she didn't like any of them and the aunts and their families didn't like having her.

She felt ashamed as she thought about this. If she'd been a cuddly child, a prettier girl with winsome ways, it would have been easier for everyone. But her minders grumbled to the rest of the family that she was difficult, by which they meant withdrawn, unco-operative and beyond their power to help. Even June's parents found reasons not to keep her, their house being in the town where the murder was committed and people whispered behind hands.

Ann brooded and mourned, and couldn't have cared less whether her unlovely aunts and their children resented having her share their homes. She didn't protest when the game went another round and she was packed off to stay somewhere else.

She scrabbled beneath her pillow for a handkerchief but failed to find one and had to get out of bed again. There were handkerchiefs on a shelf in the cupboard. Her cousin, Lucy, a twelve-year-old prig in pigtails, had ironed about a dozen of them while Ann sat watching, neither of them talking but listening to the wireless, or perhaps only giving that impression. The wireless was a wonderful excuse not to talk. It seemed an age since the days when she ran riot with Sandy Minch, and her father was the one absorbed by the wireless, or pretending to be.

The coldness of the linoleum gave her a start and she ran on tiptoe to the cupboard and groped for Lucy's neat pile of handkerchiefs. Then, toes numb, she moved to the window and pressed her face close to the glass. Strangely, night wasn't yielding to day. She couldn't understand it at all.

Ann went back to bed and this time got in properly and wriggled right down, drawing the covers up to her chin. She was shivering, her flesh turned to ice, but only partly because of the bad cold room. The mystery of the delayed daylight frightened her. Too late for prayer and too late for hope, yet something was holding back the day.

'*If the day doesn't come, they can't hang him.*'

None of the wild ways she'd dreamed of for him to escape

execution matched this. Since he was sentenced she'd imagined exonerating evidence rushed to his lawyers; a sudden capitulation by politicians to those who campaigned to *Stop the hanging! Stop the hanging! Stop the hanging!* But what was actually happening was a magical means of saving him. The day wasn't dawning. The judicial hour would never come. Magic. Miracle. An answer to prayer, after all.

Then the clock struck seven-thirty and Ann's tentative faith in the miracle dwindled. Mechanical time was moving on even if heavenly time was not. She didn't doubt the prison had a clock and the executioner owned a watch. How else would he know it took him fifteen seconds precisely with the cap, the noose and the lever? With or without daylight, he would hang Dennis Aylard.

Ann turned onto her front and buried her face in her pillow, refusing to witness the extraordinary delaying of the daylight if it was of no practical use.

'*Easier to believe in a trick of the weather than in magic,*' she decided, weary and despairing.

When the church clock stirred again, ready for eight, absolute horror overwhelmed her.

'*It's now. They're hanging him now!*'

She flung herself onto her face and bunched the pillow against her ears to rule out sound. But the stroke of the clock was inescapable. Real or imagined, it reverberated in her skull.

'No! No!'

She was groaning the words aloud. The lapse scared her and she sprang up, alert for footsteps outside her door. But the only sound was her own jagged breathing. Her lungs were bursting with silent screaming, her throat ached and sweat dampened her forehead. She tore the nightdress away from her neck but it was no help. She felt herself being choked.

No one moved in the house. After a minute or two the crisis was over and Ann crept to the window. Instead of seeing a brightening of the eastern sky, the usual pinpoints of yellow light in village houses and the roaming lights of a car in the lane, she looked into the opaque grey-ness of fog.

Daylight made a late entrance on the morning they hanged Dennis Aylard. By the time Ann could pick out the reddish roofs of cottages and the white streaks of wintry hedges, he'd been dead for an hour. She turned away from the window when the clock geared itself up to strike nine.

An unexpected calmness enveloped her, now there was nothing to be hoped and nothing to be gained. The event had happened. They had done it. The police and the lawyers, the jury and the judge had connived to have him killed. It was wrong and the blame was theirs.

Their job was to find the truth and, in her secret soul, she'd trusted them to do it. Sandy Minch had said: 'They'll let him go, you'll see.' And: 'It's the law that the judge and everyone has to do what the jury says.' And: 'Whoever they say did it will have to be hanged.'

CHAPTER FOURTEEN

'The police didn't spend long enough on those two little girls,' Gillian Spry said.

Richard King snorted. 'But the kids wouldn't have kept quiet and let an innocent man be hanged.'

'No, I suppose not.'

'They were *girls*, Gillian. They weren't rough little monsters. They were a couple of nicely brought-up girls.'

'So was I and look what happened to me. I ended up with a life of crime.'

He said: 'Ann's family were so bloody genteel they couldn't even face the shame of living in the town afterwards. And they were the *victim's* family, not the killer's. That's the sort of decent kids we're dealing with.'

'Yes, I know. I know all that, but it's what I *don't* know that's bothering me. Think of this, Richard. A man at the party sees Sandy Minch in the garden and thinks, but isn't sure, that Ann is there too. It isn't an illogical assumption because the girls were usually described as inseparable, and the party was in the garden of the house where Ann lived.'

Holding up a hand, he brought her to a halt. 'To be precise, the party was in the other half of number seventeen, not the half Ann's father rented. If Sandy was there, it could have been because she was invited by one of the people giving the party or by a guest. You can't automatically assume she was there with Ann.'

Gillian conceded. 'Fair enough, I won't. But the man who saw Sandy did make that assumption. Sandy was quite familiar to him and he was positive he saw her running through shrubs at the far end of the garden. She wasn't joining in the party, she was on the fringe and actually hiding when he noticed her.'

'Kids do that. In an adult it might look furtive but when you're a child it's what you do. You have a separate party of your own, enter a make-believe world and leave the grown-ups out of it.'

'Fine. But when Ann was questioned by the police she originally said Sandy was present and later denied it. Sandy *always* denied it. She still does, she denied it when I called on her the other day.'

The interview had been brief indeed, the two women disliking each other on sight. Gillian's unkind first impression of the estranged wife of Mr Eliot Brown, company director and one time teacher, was that she'd grown into a hard-faced rich bitch. Her skin was evidence of hours of foreign sun or maybe sunray lamps, and her hair was an unconvincing shade of yellow. Asked to hazard a guess, Gillian would have said her twin hobbies were slimming and drinking.

Sandra invited her into the hall of the house among the trees off Uffington Road. They talked there, standing, which made it clear the plan was for Gillian to be out on the drive again almost before she knew it.

The hall was lavish. A chandelier, oak panelling, reproduction oil paintings, squashy carpets, marble tables trimmed with ormolu, and a curving staircase to a stained-glass window. Gillian calculated the considerable sum of money that had been splashed around. She'd now been into the homes of three women in the case – Anna, June Foley and Sandy Minch – and, to her mind, this was the least likeable.

The decor of Anna's charming terrace house reflected the same care she devoted to her personal appearance. June's inheritance of fading furniture and rugs created the mildly shabby look the English have always been comfortable with.

By comparison, Sandy's home was a gleaming, off-the-peg horror that said nothing of the owner's personality but stipulated the size of her bank balance. Gillian had the wild idea that things would improve immeasurably if June's furniture were moved in instead and Anna were put in charge of choosing the colour schemes.

Sandra Brown spoke in a loud voice which she didn't lower although they were standing close. 'I really don't see why you've come to me. That woman was killed when I was a small child.'

Gillian silently corrected that. '*Not small. You were nine. You're bound to remember.*'

Aloud she said: 'I understand that, Sandra, but let me try one or two questions, if you don't mind.'

'You're wasting your time.'

So Gillian proved her right and wasted her time with a series of questions Sandra fended off with a tired-sounding no.

'Were you at the house earlier on the day of the party?'
'No.'
'Were you there the evening Rita Morden was killed?'
'No.'
'Do you remember anything about the murder.'
'No.'

A few more questions before, finally, 'Would you like to hear from Ann Morden now?'
'No.'

A couple of minutes later, driving out of the gateway into Uffington Road, Gillian began to smile. 'A good thing Sandy refuses to see Anna. I think Anna would be appalled by her.'

She didn't tell Richard every detail of her visit. Sometimes she liked to outline her impressions of people and places, but her interview with the former Sandy Minch was so empty there was nothing to add to the fact that the woman denied everything.

Gillian stressed, while she and Richard were arguing about whether or not Sandy was sighted at the party: 'Nobody pressed those girls for the truth although, if they were in that part of the garden at the time the guest says he spotted Sandy, they stood a better chance than anyone of seeing whether Aylard or his car were there or even, God help them, if he had a row with Rita Morden.'

Richard was shaking his head. 'No, no, that hinges on the timing of the man's supposed sighting of Sandy. What he said was he noticed her *after he'd been there twenty minutes*.'

'And that he came late, about nine.'

'Is that corroborated?'

In reply he got her ironic laugh. 'In the Rita Morden case, nothing's corroborated.'

After pondering she added: 'You know, Richard, everything comes down to timing. The time Sandy was seen in the garden; the time the police claimed it took Aylard to drive from home to Rita's house and kill her; the time it took him to drive back again; the time of Rita's death; the time she was last seen alive . . .'

Cutting short the list, she said that when you looked closely at the witness statements, the lack of corroboration was glaring. 'It's as though everyone is at a different party. Only one person sees Sandy. Only one hears a car engine on land behind the garden. Only one sees Rita Morden after ten to nine. Et cetera.'

Richard brought them neatly to consideration of the pathologist's role. 'This lack of corroboration was one factor that made Winterlea's forensic evidence of paramount importance. He estimated she died between 9.30 and 10.00, in effect after the neighbour heard a car arrive.'

'Quite. But at 9.30 and again at 9.45 a woman crosses the land where the car is supposed to be and doesn't see it. Or Aylard. Or Rita. Or anyone.'

He asked her the time of the last sighting of Rita Morden, the one reported to the local newspaper journalist.

She said: 'Nine-thirty when Rita comes out of the side door of the house. The witness called by the prosecution was a Mr Jermyn who says he saw her in the garden half an hour earlier.'

Richard grimaced. 'They're guessing, aren't they? I mean, you don't look at your watch and make a mental note whenever you see anybody or hear anything. And at a *party*, for heaven's sake. You've got all that drinking and joking to do, how can you be clocking everybody's movements?'

Gillian walked over to a flip-chart in the corner and sketched a big oblong. 'Let this be the garden of number seventeen. And this is the spare plot behind it, the unofficial car park. And this the house. Now here's the side-door Rita came out of at 9.30. And this . . .'

She filled in the positions of people and the times they were supposed to have been there, according either to evidence given in court or in private interviews.

'Pretty,' Richard said, 'but does it demonstrate anything you didn't already understand?'

'Not a thing.' She tossed down the crayon and went to the window. Another dull day. On the pavement below a woman unfurled an umbrella.

Gillian stiffened. 'Yes, wait a minute. There was a sudden, very heavy shower that evening.'

'When?'

She hurried to her desk, tapped eagerly at her computer. 'Yes, here we are. Shortly after ten. That was checked with the local weather office after the murder. Storms had been forecast, to swing in from the west, and *woosh* there it was, the first of them. Described as a sudden downpour.'

Richard was studying the flip-chart. 'Presumably everybody ran indoors to shelter, and by ten-fifteen there wasn't a soul out there.'

'Actually, a number of guests who lived nearby took the opportunity to go home instead. That includes the woman with the child at home alone, which means she crosses the car park for the *third* time without seeing Aylard, Rita or a car.'

'Another gate?'

But Gillian had thought of that. 'I snooped around checking the premises and I consulted an old plan. There was, and is, only one rear entrance to 17 The Avenue. If the other evidence about timing was correct, then any of the neighbours who left by the back way after the rain started would have stumbled over Rita's body lying by the path or discovered her fighting for her life in the car park.'

He muttered that it was increasingly obvious the rest *wasn't* right. 'You know,' he added a moment later, 'I'm beginning to feel sorry for the police. Forty people at a party and nobody sees Aylard and hardly anyone notices Rita.'

Gillian caught her breath. 'Richard, they had a bonfire.'

'So?'

She picked up the crayon and scribbled a bonfire on her sketch. 'For safety, it was well away from the house. But it wasn't far from the trestle tables with the drinks and snacks, and it was on the side of the garden the Mordens' neighbours used. Therefore it must have been about here.'

She turned to him with a triumphant smile. 'That could explain why people were peculiarly unobservant. They had a bonfire to watch, and you know how people do gather round and gawp at a fire.'

He contrived a look that said he admired her deduction but was dismayed the significance of the fire hadn't impinged on either of them earlier. All they'd previously talked about were the reasons for it: the man who held the party decided it would be welcome once the day cooled and grew dark, and it spurred him to clear the garden of fallen branches that had littered it since gales the previous spring.

Enlarging Gillian's point, Richard said: 'The fire kept people away from the path and the car park end of the garden. When you come to think of it, a fire is a pretty noisy and distracting entertainment. Possibly it prevented them hearing a row in the car park. Look.'

He trailed a finger over her sketched garden. 'The woman who hears a car happens to be near the end of the garden. That's why she's the only one who does. And look at Rita Morden coming out of the side door. She goes straight on down the path to the gate without meeting any other guests.'

Gillian cautioned him, although her own excitement was growing. 'Don't forget this is only my rough picture of where they were.'

'But the salient points are correct. Mr Jermyn sees Rita walking away from the fire and towards her house at 8.50, when he's returning from using the lavatory in the adjoining house. Forty minutes later another man sees her leaving her house by the side door and walking ahead of him into the garden. Doubtless he turns towards the party gathered around the tables and the fire.'

'I imagine so, but all he says is he lost sight of her once they reached the garden.'

'Which he might well do if she goes to the gate.'

There was a hiatus before Gillian said gently: 'What we're doing, Richard, is finding reasons for the murder happening the way the police said it did. Aylard drives to the rear of the—'

The telephone rang, forcing them to drop the subject. He didn't mind, they were spending too long on it for his liking. Unfortunately, every time he started to suggest this something revived her interest. He preferred to stick to Marcus Winterlea, but it was no use phrasing it like that because she would insist this *was* a Winterlea case. And if, as they suspected, Dennis Aylard hadn't had a fair trial, this case might become an important item in the CJI dossier on Winterlea.

Richard put a kettle to boil, realised they'd forgotten to pick up a carton of milk, switched it off again. Looking out on steady rain, he listened to Gillian's call.

She was protesting: 'No, I assure you the information didn't come from anyone working here. We're meticulous about respecting confidentiality.'

A woman's voice chimed in.

Gillian waited and then: 'She made contact with us, it's true. But we definitely haven't provided her with information.'

The voice cut in again.

After two minutes, during which Richard tried without

169

success to catch her eye and ask the name of the caller,
Gillian repeated her reassurance about respecting confidentiality. She seemed poised to ring off but the tenor of the
conversation changed. Instead, Richard heard her saying:
'Tomorrow, if that suits you.'

He opened the desk diary. Tomorrow? It was booked
solid. He gesticulated at her but she chose to ignore him.

Setting down the receiver she announced: 'June Foley.'

'Oh. Anna's cousin? The one who kept you on the
doorstep the first time and wouldn't open the door the
second time?'

'That June Foley. Yes. Guess why?'

'Give in.'

'Dennis Aylard's daughter telephoned her.'

His eyebrows shot up, emphasising his owlish look. 'But
. . . I don't wish to be unkind but what does she think you
can do about it?'

'Nothing, now I've convinced her I didn't set Meryl
Aylard onto her. But she's decided to talk to me about
the murder, after all.'

'Setting things straight, putting matters right, that sort
of thing?'

'That appears to be the idea.' She couldn't help smiling
with pleasure at June Foley's change of mind.

'Does she still think you make television programmes?'

'I suppose so. She didn't say otherwise.'

She went to stand by the window. Umbrellas floated
below. 'Let's go to Giovanni's for hot chocolate. I'll pay.'

'Gill, you always complain it's an expensive rip-off and
you can't hear yourself think.'

'True, true. But I feel I've earned a modest treat. Besides,
I don't *want* to think. I do too much of that, as it is.'

She crossed to the door, lifted her mackintosh off a
coat-stand. 'Coming?'

'Er . . . yes.'

He was having trouble adjusting to her switch of mood.
After setting the answering machine, he followed her out.

Downstairs, by the street door, she hooked her mackintosh

up over her head like a cape and ran the few yards to the café.

'I think,' she said, shaking rainwater over Giovanni's tiles, 'this is the best idea I've had in ages.'

Richard, getting spattered, stepped smartly out of range and went to the counter to order. On days when Giovanni was in a good mood you were served at table, on others he ignored you and eventually you realised he'd declared it a self-service day. Richard was taking no chances.

Gillian settled at a table near the window and inspected the umbrella-carriers at eye-level for a change. She was mulling over June Foley's telephone call, the unexpectedness of it and the timing. Although Meryl Aylard's butting-in was unfortunate, it had given June the shove CJI needed.

'June Foley?' Richard guessed, setting two cups of froth on the table.

'Yes. The why and the what next.'

'Why is easy: she would rather talk to you than Meryl Aylard. And so would I, for that matter.'

Gillian made a face at him. Then: 'But what does she want to say? She's already told me to mind my own business, so it can't be that again.'

He appeared to consult the ceiling before replying. 'She thinks Meryl is likely to uncover facts we haven't, and she prefers to tell us herself first.'

Gillian quoted his own words back at him. 'Setting things straight, putting things right. Yes, but what things?'

He began spooning froth, piling it into a peak. 'Remember, if she tells you anything about the murder, it's second-hand. She wasn't there, she was on holiday.'

'I do remember. I'm trying to decide whether it's possible she'll tell me the family believed Aylard innocent or whether she means to reinforce his guilt.'

'Guilt, I should say. Victims' families always need to believe the culprit has been brought to justice. How often have we seen that? Campaigners, lawyers and most of the country will accept there's been a wrongful conviction, but the victim's family can't face it.'

She agreed, the pattern was established; and yet that didn't mean it applied in every case. Gillian sipped her coffee. 'Tomorrow,' she said. 'I only have to wait until then for all to be revealed.'

Richard lifted the top half-inch of foam off the pile and ate it. 'I wonder whether your meeting with June isn't actually Anna's idea? It's such a *volte face* for June, and Anna has been quite forthcoming.'

'Except she didn't tell us much. Pleaded she was too young and too forgetful whenever we drew near to the bones of it.'

'Still, I wouldn't rule out her orchestrating June.'

Gillian grunted agreement. They kept coming back to Anna Foley who had been Ann Morden, eight years old when her mother was murdered. Unlike her cousin, any information she was willing to give was first-hand because she'd been there when it happened. In a bedroom, apparently, hiding from fireworks because she was nervous of the bangs. But maybe not. To begin with she'd said she was with Sandy Minch in the garden and they'd run indoors when it rained.

Excluded from her thoughts, Richard coaxed: 'Come on, tell me.'

'Sorry, I know I said I wasn't going to think about it but I can't help it.'

'Go on.'

'It's nothing.'

'Oh, yeah?'

'I mean it isn't what you want to hear.'

'Gillian . . .'

'All right. It's just that I feel myself circling Anna, as though she's the pivot. Whenever I try to move on, there she is again.'

Richard was wishing he hadn't raised the question of Anna being behind June Foley's change of heart. He thought carefully before speaking.

'Look, Gill, don't you think you're a bit hung up on her? I know it's bugging you that she doesn't remember much,

172

especially as she's the only person we've got who was on the spot. But that's the way it is.'

Gillian agreed. 'But that doesn't necessarily make me wrong. You know what she sounds like on our tapes – the way she wriggles away from subjects she finds sensitive. There must be a reason for that.'

His voice was more exasperated than he intended. 'She was a *child*. A little *girl*. Having your mother bashed over the head and left to die in your back garden is bound to be a sensitive issue. Now come on, admit it.'

She threw up her hands in surrender. 'I do. I really do. But you asked me what I was thinking and the fact is I can't help suspecting that nicely brought-up little girl knows more than she's telling.'

When he asked 'What does it matter?' she jumped in with: 'If Aylard was innocent, it matters very much indeed.'

Richard backed down. She was correct. Their dossier on Winterlea proved it. His evidence had convicted a man against whom there was no other evidence. Prejudice, yes, but not evidence.

He said: 'Look, I accept that a child who lied or withheld information in that situation was playing a dangerous game. But would a child of eight appreciate that? Don't kids take the short-term view, rather than consider consequences the way adults do?'

She shook her head. 'Who knows? As a country, we change our minds about that. We upped the age of criminal responsibility from eight to ten in 1963, but from the Middle Ages until the beginning of the twentieth century it was fixed at seven.'

He was sorry they were digressing because it was child psychology rather than the law that interested him. Trying to hurry through it, he got in a mention of the current dissatisfaction with *doli incapax*, the presumption that children aged from ten to fourteen are incapable of doing wrong because they are unable to understand the seriousness of their actions.

He was going to swing them back to the mysterious

mind of the child but Gillian cut in. 'You underestimate the wickedness of children.'

'*Wickedness?* That's a bit strong.'

'No, not at all. I mean the latent talent we all have for deliberate cruelty. Some children *are* the innocent little creatures you like to believe in but others aren't. It's an individual thing, the same as with adults.'

Richard argued that children who committed serious crimes – and cases of murder, manslaughter, rape and arson sprang to mind – were almost without exception the victims of physical, sexual or emotional abuse. 'This isn't what we're talking about in the the Rita Morden affair. We just have a girl who, in your opinion, kept silent when her evidence might have influenced the outcome of a trial. I don't think it's fair to assume she fully understood the implications of keeping her mouth shut.'

Gillian watched the umbrellas passing the window. Her voice was soft when she spoke again. 'Richard, it was a matter of life and death. And I can't believe Ann wasn't made aware of that.'

CHAPTER FIFTEEN

As soon as I heard her voice I suspected trouble, but before she was ready to tell me why she was ringing we had one of our silly conversations. I'm afraid I was short of patience, because this was the latest episode in a frustrating day.

The telephone had been ringing as I let myself into the house and I leaped for it. It was hot in the sitting-room and I began undoing coat buttons while I fumbled with the telephone.

'Hello?' My voice was a gasp.

'Anna?' I identified an underlying anxiety in June's voice.

When she went on, her tone was accusing. 'I was about to hang up. I've been ringing and ringing your number all afternoon.'

'But I've been at work, June.'

I rolled my eyes skywards, one of those silent comments you're free to make when someone is cross on the telephone but which you wouldn't dream of face to face. June seems unable to grasp I have to work, even though she's retired, and my work takes me out of the house. We've been around this course several times, with her phoning at impossible hours and later complaining I was out. Sometimes she compounds the folly by begging a mid-week visit.

She said 'Oh,' slightly chastened, and rambled about never being able to remember which particular days I'm busy. This made her appear aged and inattentive, and perhaps she realised this because suddenly she switched tack and came rushing out with her news. I was riveted and, for a few seconds, quite incapable of speech.

This is how she began, pouring it out as though her nerve might give way if she faltered. 'Anna, I've been speaking to Dennis Aylard's daughter. Her name's Meryl Aylard. Yes, she still uses Aylard. I was taken aback when she said who she was. I mean, I never dreamed anybody in his family would have the temerity to approach any of us. But, well, there she was on the phone, being courteous and pleasant and asking if she might see me. If it wouldn't put me to too much trouble, she said. Well, of course, I asked whatever for, which was straight to the point if a shade rude. And then she recited a formal little speech about her family begging my help because they're campaigning to clear his name. The way she trotted it out, it sounded as though she'd tried it on heaps of people before me. Anyway, I was brusque, more or less asking how on earth they hoped to do *that*. But she didn't take offence. She told me the main thing they're going to do is have certain pieces of evidence in the case re-examined, by using modern scientific methods, and they're convinced this will prove his innocence.'

There was a pause inviting my reply but my mouth was dry. The most she heard was a croak.

June swept on. 'The statement her father made to the police is one of the items they're looking at again. According to her, Aylard claimed the incriminating passages weren't written by him. I didn't know that, did you?'

Confronted with a question, I spoke at last. 'No, I've never heard that.'

My gratifyingly calm voice came to my rescue again. Unable to see my pallor, she couldn't guess how badly her news had rattled me.

It emerged that Meryl Aylard called her the previous day and June spent the interim wondering what and whether to report to me.

'I wasn't sure I ought to bother you,' she said, in a tone suggesting she remained undecided.

'I prefer to know anything of that sort.'

'Well, as long as it doesn't upset you.'

A faintly patronising note had crept into her voice, as though I was eight years old again and not to be upset by the horrible adult business going on above my head. I told myself not to be ridiculous, to stop being impatient and critical. The day had worn my spirits down and I was being unfair to June.

Also, I was being deceitful because I hadn't mentioned I already knew of the Aylards' campaign, although *all* I knew was that there was one. Gillian Spry hadn't explained about re-testing documents or whatever else they might try.

'What,' I asked cautiously, 'did you say to a visit?'

'Oh, I refused her, of course. Point-blank. On the entirely sensible grounds that I wasn't in town at the time of the murder and there's nothing I can tell her about any of it.'

'Does she accept your decision?'

'I was extremely firm, so I should hope so. I made it clear that if she arrives on my doorstep, she stands no chance of changing my mind.'

Despite everything I smiled, at June and her firmness. She prides herself on it and, whenever she has lapses, she bounces back with greater determination. Then I took the plunge and confessed I knew of the campaign and had already rejected an approach via Gillian Spry.

June said 'Mmm' and 'Oh' a few times, but didn't probe which spared me having to describe my meeting with Gillian in the hotel.

I ended with: 'It didn't enter my head Meryl Aylard would pester you. I feel now I ought to have warned you but I didn't want you to be troubled.'

June retorted she wasn't troubled, that she'd dealt with the matter as best she could, and was confident she would hear nothing further from the woman.

She had a comical thought. 'If she bothers me, do you think I could report her for stalking?'

I said, and only partly in jest: 'You could try. With such a new offence on the Statute Book nobody knows for sure what they can do with it.'

But any notion of us falling back on the stalking legislation, to rid ourselves of campaigners and researchers, was fleeting indeed. Attempts to use the new law were attracting enormous public interest and guaranteed newspaper and television coverage. If June and I wished to make ourselves thoroughly famous, all we need do was make an accusation of stalking. Like several of our laws, it protected us in theory but was impractical.

June said: 'I'll wear my black suit to go to court. One doesn't wish to appear frivolous.'

'Court?'

'Our stalking case, dear.'

'Oh. Yes.' I laughed again, to oblige.

We talked about inconsequential things then. At least, they were that to me. June was fairly cross about the grocer 'forgetting' to deliver her biscuits while featuring them on the bill. Her spaniel was another concern. Frisky's paw was tender and June was trying to arrange a visit to the vet.

'Not easy when you're housebound,' she grumbled.

'But surely . . .'

Fortunately, I broke off before blundering on with the rest of a remark to the effect that it was relatively easy to get people to help out an animal in trouble. The trouble? I recalled the click, click, click of Frisky's overgrown claws on the kitchen tiles and drew conclusions. And where was Mr Tompkins, the considerate neighbour who walked Frisky to the churchyard?

'Sorry,' I said, struggling to extricate myself. 'I have to go, there's a knock at the front door.'

With rapid goodbyes we hung up. The lie, the escape, allowed me time to rearrange my thoughts about her contact with Meryl Aylard. I knew I'd have to ring June back, either this evening or the next day, but I needed to think. I was facing decisions and there was no sense in making them off the cuff, and especially not while I was recovering from her disconcerting news.

I plucked the free newspaper out of the letter-box where the delivery boy had jammed it a couple of minutes earlier, hung up my coat and poured a glass of wine. If I'd felt seriously in shock I would have opted for brandy, maybe whisky, but I was over the worst and I find a glass of full-bodied red wine comforting. I'd opened a bottle the previous evening when my friend, Susie, called in for a respite from the trials of her home life.

Don't worry, I shan't burden you with Susie's woes, and I promise to stick to the subject instead of sloping off. The thing is, it's so extraordinary for me to be talking about it that now I've started I want to put everything in.

Anyway, what I should be saying is that I had to choose whether to let June handle matters in her way or to interfere, tweak the strings. It wasn't as clear-cut as that. It never is.

If I'd believed for a fraction of a second that June had deterred Meryl Aylard, there would have been no problem. But my instincts, my experience, convinced me otherwise. You see, what kind of campaigner quits after one call? Admittedly, Meryl showed naïvete in telephoning instead of appearing in person but she would soon stop making that mistake. Families who campaign to right wrongs are commendably tough. When there isn't a hope in hell, they go looking for one. And when there's a spark of hope, they fan it into a distinct possibility. Professional investigators are allowed to give up and drift on to other causes, but families sacrifice their lives to the fight.

Most don't wait forty-five years to begin.

What prompted the Aylards to start now? Was it, as Gillian Spry claimed, because they'd made a connection between her work and Marcus Winterlea giving evidence against Dennis Aylard? Or was there another element, one nobody had mentioned to us?

Neither June nor I distinguished ourselves in these encounters with the Aylard campaign. June was busy being firm and I was busy being astonished. Had we demanded more information, we might have gained it.

I played with the idea of coaxing Gillian Spry, but she was the professional secret-holder. She would give away nothing worth having.

Then I wondered about approaching Meryl Aylard, giving myself the advantage of surprise and squeezing information from her while she was unguarded. But perhaps she was never off guard and, anyway, I didn't know where to reach her.

I refilled my wine glass and considered the dilemma from various angles. On the face of it, I wanted to protect myself and June in particular, and our family in general, from the distress caused by a reopening of ancient wounds. Privately, I was concerned to see any attempt to exonerate Dennis Aylard founder.

What is the point, years after an execution? It's a cliché that justice delayed is justice denied, but if an innocent person has been executed that's a wrong that can't be rectified. It's justice denied for ever. What would it profit Dennis Aylard to have police, the judge and the jury step forward and confess they were wrong?

Believe me, I'm not so heartless I don't sympathise with the Aylards. Theirs isn't an extremely common name and the case became widely known. It remains so to those who enjoy reading articles or books with titles such as *Famous Cases of the Past* or *Murder in the Fifties*. The Rita Morden affair – which is how it was referred to at the time, I suppose because of the play on the word affair, and is how it appears in indexes today – featured prominently in an especially lurid anthology of twentieth-century crime. One day, when I feel mischievous, I will casually show June a copy and see what she makes of it.

Yes, I do pity Meryl Aylard. In a way, we shared a common fate. My mother was branded a wicked slut and her father was convicted of murder. They both became outcasts, their names whispered with dread. Each of us lost a parent in the most horrific and public manner. I was eight, she eleven.

We lived in the same town although, to my knowledge, we didn't meet.

But it happened half a century ago. Surely the hurt has faded? Or is she like one of those old women who revive memories of youthful anguish and can't let go? You know, the ones who become fixated on early pregnancies that resulted in abortion or adoption, and drive themselves to neuroses. The past can't be re-entered, it can't be changed.

Whatever Meryl Aylard wishes to achieve, she ought to understand it will all be for nothing. She can't wipe out the years of ignominy because she's already endured them. She can't resurrect an innocent father from the prison grave because, well, because you can't. The maximum effect she can hope for from a successful campaign is a few paragraphs in the newspapers, a brief item or two on the television news, a footnote in those books about true crime, and the personal satisfaction at altering an official record.

I wonder whether it's enough for her?

I don't doubt she would say yes, that vindication is all the family requires. It isn't though, is it? After the vindication comes the totting up. What's it worth financially to grow up without a father, without a husband, a son, a son-in-law? People invariably bring it down to cash nowadays, hitting authority where it hurts, in the budget.

Well, they might possibly make the Home Office ache with the cost of compensation, but nobody who accepts it ever says it's made the agony worth while. Receiving an award, I think, is striking a blow in return but it does nothing to soften the impact of a father judicially murdered for a crime he didn't commit. If Meryl doesn't know that, somebody should tell her.

I went into the kitchen and put a pizza in the micro-wave. There was salad in the fridge but I chopped and dressed it with the absent-minded motion of a woman in a trance, my mind engrossed by June and Meryl and what to do next. One idea buzzed around in my head. For a while I discounted it but, once I noticed how persistent it was, I gave it serious attention. The longer I thought it over, the more it seemed the only possible solution. No, maybe it wasn't a solution, maybe it was no better than a logical next step. Either way, it was increasingly appealing.

I was tempted to telephone June at once and set the plan in action but a natural caution held me back. It's best to sleep on brilliant ideas, especially those brilliant ideas conjured after three glasses of wine before supper. I didn't ring her that evening. After my pizza I went to bed early and watched television until I fell asleep.

My call to June next day was delayed by a flurry of activity on my telephone. First, one of my clients wanted to bring forward our next meeting, and to satisfy her I had to switch a less important session with another client. Then Kate rang to say she'd wangled tickets for Covent Garden, quite a feat as they were declared sold out when she tried previously. No sooner had she gone, leaving me exhilarated, than Susie rang in tears over her latest domestic catastrophe and I was cast into gloom. Susie's the antithesis of Kate, distinctly *un*steady, excitable to the verge of hysteria. Kate revives me, Susie exhausts.

I arranged to see Susie that evening, at my place rather than hers, of course, because hers is a battlefield. Then I hovered by the telephone ready for it to chirrup again. After a few seconds reassuring silence, I felt free to abandon it and make a fortifying cup of coffee. A little respite was needed before I rang June.

In the critical light of morning, my plan still seemed effective, if not as brilliant. In any event, it was the best I could do and I was ninety-five per cent sure it was worth trying. The percentage varied but was always in the nineties and I encouraged myself to believe this was easily good enough. After all, how can you ever be one hundred per cent sure of an outcome?

So, perked up by the coffee, I rang June. I was completely unprepared for the machine which answered me. There didn't seem any sense in leaving a message, because I was about to drive off to work, and I couldn't think what to say except I'd rung. I resisted that because she might spend the day wondering why, and I couldn't guess what track her thoughts would run on.

When her recorded message ended, I waited to see whether she was actually there, filtering out callers as people often do. Silence. I hung up.

I felt disturbed. June was housebound, she hadn't had an answering machine until now, so where was she and what was going on? One reasonable answer was that she'd taken the spaniel to the vet for its paw to be treated, but I wasn't content to assume anything mundane. For several minutes I was convinced she'd fallen and was unable to reach the telephone. I badgered myself to remember who her neighbours were so I could hunt down their telephone numbers and send them to her rescue.

'Or I could call the police,' I thought, although that would definitely be the last resort.

I decided to ring her number once more before I left the house, and composed a message for her puzzling machine. Before I dialled, the chirruping began again. First it was a man trying to sell me a kitchen. Next it was June.

'Anna, so glad I've caught you. I was afraid you might have dashed off to work.'

'I'm poised for the dash. Are you all right? You sound breathless.'

'Oh, I've been hurrying around, that's all. You rang me but you didn't leave a message.'

'I was so amazed to hear a machine, I couldn't think what to say.'

'It's my latest novelty. I dropped my telephone the other day and it broke. The telephone people said I had to have a modern one instead of a dial, and they suggested I might find an answering machine useful.'

I agreed it was a good idea.

She said: 'Well, it would be if people would only leave me messages. No one has yet, they've been too shy. I have to tap 1471 to see who's been calling.'

The machine, I realised, was the most modern piece of

equipment in her house. Might she acquire a taste for modernity, swap the Aga for a microwave, junk the mains radio for a Walkman . . . ?

I stopped thinking nonsense and got on with what I had to say.

'June, I've been thinking about Meryl Aylard and her family's campaign.'

'It's worrying, isn't it? We don't want all that unpleasantness dredged up.'

'I've been trying to think of a way of heading her off. Whatever we say won't deter her, but if we say nothing, that won't, either. As I see it, we have two problems. CJI as well as Meryl Aylard. How do you feel about getting them to squabble?'

She was at her driest as she replied: 'I think they deserve whatever we can do to them. What do you have in mind?'

'I suggest you complain to Gillian Spry about foisting Meryl Aylard on you after you refused to speak to Gillian herself. Play the hounded old lady, June. Persuade Gillian you're convinced Meryl is working in cahoots with CJI, and you're sending for your solicitor if either of them delves into our family business again.'

It wasn't masterly, I knew that, but it could cause mayhem and prevent them working in concert.

June disappointed me by sounding dubious. 'Oh, dear. Do you really think that's our best course?'

'Yes.' I explained about the mayhem. 'We haven't any power to stop them but we can make them fear it would be more trouble than it's worth. Don't forget, CJI claim to be investigating Marcus Winterlea, not Dennis Aylard. As far as Gillian Spry and Richard King are concerned, Aylard's a sideshow.'

'Oh, dear.'

She was being faint-hearted. I urged her to see the picture from what I trusted would be CJI's viewpoint.

'June, Criminal Justice Investigations is a charity. It depends on goodwill for its funds, and Gillian Spry won't want the public's perception of it damaged by a fuss created by us. Our line, of course, must be that she set Meryl onto us. And for all we know, she did.'

Waiting, I heard a sigh. I tried again.

'Look, June, I would do it myself but it's far better coming from you.'

She interrupted. 'It isn't that, Anna. The difficulty is I've asked Gillian Spry to come to see me today. I've told her I'm willing to talk.'

'Oh, God.'

I don't know whether I spoke the words or only heard them in my skull.

June was saying: 'I decided what should be done and I'm going to do it. And I decided not to trouble you. I'm sorry if you think it's the wrong decision, Anna, but it's too late to change it.'

Her voice was running on and on, saying she regretted not telling me the previous evening, saying she had her mind firmly made up and I was to rely on her and not worry about anything.

I worried. I listened with half my attention and gave the other half to mounting panic. I wanted to insist on being with her while they talked but my day was full. There was no chance of my getting there.

It isn't that I think I'm brighter than June or that she's incapable. Far from it. But her interests and mine don't fully coincide and what looks good to her is, to my eyes, riven with flaws. June sitting down to talk to Gillian Spry about the Rita Morden affair is a perfect example. But I would never be able to explain that to June. She has her perspective and I have mine. Never the twain.

When I came off the line I was hysterical, laughing uproariously at this unimaginably bad turn of events.

Once the laughter abated, as abruptly as it began, I rushed to the kitchen and poured a glass of mineral water, icy from the fridge. I had a notion that the coldness of the water would cool my over-heated brain, slow my racing heart, and quell my spiralling panic.

The shock of the coldness forced a little clarity into me.

I sat at the kitchen table, weak from the swings of emotion and waited to see where the pendulum would stick. It stuck on bitter resignation. June would do what June had planned and there was no hope of putting into practice any part of my cunning plan.

Meryl Aylard might or might not stay away from June, but there was nothing to impede her pursuit of me. In fact, I was having such a dreadful day it would be entirely in keeping if she pitched up on my doorstep right away.

'Keep calm,' I muttered. 'Don't get hysterical again.'

But I wasn't hysterical, I'd accepted that everything was terrible and growing worse. Gillian Spry, for instance. How dare I hope she would hear June out but not come after me again? She'd already seen me three times: in the churchyard, at my home and in the hotel in the town where Sandy Minch lived. Yet she persisted in inviting me to believe she was focusing on Marcus Winterlea! She was preposterous. Everything was preposterous. I might as well . . .

Rising, I went to the sitting-room window and flicked a lace curtain aside to peer down the alleyway. A couple of people crossed the end of the passage. I let the curtain fall.

'I might as well,' I repeated, but finished the sentence with a fresh and sensible thought, 'go to work.'

Behind my house there's a garden and beyond it a cramped car park serving me and my neighbours. I can reach it the back way, but that means leaving my garden gate unsecured because I haven't replaced the bolt with a lock. The result is that when I use the car, I walk down the alley.

As I was nearing the end of the terrace, a teenage girl shot round the corner and cannoned into me. She swore, furious that I was in her way, and flung me against a window-sill. Then she thumped on a door and was immediately admitted to a house, presumably by somebody who was waiting for her.

While I was getting my breath, two policemen ran into the alley and slithered to a halt.

I pointed. 'In there.'

'Cheers.'

They knocked on the door. They were still knocking when I turned into the street and, for a few yards, joined the mid-morning activity of the town. The police didn't need me, they knew the gang of girls they were after. Shoplifters. Street fighters. Suspected drug pedlars. It was a sad day for the terrace when the Greenes went abroad and put their house in the hands of a letting agent. The rest of us were mystified that their tenants hadn't been thrown out.

By the car park a middle-aged woman hurried forward, purposeful as a market researcher but without the clipboard.

'Excuse me? Are you Anna Foley?'

I frowned, taking in the intensity of her blue eyes, the unnatural auburn hair, and the good cut of her loose jacket. An acquaintance I'd forgotten?

'Sorry, I don't think I . . .'

'No, we haven't met but you'll know my name. Meryl Aylard.'

Stupidly, I gaped.

She filled the silence. 'Please, I'd very much like to talk to you.'

'No, no.' I was shaking my head vigorously.

'We can't talk out here. Is there somewhere we could go.'

'No, really. I don't wish to . . . I don't think . . . No, I . . .'

'It's very important. I wouldn't dream of troubling you if it weren't.'

My hands were trembling as they clutched my car key and bag. I made a huge effort to be cogent.

'As you see, I'm on my way to work. I'm late and I can't possibly spare the time. But, in any case, I have nothing to tell you.'

She was wearing a sympathetic expression but I hardened my heart against wheedling.

Meryl said: 'Gillian Spry warned me you would say that.'

'Then you should have believed her. Honestly, it's no

good you or Gillian or anyone else going on at me. I was eight years old when my mother was murdered. I knew very little about it and I certainly can't be of any use now.'

Her expression didn't alter but I couldn't afford to be swayed by pity for her. I took a few steps towards my car. She walked beside me.

She said: 'I appreciate what you say, Anna. I was only ten myself at the time of the murder. Eleven when they hanged my father. I understand you don't know much but I want to tell you about my family's plans. I feel it would be discourteous not to keep you informed.'

This was intolerable. I wanted to say a letter would do and she was never to approach me again. Instead, I demanded: 'Did CJI tell you where I live?'

'Oh, no. They wouldn't tell me anything, which was really frustrating but I can understand they have to respect confidentiality.'

'Then how did you trace me?'

She was between me and my car, making it awkward for me to get closer without pushing her out of the way.

'I didn't. I'm no use at that sort of thing. I hired a private detective.'

'A *detective*?'

My outrage amused her. 'Yes, a real private detective. He's very efficient.'

'So I see.' I wondered whether he'd been efficient at a paper chase or whether he'd asked people about me. Worse, had he followed me around? With a sinking feeling I realised what she was going to say.

'He traced your friend Sandy Minch, too.'

I got a grip on my nerves. 'Have you been to see her?'

Meryl denied me an answer. 'Look, why don't we go where we can talk properly?'

'I've told you. I'm on my way to work and I'm late.'

Sweeping past her, I unlocked the car door, adding as I did so: 'And I'm not prepared to discuss this further.'

My determination made me sound pompous although I doubt that bothered her. She was thick-skinned, not a woman to be cast aside. I slid onto the driver's seat and said a cold goodbye before closing the door.

She stretched out a hand, futile as I responded by locking the door. Her eyes stayed on me while I fastened my seat belt and started the engine. I didn't look at her until I lifted a hand in a faint gesture of farewell. It wasn't until then she admitted defeat, stepping back and letting the car move off.

For a few minutes I drove automatically, going through the motions of real life but numbed. When I was on the ring road insistent thoughts thrust themselves upon me.

Meryl Aylard came for me. She had a detective root me out. He found Sandy. June's talking to Gillian Spry today. I'm powerless to stop them doing whatever they fancy. Any attempt to manipulate them will make it worse.

Round and round they went, in a giddy whirl of anxiety.

Feeling sick, I pulled into a layby. Gigantic lorries lurched past inches away, buffeting the car. If I opened the door and got out I could be crushed. Cars slowed in a tailback and drivers looked idly at me. Was one a detective? I turned my head away and looked without seeing at the ragged hedgerow and dumped garbage.

'I wish they would all go away,' I blurted out, my voice petulant. Despairing, too, because none of the actors in the drama had any intention of leaving, and the underlying problem never went away. Yet the sheer hopelessness of it helped because it meant it was no use laying plans, none whatsoever worrying. I must face things as they arose, and meanwhile I ought to put it out of mind.

Driving on, I concentrated on the meeting ahead of me. The client was one of my best ever and a personal friend. It's a bonus when you work with a person you admire and who trusts your instincts.

A year back she'd offered me a staff job, which was excellent for my morale, yet I turned her down. My excuses were inventions: the distance was too great for daily commuting and I didn't wish to move house. She didn't press me too much. Women readily accept you might live in a house you love, or that other domestic arrangements might be your chief concern. Anyway, she wasn't losing me. Our business relationship continued as before.

Eight miles out of town this journey takes me over a flyover. It's a busy junction where I usually crawl while heavy vehicles lumber up to motorway access roads. This day, though, as I was late I'd missed the worst. I reached the roundabout and was pulling into the centre lane when I was hooted at and blocked by a speeding van. The van hurtled past me onto the roundabout. I heard a bang and saw it tilt as a car coming from the right crashed into it.

Behind me another horn sounded. I put my foot on the accelerator, sped down the access road and away up the motorway. In a great rush of adrenaline, I'd escaped. I was free. I'd cut myself off from everything. I could go anywhere I chose. Whose business was it but mine? I was *free*. I didn't have to explain or justify myself. If I wanted to go away, then I could. So that's what I was doing.

I had no idea where I was heading, and that was the joy of it. Just to be here now and a different place in a while, was enough. Hating the past and fearing the future, I decided to have nothing more to do with either of them and to live in the present. All that mattered was to have petrol in the tank and a road to drive on. I drove. On and on, I drove.

I passed under bridges where cows and farmers were a frieze against the sky. I skirted towns where warehouses looked like temporary camps on fields beside the motorway. I passed lorries and was overtaken by expense-account limousines. For a spell, I noticed horse-boxes, and then read directions to a race course. Sheep stuffed woolly noses through gaps in the sides of cattle trucks. Children pulled faces at me from the rear seats of estate cars.

On and on I drove. I squinted at sun angled through the windscreen. I played my wipers double speed in a pelting shower. I gazed dispassionately through long grey stretches of the day. When I noticed I was hungry, I swerved into a service station and ate mysterious soup followed by a plate of fried food with chips. Then I lingered over dark coffee, treacherously hot. Outside the window by my table the cars flashed, the lorries, vans, horse-boxes, cattle trucks and cars, cars, cars. Everyone was going somewhere. Everyone except me knew where they were going.

A teenage boy with spots pushed a trolley alongside me and clattered dirty dishes out of my way. I thanked him with a smile but he was gazing out of the window at the lorries, the trucks, the cars, the cars, the cars.

I went into the shop, planning to stock up on chocolate, sweets and mineral water. They catered for forgetful travellers so I bought toothbrush and paste, and tried to look like an inefficient packer rather than a runaway.

That's what I was. A runaway. A shucker-off of impossible predicaments. A puller-of-plugs on awful situations. As I couldn't change the predicaments or improve the situations, I was running away. It was utterly reasonable.

I felt like a child again, seeing the direct way out of a difficulty and seizing it, without being hampered by the iffing and butting of adult considerations. Like the girl on the window-sill who watched the funeral car, I was guided by a simple logic. For a few minutes in the car, for a few miles of motorway after I left the service station, I felt us merge into one. She had once been me. I'd thought I could never become her. But that day, for a time, I did.

CHAPTER SIXTEEN

The little red car was maintaining a steady pace, three vehicles behind me, never more and never less.

I put my foot down, scooted past a French truck, cut back into the centre lane and well and truly broke the speed limit for half a mile. The little red car was behind me, three cars away.

Coming up to a service station, I moved to the inside lane. When the exit was flagged, I indicated I was turning off. At the last safe moment, I flicked off my indicator and charged on instead. There was congestion ahead. Traffic was filtering in from the service station and messing up the free flow. I changed lanes for a few hundred yards, dropped back to the inside lane and checked my rear mirror.

Damn. The red car was right there. Three vehicles behind. Always the same distance away. Always with me.

I first noticed it how many miles ago? Eighty? Ninety? But how long was it hanging there before it caught my eye? Ever since I left home? Or since I joined the motorway? She'd told him and he'd come pell-mell after me.

'Watch her,' she'd instructed. 'I want to know where she goes and who she sees and what she does and, this is the priority, mind, *I have to know what she's thinking*. She won't tell me, you see. Won't tell anybody. Never has. So it's up to you to find out. You're a detective, aren't you? Well, then, find out.'

I heard her voice as clearly as I'd heard it when she accosted me by the car park. My car park, I mean. The one behind my garden. Oh yes, I heard Meryl Aylard putting him up to it.

'I don't care what it costs or how long it takes,' she was saying, 'I want the job done. It's a matter of life and death, you see. My father's life and death. Oh, and her mother's life and death, although I don't care so much about that. Got it? I want to know what she's doing and where she's going and, above all, *what she's thinking*.'

Around the next town the motorway grew busy. We bunched, we slowed, we swerved from one lane to another which caused more slowing and bunching. We ignored speed restrictions and honking flat-bed drivers and we swerved and bunched and slowed. Through it all, the little red car stayed behind me.

Another thought: was the driver Gillian Spry? She'd followed me once, I suspected, and I wouldn't put it past her to do it again. But did she have a red car? I seemed to recall green. Oh, but she would use a different one to put me off the scent. Then I remembered it couldn't be her because she was interviewing June, and nothing on earth would prevent her doing that.

I wove my way through, like the free end in a knot of string. Then, in the outside lane and cruising way above eighty, I pulled ahead, putting space between me and the rest. When the distance was far enough and the traffic was quiet enough, I flashed an indicator and flew across three lanes, making for an exit. I raced up it, screeched to a stop at the top, gave way to a line of vehicles inching around a roundabout, and then I went at a sedate pace down the access road on the other side, rejoined the motorway and settled down for the long, long drive.

He was behind me. Three cars away.

By now my anger was boiling. What had he done? Pulled over onto the hard shoulder and waited for me to emerge again? But I didn't care how he'd done it, I was too angry. He had no right. At least, I didn't think so. He wasn't the police, he was a private detective. Meryl Aylard's private detective, that's all. He didn't amount to much but he was buzzing me, making me burn with indignation, making me do things I didn't wish to do.

I decided to change my tactics, to give up trying to outpace him or fool him. Instead I would slow right down and force him to overtake, which he would have to do if he was to retain any semblance of being a driver on a normal journey. In fact, I might stop altogether.

My speed gradually dropped. I felt calmer. I drove sensibly and with consideration for other road users, safely and normally. Soon I let my car slow, slow, slow. The car behind pulled out and overtook. The one behind him followed. There was only me and a small red car quite some distance behind.

'He isn't closing the gap. A giveaway, a complete giveaway.' If ever I'd doubted my instinct, this vindicated me. I was almost pleased he was hanging back, trailing a steady distance behind.

'Well, at least I know where you are,' I thought. And for a few hundred yards that was a consolation. If he'd been switching vehicles to trick me, I wouldn't have known where danger lay.

It's always good to know where the danger lies. I haven't always known, not all through my life, and I've had bad experiences because of it. But no, I won't dwell on that. Those things are past. Long gone and buried. No use in digging for them. I mean, what for? To see whether they have the power to hurt me as much as they once did? To test whether their threat has diminished or I've grown tougher and learned how to combat them? No use. Leave them there, leave them buried.

Daylight was fading. I didn't choose to stop again but the petrol gauge was low. While I waited at the pump, I saw him. He was about thirty-five with crew-cut hair and a pinkish wind-whipped face. The red car drew up at a pump away to my right and I saw him plainly as he got out. I watched him while he refilled, and I was forced to admire the fact that he was so controlled he appeared to ignore me. Nobody would have guessed he'd chased me for hours.

Without a backward glance, he walked to the office to pay. By the time he came out, I was filling my tank. His eyes swept over the forecourt but he didn't show recognition. That was the only glance he risked in my direction.

I didn't see him when I left the pumps or drove down the access road, but I was too wary to assume he'd abandoned me. Two miles on, I caught a glimpse of red in my rear-view mirror. Recognition was almost a relief. At least I could stop wondering what had become of him.

Traffic was sparse for the first half-hour, then there was a build-up near a city, then it dwindled again. Through thick and thin the little red car was there, as though I'd learned a trick for long-distance towing. I began to be afraid what he might do when it got truly dark.

While the next big town was only an electric glow on the horizon, I decided to get off the motorway. I plunged up a steeply rising exit, took the first road on my left without a pause and careered down a well-lit dual carriageway. My pursuer seemed not to have followed. I had a long stretch of road to myself, a quarter of a mile perhaps, before a vehicle's headlights blinked distantly in the mirror.

Unfortunately, I met speed limits and a sinuous village with local traffic pottering along. There was nothing I could do except slow down and sense my crew-cut detective catching up on me.

On the far side of the village I ran into winding country lanes and soon became aware of his headlights. Our lights flashed over lonely barns, majestic trees and empty fields. I hardly saw the car and when I did the darkness deprived me of its dashing red.

He had me at a disadvantage because I didn't know the road and dared not go fast. I tried other means of throwing him off. When I spotted a pub at a crossroads, I drove through its car park to turn left rather than pull up at the junction. Soon lights were gaining on me again. I thought about stopping in a layby but immediately realised

I'd be putting myself in danger. Instead, I swung into a service road in front of a terrace of shops in a village and crouched down out of sight, which was a mistake because I didn't know whether he'd sped by or was lingering and looking for me.

A few minutes later, I chanced driving on. Before many miles had gone by, the villages grew bigger and closer together and then merged into conurbation. I went quietly into the heart of the town, discovering how tired I was. Anger and fear are exhausting and I'd suffered them most of the day.

A choice. Left to the port or right to the town centre. I wanted to go to the port, to cross the water and vanish into the confusion of the continent. I hesitated. An impatient motor-cyclist manoeuvred around me. I desperately needed to get on a boat, but did they sail through the night? Well, I could ask. I jerked the steering-wheel to the left, then hesitated again. Would a boat take me out of the country without a passport? I thought not, and drove towards the town centre.

Soon I saw a hotel sign and booked myself in. As the receptionist handed over the room key I said to him: 'I'll fetch my stuff from the car later. I have to go out again, anyway.'

He wished me a goodnight. I wonder whether he could see I was too shattered to go anywhere except to bed, and whether he knew there was no luggage in the car. Probably. They develop a sense for our little shifts and lies, don't they?

The room was clean and comfortable in that cheerful mock-up of the English country-house style. I kicked off my shoes, dropped my coat on a flowery armchair, pulled back the padded quilt and stretched out. That's all I remember for hours.

My mother was in my dream. Rita was laughing at me, scoffing. I'd done something wrong, I don't think I understood what, and she was telling me I was stupid and laughing at me. I was desperate to escape and battled to unlock a door but, when I succeeded, it proved to be the door of her wardrobe rather than the way out of the room. She loomed over me. She was wearing the dress with the butterflies on it.

She was laughing but what she was saying wasn't humorous. I covered my ears with my hands and tried to block her words, but they savaged me all the same.

'I'll kill you, you little bitch. If it wasn't for you, I wouldn't be here, stuck in this stinking hole. You know that, don't you? It's all your fault. If it wasn't for you . . . I'll kill you. Little bitch.'

And it echoed like a song, the identical phrases over and over, the order changed to suit the mood but the same wicked words.

Her face was thrusting at me, its ugly grimace an offence. I stepped back, suddenly nervous she was going to bite, but I stumbled and grabbed at the door-frame. With a downward slap she loosened my grip and pushed me into the cupboard, smothering my face against the tarty clothes her lover bought her. The stink of them choked me. Dried on sweat. Stale perfume. Scummy make-up traces. Tobacco smoke. Heaving, I recovered my balance and tried to back off. But she shoved me face first into them again, and she held me there.

Throughout she was screaming at me. *Little bitch. Kill. Bitch. Kill. Kill. Kill*. In the torrent of her fury, those were the words that seared me.

The door slammed. The key turned. The odour of the garments sickened me. I vomited, down the sophisticated black grosgrain dress.

With a start I woke up, disorientated, knowing nothing of the hotel and my journey to it. I lay, frightened, worn out, lost.

Light seeped beneath the door from the landing. Gingerly, I stood up and moved towards it. My leg brushed against an armchair. I felt along a wall and, on my progress towards the band of light, I touched a switch. The room leapt into view.

Everything came back then, with a rush. June and her folly in talking to Gillian Spry; Meryl Aylard and her pursuit, and the detective and his; the town and the hotel. Which town? What hotel? I picked up a folder on the dressing-table and discovered where I was. It was a very long way from anywhere I'd previously been in England.

'I've run away,' I thought. 'Nobody here knows me. I've run away and I'm never going back. I'm never going back because I don't want Sandy Minch to find me and because I know it won't be over as long as Meryl Aylard is alive.'

But at that second I heard my mother's sneering voice. 'It's all your fault . . .'

I spun round, fearful of finding her in the room. Often, after she died, my mind played tricks and persuaded me she was walking down the street, or going by on a bus, or caught in the background of holiday snaps a friend was showing off. Since she died she's been on television, taken part in an Australian soap opera, won a lottery ticket, posed by numerous well-photographed monuments and once, spectacularly, she figured in the tearing down of the Berlin Wall. I've seen her everywhere.

I've seen her everywhere and, in my dreams, I've heard her. But the dreams, what are they? Imaginative flights or fragments of a life relived? The locking in the cupboard was real. The vomiting on the black dress happened. The wicked words were burned into my memory, although I only listen to them in my sleep.

How can I say what's real and what's elaboration? I'm no longer the child who endured and I can't slip back inside her to check. If I, as an adult, ache for her unremitting suffering, it's because that's what an adult feels when a child is wronged. I honestly don't know how those scenes weighed in *her* scale of things. Were Rita's tantrums harder than having a father who took no notice? Were they both worse than the disloyalty of a friend? My scales aren't hers, our opinions may not coincide. And I come back to it, always: her feelings are a secret from me. She is a stranger.

I washed, and opened the bottle of mineral water on the hotel room dressing table. Hungry, too, having eaten nothing since afternoon, I ate the packet of three biscuits on the tray with the kettle and instant coffee, the tea-bags and plastic pots of milk. Then I hung up my coat, blouse and skirt, left my underwear on the chair and I fell into bed.

Whenever I closed my eyes and drifted sleepwards, that dreadful laugh brought me shuddering awake. Rita challenged me in the turquoise blue shantung suit which was mentioned at the trial. She attacked me in the dusty pink that made her as dumpy and dull as a blancmange. Finally, she accused me in the black grosgrain with sour streaks of vomit down the skirt.

'I'm dead and it's all your fault, you little bitch.'

Sleep was impossible. Lying awake, rest was too. My brain seethed with images, recriminations, memories and fantastic wishes that could never be granted. Hounded by guilt, I fought back with accusations. For hour after hour, the arguments raged silently within me. My limbs were leaden, as though all my strength was being spent on fighting the old battles, fending off the foes that threatened to overwhelm me.

Dennis Aylard grinned at me, the loose-lipped smile that had made me cringe whenever he turned it my way. He put a hand to his throat, unbuttoning the uncomfortable shirt collar and sliding down the knot of his tie. He moved towards me, hand outstretched. It was a podgy hand, on one finger a thick gold signet ring embedded with flashy stones. Red, white and blue, a patriotic colour scheme for a swindler and a smuggler. I watched the hand getting nearer and nearer to me but I stood my ground.

Sandy Minch had said I was silly to run away from him, that I ought to stand up to him and tell him to go away.

'Go away,' I said, in a thin little voice, when the hand dropped on my shoulder.

His eyes disappeared into folds of flesh as his smile tightened. 'Go away? Is that what you said, Ann? Go away? You don't mean that.'

We were in a tableau, he waiting to see whether I was going to squirm out of his grasp and I discovering I was paralysed, as usual.

I didn't have any power. Not over him. I could make a grown-up person angry to the stage of frenzy, as I'd done to Rita, but that was as far as it went. I couldn't make an adult respect me.

Sandy had said I wasn't to put up with it. 'Girls mustn't let men do what they like, because afterwards they don't respect them.'

'Who said that?'

'Everybody says it.'

She was speaking in her superior manner but I gathered it was merely talk she'd overheard. I doubt whether she realised there was a specific meaning, and I certainly didn't. She applied the advice generally. I applied it to defending myself against Dennis Aylard.

So I tried a second time. 'Stop it. Go away.'

My voice was slightly louder but the tone was wrong. I wished I sounded threatening, fierce, like a troublesome girl who's got a fine pair of lungs and is ready to scream until she bursts.

But who would save me if I screamed? My father glued to the wireless in the kitchen? My mother drenching herself with French perfume and body lotions, in preparation for an evening with this monster? I pictured her upstairs, jiggling her breasts into a tiny lace brassiere he bought her, wriggling her behind into the lace knickers, rolling the fully-fashioned stockings up her legs and looking over her shoulder into the mirror as she straightened the seams. She was going to a business meeting with him, she was too busy to listen to me. I didn't scream.

He knew I wasn't the screaming type. He'd known it for months. I was frozen as he moved in closer, ran his hand down my front and felt where my breasts would grow one day, and moved his hand further until he lifted my skirt and felt between my legs.

'Go away?' he repeated, pinching my bare thigh. 'You know you like it.'

His voice had changed, become breathy and his face was very close to mine because he had to get down low. A sort of dreaminess had come over it, as though he might nod off to sleep.

A door closed somewhere in the house. He rose and moved away from me so fast that, if anyone had come into the room that very minute, they would never have guessed. I believe he was confident I wouldn't tell them, anyway. I hadn't the first time, you see, and after a while it seemed impossible to do so. Whoever I told would ask why I hadn't mentioned it before, besides which they mightn't believe me. When I complained to my mother about him pawing Sandy's knee, on one of our outings in his car, she called me a liar.

My solution was to avoid him and I became efficient at it. This day I made a mistake, letting him indoors to wait for Rita and not thinking he dared touch me while he was in our house. It was my mistake and I felt that made it my fault.

I didn't tell anybody and that included Sandy. All I admitted to her was he plonked his hand on my shoulder and patted me, and that he gave me the creeps. True, although not the full truth. When I started to tell her I intended to spill out everything, but the quickening interest in her eyes persuaded me I would regret it. Sandy was a gossip.

So I didn't tell anyone and then, amazingly, Dennis Aylard did! Drunk, he taunted Rita with it.

She burst into my bedroom in a drunken rage while I was asleep, flew at me with her nails, screaming that I was a slut. 'Slut! Slut! Dirty little bitch. I'll kill you.'

I was howling that I didn't know what I'd done. She spelled it out, regardless of the fact I didn't understand the vocabulary or the concept. According to him, I was supposed to have sidled up to him, fondled him, said all manner of things that were mysteries to me, and tried to interest him in using me sexually.

All I could think was they'd gone mad, the pair of them. She had an uncle who'd grown paranoid and violent so perhaps that was it, madness in her family. But Aylard? Did he have a mad old relation, too?

Next morning Sandy called for me. The appalling scene was recorded on my face by Rita's nails. There was no chance of not discussing it with Sandy when the evidence was in front of her. Besides, I felt an urgent need to talk about it.

'I don't understand it,' I repeated.

She looked terribly wise and said I was to make an end of it. 'You put up with too much, Ann. It's time you put your foot down.'

'Yes,' I wailed. '*But how?*'

Sandy tipped her head on one side and regarded me seriously. Then she told me.

In the hotel room I staggered to my feet, knocking a bedside lamp to the floor and breaking the bulb. Then began a restless wandering in the dark, while I grappled with the demons tormenting me.

It was too much. I'd endured too much. I couldn't take any more, I had to put my foot down . . .

The demons threw at me Sandy's words, my mother's accusations, Aylard's sliminess, my father's acquiescence . . . They shrieked that it was *my fault*. Sometimes they used Rita's voice. Then it would be Sandy's or Aylard's. Practically anybody I'd ever known was pressed into their service.

My eyes adjusted to the dim light. I tramped the space from the bed to the window. I found myself in the bathroom. I circled the armchair. I tried sitting down but I couldn't be still. I was frantically trying to evade the hounding voices. Once I saw a red car out of the corner of my eye, over by the dressing-table, but when I whirled round to catch Meryl Aylard's detective in the act of spying, there was nothing but a dressing-table.

With unsteady hands, I poured a glass of water and drank it carefully, the glass clinking against my teeth. The demons were chanting things I hated to hear.

'I won't listen,' I said aloud, my voice a weary whisper.

'Oh, but you will,' they said.

I threw myself on the bed and covered my head with the pillow to shut them out. But I smelled stale perfume and vomit and I dropped the pillow over the side of the bed and began to weep.

For hours I wept. My tears provoked memories of earlier tears. My secret horrors the night before the hanging. My noisy outburst when they told me my mother was dead. Lots of tears, for lots of reasons. Crying I remembered them all, and remembering made me cry more.

My life seemed hopeless. I tussled with one disaster after another and yet, after all these years, I'd achieved nothing. I couldn't leave the childhood tragedy behind me. It had always burdened me, although I succeeded in pushing it out of my consciousness apart from those three anniversaries; but an Aylard family campaign and a CJI investigation were about to expose the case, dangle me before the public, make it utterly impossible for me to carry on as I'd managed for the last few years.

Death seemed my only escape. I lay there planning how to do it. I compared methods, one with another, and selected the means of my own death. At the time this didn't seem absurd or self-indulgent. I believed I was the only one who mattered and I was prepared to act in the way that guaranteed me least pain. If avoiding further anguish meant dying, then I was ready for it.

The plumbing disturbed me. The guest in the next room had a weak bladder and went to the bathroom three times in the hour before dawn. When light broke, I pushed back the curtain and looked out, curious at last to know what it was like, this town which would be the last place I ever saw.

A beach, grey in dawn light. The whiteness of breakers rolling out of darkness. Shapes that suggested boats moored in a harbour. A gull landed on my balcony, its flapping wings obscuring my view. Waggling a hand, I shooed it away so I could watch a figure walking along the beach.

The sky was brightening, revealing miles of sea and the muddled streets of the town. Fishing boats were lurching back to harbour. Loose lines were flapping on anchored yachts. People were being towed along the pavement by their dogs. A fat man was jogging. Sporadic cars and bicycles tootled by. A paper boy lugged his load from letter-box to letter-box. A sentimental sun was scattering gold and dabbing the sky with pink. As it rose higher, lengthening shadows created the impression that everything in sight was waking up and stretching, ready for the new day.

All at once, I was eager to be out there, too.

CHAPTER SEVENTEEN

'Worth the detour?' Richard King enquired, bouncing into the CJI office the morning after Gillian Spry's visit to June Foley.

'Yes, thanks.'

He chivvied. 'Well?'

'I'm holding on until you sit down, in case you fall over with astonishment.'

He strode round behind his desk. 'Right, I'm sitting.'

'Dennis Aylard is innocent and John Morden murdered his wife.'

'Good God. Did he? Morden, I mean. Did he do it?' When his eyebrows shot up in amazement he looked extremely owlish.

Gillian smothered a smile. 'Miss Foley says so.'

'Wow!'

'That's roughly what *I* said.'

He whipped off his glasses and began swinging them about by the arm. 'What did she offer for proof?'

'Only a confession.'

'*Confession!*'

Gillian looked over her shoulder. 'We seem to have an echo in the room this morning. What's more you're talking in exclamations.'

He shot her a look. Then: 'Come on, out with it, Gillian. I want it line by line before I'm prepared to believe a syllable of it.'

'And I want a sustaining cup of coffee while I tackle the task of convincing you.'

She put the kettle on to boil and fiddled with the mugs and things, letting Richard absorb what she'd already told him. The little smile playing around her lips was unavoidable.

A few minutes later she was happy to begin the tale, much as she planned it in her head in bed the previous night. This time it was essential for him to understand everything. Ideally, he would have accompanied her but they were overstretched and, anyhow, June had invited her alone. It had seemed rash to risk taking him along. With hindsight, that was the wrong decision but how could they have guessed what the formerly reticent June Foley was about to reveal?

'Here we go,' Gillian said, flipping open her notebook once the coffee mugs were on their desks.

She began with her driving up to June's address, and summed up the old bay-windowed house overlooking the park as tattered Edwardian-suburban. Richard had never seen it and she felt it was important to set the scene.

On her other two visits she stayed in the porch. Yesterday, having rung the bell twice she began to worry that June Foley had changed her mind yet again, and wasn't going to open up. Then there were sounds the other side of the door, a chain was being removed and a key turned.

June Foley dressed for the occasion in a jersey suit a gentle shade of green and took extra care in pinning back her grey hair. She was spindly thin which Gillian thought lent her an elegance many younger women would envy. The effect was spoiled, though, when June led the way down the hall and her awkward gait and clumpy shoes proved she was partially disabled.

They went into the sitting-room. June seated herself in her usual chair and left Gillian a choice of four others. Gillian picked one which gave her a sporting chance of seeing her subject's face in daylight.

'Do you think it's too early for a sherry?' June asked, but

in a way that suggested it would be as naughty as spoiling a child's fun to say yes.

'Sherry would be lovely.' Gillian didn't care what the hour was or what they drank providing June eventually told her something that made the long drive worth while.

The sherry was remarkably dry, so dry her tongue felt singed by the first sip. However, Miss Foley coped and Gillian couldn't see any way to avoid matching her. She wondered how Ann Morden fared, whether she avoided the sherry or endured it. It was virtually impossible to imagine her enjoying it.

'Did you have a reasonable journey down?' June asked, stalling.

Gillian nodded. 'Except for a tailback on the ring road here.'

'The council says the changes to the roads in town are an improvement but I've yet to meet a driver who agrees.'

After another, cautious, sip of sherry Gillian urged her on. 'Of course you've known the town all your life. You were here when the murder happened.'

Correcting her, June engaged with the subject at last. 'No, I wasn't. I was on holiday.'

'Yes, I know. What I meant was that this was your home.'

'We all lived around here, all the Mordens and the Foleys. Rita was the youngest of my father's three sisters, you know. Patch – well, her proper name was Patricia but in the family she was known as Patch. She married an American and emigrated to the States. Nella, who was really an Eleanor, married the ironmonger's son and they lived over the shop in Church Street.'

Gillian was patient with the family history, trusting there wouldn't be too many Foleys and Mordens to chart before they could think about murder. 'What did your father do, June?'

'He was an accountant, working for a firm that used to have premises next to the Red Lion. It's gone now. He was Stewart Foley, named after his father, and he was the eldest. My mother, Jean, was the daughter of a widowed schoolmistress who inherited a couple of rather decrepit cottages in Church Passage.'

She hesitated, then hurried on with the story of the cottages. 'That bequest caused a bit of bother because the Foleys thought she ought to let Nella and her young ironmonger live in one. It would have been extremely convenient for them, a step away from the shop, but my grandmother refused to throw out the existing tenants. My poor mother was driven to distraction by the Foleys bemoaning Nella's bad luck in having to raise a family of four in two rooms over the shop.'

While June was using words like imposition and grudge, Gillian was revising her opinion that the Foleys of the Fifties were a close-knit clan wrecked by the tragedy of murder. She'd imagined she understood June's earlier claims to be defending her family but now she was less sure. Wherever this family saga was leading, it wasn't where she'd expected.

'What about the Mordens?' she wondered, coaxing June.

June dismissed them with a sweep of her hand. 'I'll explain about Rita first. I'm sure you think your research has taught you as much as you need to know about her, but let me give you my version. I was eighteen when she died. I liked her because she was amusing and adventurous in a way women weren't allowed to be then.'

Gillian had a hilarious suspicion June was about to declare Rita Morden an early feminist. She wondered how she would manage not to laugh. Luckily, June's story was nothing of the sort.

'She was the family pet, spoiled, the one who could do no wrong in her parents' eyes. My father was rather entertained by her antics for a long while but Patch and Nella resented the attention she got. Within the family, that is. What happened later when she fell for Dennis Aylard was quite different, yet I imagine that if you analysed it you'd decide it was all of a piece with her behaviour while she was growing up.'

She broke off and topped up Gillian's half-empty glass then refilled her own. The door eased open and a fat spaniel blundered into the room. He sniffed Gillian's shoes, veered away leaving a strong whiff of dog in the air, and sank down beside June. Gillian made an effort not to wrinkle her nose.

June, patting the dog, recounted how Rita married John Morden in defiance of her parents and settled down to be a faithful wife during the war, while plenty of local women were otherwise.

'The Foleys considered John Morden an uninspiring man who went where Rita led. They thought she should have done better for herself, as she was pretty and enjoyed dress-making.'

June made one of numerous historical digressions to ensure Gillian fully appreciated what she was hearing. 'The only way ordinary women could get clothes without coupons was to make them. Either you did it yourself or you had a good friend who did it for you. Nella and Rita had great rows over the sewing-machine, it became a family legend.'

Digression over, she told Gillian how John Morden's personality was changed by the war, and this had led directly to the tragedy. Gillian was feigning greater fascination than she felt. Despite June's conviction that all was new to CJI, most of it wasn't.

Pushing the spaniel's head away from her lap, June said: 'He wasn't physically injured but he was with comrades who were blown up and it affected his mind. He became withdrawn. I suppose these days he would be diagnosed as suffering from post-traumatic stress disorder or, at any rate, depression. Back then people learned to live with it.'

Growing aware how much time she was spending and how little of her journey she'd covered, she sped on, rattling out facts rather than meandering wordily from one point to the next. She described how, for several years after Ann was born, Rita continued to be the loyal wife but when it became apparent John wasn't going to improve, she began to lead her own life.

'My parents were shocked at how badly she reacted, railing that her life was being ruined and she didn't see why she shouldn't have some fun. The next stage is the part everyone knows about: other men and finally Dennis Aylard. The part that gets overlooked is that Rita was earning money and John was relying on her to do it. He had nothing, although the pair of them encouraged the family to believe he bought that house in The Avenue with a legacy and they were living on the rent from the other half. It was a face-saving fiction.'

'A lie. But why? Wouldn't their families have helped if they'd known the truth?'

'That was Rita's pride. We don't think John was up to making decisions, he just went along with the subterfuge.'

'And sat at home while she went about her doubtful work?'

'Until Aylard her work was legitimate. We knew the people she was involved with in town. To begin with she worked for a man who owned a small factory behind the old police station. Then she had a spell on a market stall. After that she was a sales rep for a knitting wool company. The significant job, though, was the one for a builder because it was when she visited a site with him that she met a property developer called Dennis Aylard.'

Gillian ventured that Aylard's property deals were few and far between, and the received opinion was that they were a cover for a variety of swindles.

'Yes,' June said. 'I don't dispute he was a con man, but Rita was one of the people he conned. That's the family view, anyway, that she didn't see through him or realise her job amounted to being his escort, rather than his personal assistant or whatever she fancied she was. My father quite sourly remarked that she ended up as a gangster's moll, and he wasn't far wrong.'

Gillian reminded June the jury had heard Aylard killed Rita because she *had* realised his business was crime.

Before replying, June absently stroked the spaniel whose head was in her lap again. 'No,' she said quietly. 'Dennis Aylard didn't kill her. John Morden did.'

And while Gillian was absorbing the surprise, June hurried on with an account of John waiting in the garden until Rita walked down the path, returning from an outing with Aylard.

'John told my father, you see. Father went to visit him and John told him. Oh, this was three or four years after Aylard was hanged for it. We none of us had any idea until then. But that was the truth of it: they hanged an innocent man.'

Gillian was enjoying the familiar thrill she felt whenever the lock on a mystery sprang undone. She kept up a regular supply of questions, eager to extract what she could lest June backtracked. Experience had taught her the unpredictability of people, especially those with dramatic tales to tell.

June's answers were fluent. He used a starting-handle he found on the land behind the house but he didn't know it was Aylard's. He was back indoors for half an hour before the last of his party-giving neighbour's guests discovered the body. He didn't explain why he killed her, but June's parents thought that was obvious.

'It makes sense to me, too,' June added. 'He was ridiculously tolerant but one day he'd had enough. There wasn't a row between Dennis Aylard and Rita that evening but there was a fatal one between Rita and her husband.'

She was hurrying along, confusing Gillian about what came first-hand from John Morden to Stewart Foley, what was deduction by Stewart and Jean Foley, and what was June's own latter-day interpretation. Gillian was anxious to separate the strands and, with a little patience, succeeded.

Reporting next day to Richard King, she was meticulous about stating what John Morden was said to have told his brother-in-law.

'We don't have their exact words, needless to say. The story goes that Stewart was visiting him in a convalescent home three or four years after the murder. John was ill on and off after Rita died. Or perhaps it's correct to say he was worse, because there are plenty of indications that he was fragile since coming home after the war. Out of the blue he announced to Stewart that he killed Rita, using a starting-handle lying on the waste land. Apparently, Stewart had the presence of mind to press him for details after which John claimed he waited in the garden shed until she came down the path after meeting Aylard.'

Richard went over to study the sketch on the flip-chart. 'Yes, if she could walk from the house without being seen by people at the party, so could he. But didn't people give him an alibi? He was said to have gone into the adjoining house when it rained, wasn't he? And to have stayed there until the party finished?'

She bit her lip. 'Timing, again. It depends when she was attacked.'

Richard jabbed the drawing with a finger. 'If he went into this room, the one with the radiogram up at the window, he could have looked across the garden and noticed her on her way to meet Aylard. Then he could have hung around outside until she returned.'

'No, impossible. He couldn't have seen her because the outside lights were switched off for safety once it started raining. They'd only hitched up a length of wire and bulbs, a dangerous arrangement in a downpour. That was cleared up at the trial: the lights were off.'

'Oh. Yes, I remember now. Hmm.' He twirled his glasses round and round while he considered how John Morden might have managed to kill his wife and get away with it.

'I'm not happy about the starting-handle,' Gillian admitted. 'By the time John's mentioning it, it's common knowledge the jury was told the weapon was a starting-handle.'

'Aylard's starting-handle. With his palm print on it.'

'Yes. Not John Morden's palm print from gripping it while he struck her. And the other thing, don't let's forget, is Winterlea's original opinion that she was whacked with a hunk of wood. Splinters in the wounds, he wrote.'

She stood up from her desk and walked to the window. Below, passers-by were clutching at hair whisked by a mischievous breeze. Richard was saying it was unfortunate for the police that the scene of the crime was muddy and soaking wet. Collecting evidence had been described, by one officer involved, as a nightmare.

Gillian's thoughts were taking a different tack and she interrupted him with: 'Wait a minute. Do you recall what was said at the trial about the police finding the starting-handle?'

'Not precisely.'

She tapped at her computer keyboard, then: 'Got it. Listen. The police said it was found on land to the rear of the garden. Aylard insisted the police took it from his car when they searched it the day after the murder. If his story was true, the police were fitting him up and Winterlea was adapting his evidence to suit.'

'Which is what we know happened in a number of other cases.' He shrugged. 'I don't wish to sound unduly stupid but how does any of that help us assess the likelihood of John Morden's confession being genuine?'

'The point is he doesn't say anything not said in court. And we can be certain he's drawing on what was claimed at the trial because we also know some of those things were false. Therefore his confession was false, if he made it at all.'

Richard grumbled that with John being dead there was no means of getting at that particular truth. 'When did June say he popped off?'

'Early seventies. He went to live abroad and stayed there until his death. She didn't cite the year.'

They thought it over for a minute. Then Gillian spoke for both of them. 'It's too convenient, isn't it? Now that Dennis Aylard stands a chance of being proved innocent, out of the hat comes a confession by a man who's already dead.'

He retorted that his word for it wasn't convenient, he called it downright frustrating. 'The ideal means of proving Aylard innocent is to advance the real killer's confession. But, under these circumstances, Morden's story, genuine or not, can't be tested.'

'There's one avenue open to us. Suppose we see whether we can find anybody else who heard Morden confess. June Foley's story is second-hand but there's a chance we could track down a first-hand account.'

She was thinking of staff or patients at the hospital, maybe a confidant among the Morden family who also visited him when he was ill.

But Richard said: 'Anna? You always suspected she knows more than she admits.'

Gillian thought his idea shockingly distasteful. 'But not *that*. I can't believe her father would curse her with the secret that he killed her mother and sent an innocent man to the gallows.'

Richard said she ought to know better, that their job taught them people were capable of the most unfeeling acts.

In reply she accused him of pedantry. 'All right, I *can* believe it. But I resist it.'

'Did June throw any fresh light on Anna, or Ann as she was then?'

Gillian recreated for him the scene when June Foley's conversation turned to the young Ann.

The malodorous spaniel had slumped into a snoring heap by June's chair. Without the distraction of the dog's head in her lap, she allowed Gillian to watch her face while she talked. Gillian saw in it nothing to distrust. June had already made her momentous pronouncement that John Morden was guilty and Aylard, therefore, innocent, and now she seemed to be tying up the loose ends of the Rita Morden affair, for her own satisfaction rather than because she believed she had anything especially important to say.

'Once the trial was over, the family's chief concern was Ann. With her mother dead and her father unwell, they were obliged to rally round if she was to avoid going into a home. We call it "care" nowadays but when we were young it was always "going into a home". There was a definite stigma attached to it, you know, because if a child went into a home its family were shown up as people who shirked their responsibilities. I fancy there might have been a hangover of the wartime spirit which meant you all pulled together and looked after each other.'

It was an interpretation new to Gillian but she didn't disagree with it. She encouraged June with a nod.

June explained that little Ann proved more trouble than any of them expected. 'You remember what I told you about Rita as a girl?'

'You said Rita was spoiled but from what I've heard about Ann's early life that doesn't seem to apply to her.'

'No, you're quite right, Gillian. Ann wasn't spoiled. Quite the reverse, you may think. But what I have in mind is the way she reacted under pressure. She became known as a difficult child. Tears and tantrums when she wasn't silent and sulky. She simply wasn't nice to have around and so the family shared the burden by taking it in turns to look after her.'

Gillian wondered whether June's parents took Ann in.

'Yes,' June said, 'we had ample space because my brother had grown up and left home. Both my parents expected her to be comfortable here, thinking it was best for her to stay near her friends. Unfortunately, after a few weeks they were forced to change their minds.'

'Because she didn't settle?'

'Because of the talk in the town. It was making it difficult for us all and, naturally, Ann was at the hub of it. You see, there were strong feelings about the case. Local people were scandalised by the story of the cuckolded war-hero but they didn't accept Aylard was a murderer. There was a general expectation the jury would find him not guilty, and after he was convicted people convinced themselves his appeal would succeed. From the day of his arrest, wherever Foleys and Mordens went there was whispering.'

She encapsulated Ann's nomadic life over the rest of her schooldays. Away from the town, Ann would appear to adjust to a new household of Mordens or Foleys but before long she grew troublesome again.

'She was handed around the family like a baton,' June said grimly. 'It can't have done the girl any good, now can it? But, again, people took a different view back then. As far as they were concerned, they were doing the right thing because, however rough a ride she gave them, the family never let Ann be put into a home. Ann cut herself off from them all as soon as she was old enough to go.' She looked wry. 'I may say it's taken an effort on my part to find her, but I do see her occasionally.'

Gillian asked whether they found it easy to talk about the tragedy in Anna's past. June said she found it safer to avoid direct mention of the murder but, obviously, once Gillian appeared on the scene and Meryl Aylard followed, that proved impossible.

'I expect I'm being foolish,' she added, 'but I can't help feeling protective towards Anna. I'm sure she wouldn't thank me if she knew.'

'People don't,' Gillian replied, thinking of an entirely different situation in her own life.

June was touching on Anna's failed marriage, and what she called 'the disappointment over her child', when the telephone rang. It was on a table behind Gillian who automatically turned towards it. The newfangled answering machine struck her as odd in the dingy eclecticism of June Foley's inherited sitting-room, but perhaps there was nowhere more suitable to install it.

Brushing the spaniel out of her way, June went to answer. The machine was set to let the caller's voice be heard in the room so the conversation wasn't private.

'Hello, is that June?'

June's guarded 'Yes' made it clear she didn't recognise the woman's voice.

'My name's Susie Witham. I'm a friend of Anna Foley and I'm trying to get in touch with her. I wondered whether she was with you?'

Bewildered, June said not and added the redundant questions: 'Isn't she at home? Or at work?' Plainly the woman wouldn't be troubling her if Anna was where she was supposed to be.

'Well no, that's why . . .'

Gillian registered the caller's reluctance to spread alarm and June's growing conviction there was reason for alarm.

June said: 'Look, why don't you tell me why you're worried about her.'

'Yes, all right. She asked me to go to her house yesterday evening, about eight. When I was walking down the alley-way to it I was mugged by a couple of girls. They stole my handbag, the usual sort of thing.'

'Oh how awful for you. Were you hurt?'

'Injured pride, that's all. But the main thing is that Anna wasn't at home and she hasn't been since. I've tried every way I can think of to find her.'

A pause during which Gillian and June separately arrived at the conclusion they were being denied significant information.

June insisted. 'You must have a reason for being concerned about her.'

'Well, yes. I'm sorry to say her house was broken into. When I rushed up to the door, I discovered the lock forced. I'm afraid there's an awful mess.'

'Did you report it to the police?'

'Yes, immediately. The mugging and the break-in. I've put a new lock on the door but . . . Oh dear, I do wish I could find Anna. Do you have any idea at all where she might be?'

'None, I'm afraid. Now tell me, how did you get my telephone number?'

Susie explained she'd played through the tape on Anna's answering machine to see whether any of the messages gave clues to Anna's whereabouts, and she'd tapped out 1471 to see who rang last. June had.

'You sounded like a friend rather than a business call, so I took a chance and rang you.'

'Most enterprising. I'm her cousin.'

'Oh, you're that June. Yes, she mentions you. Well, look, I really don't want to worry you but perhaps I should tell you I rang a client of Anna's who left a message wondering why she failed to keep an appointment yesterday morning.'

The conversation petered out, leaving all three of them perplexed.

Afterwards June said, with what Gillian considered a rather beady look: 'Gillian, this is your line of country rather than mine. When we first met I thought you were a television documentary-maker but now I know you for a lawyer and something of a detective. So, how do we find a woman who's gone missing?'

But Gillian had moved on to wondering whether Anna was missing because June was naming John Morden as the killer.

Next day she related to Richard King how she gleaned what little she could about Anna's haunts when she wasn't at home or at work, and then brought the meeting with June Foley to a close.

She wanted to say to Richard: 'All at once I felt I understood Anna Foley, really understood her, and I wanted to extricate myself from June and her opinions and sift through my own.'

It had seemed all right when she lay awake the previous night thinking it over but now the opportunity arose, she ducked it, knowing he would accuse her of being fanciful.

Instead she said: 'What I want to do is get to Susie Witham, preferably before Anna comes back.'

He gave her a hard look. 'No you don't, Gill. You would have done it by now, if that were true.'

'Oh? What's the truth then?'

'That you're *not* expecting Anna back.'

Rather than own up, she gave a careless shrug.

'I'll quiz Susie Witham. I have her telephone number because she gave it to June Foley in my hearing.'

'My turn,' he said, faking resignation at once again being left to last. 'You want to know what *I* did yesterday?'

Ironically she said: 'I was relying on you to complete the Winterlea dossier.'

'Well, how's this? I heard from Meryl Aylard that the detective her family are employing has traced two alibi witnesses. They've been living in Bristol all along. Aylard claimed he was talking to them in a pub at the time the prosecution said he was driving to Rita Morden's house and killing her. He said they fell into conversation in the car park because they owned similar vehicles.'

Gillian was sceptical. 'Not much of an alibi, a conversation about cars in a pub car park.'

'But the couple do remember it, mainly because he offered to get them a new model if they wanted to trade up. Cars were one of his scams, remember.'

'Yes, but . . .'

'Gill, he gave them his name and phone number.'

'Yes, but . . .'

'And all the woman had to hand was the programme of a show they were returning from so she wrote it on that. And guess what? She's the sentimental type and keeps the programmes of all the shows they've ever . . .'

'Good lord.'

'I knew you'd be impressed eventually. Oh, and before you cavil, the time they left the show and reached the pub proves Aylard couldn't have been anywhere near the Morden house that evening. Just like he said.'

She noticed similarities with another case in the Winterlea file. 'Richard, you know what this reminds me of? Rhea and the Dancing Doll case. The police didn't find his witnesses, either, but his family turned them up years later.'

'They were police forces in different parts of the country, though. Anyway, we can't hold that against Winterlea, much as I'd like to.' But he knew she was concerned less with Winterlea's tainted evidence than with Aylard's innocence.

She gave him a searching look. 'Richard, I have only two other questions.'

'Yes?'

'Who's the Aylards' detective? And can we have him, please?'

He cleared his throat. 'You aren't going to enjoy this, Gill.'

'Eh?'

'His name is Stephen Kuyper.'

'Shit.'

'Well, we knew he was good.' He added silently: '*In fact, you were especially fond of saying so.*'

She slammed her fist on the desk. 'The moonlighting bastard.'

'Yup, he's so hot he works for both of us at once.' He couldn't resist being flippant. Months of wrangling about Kuyper's merits were culminating in farce.

'Except he's been rumbled. Richard, we must sort this out. Either he's working for us or he isn't.'

He reminded her of the loose arrangement that, in his opinion, allowed Kuyper much too long a rein. 'He hasn't a contract with CJI. We toss him a few crumbs.'

'But he needs us because it enhances his credibility. No, scrap that. He *used* to need us. After turning up the Aylard witnesses he doesn't need anybody.'

'And we, Gillian, go on needing him.'

'Unless we find him real money and a contract, our love is doomed to go unrequited. You realise that?'

'Hang on.' He looked in the grip of a bright idea.

She questioned with a raising of her left eyebrow. He'd never worked out how she did that. He could only lift both at once and look astonished rather than quizzical.

He said: 'Let's haul him in for a conference on Winterlea et al.'

'Oh, I see. Yes, that's good. He'll have to tell us about the Aylard witnesses and we can squeeze out of him anything else that's of use to us.'

'Including,' he suggested, 'whether he knows where Anna Foley has hidden herself.'

But Gillian's face clouded. Richard had been right first time. She didn't think Anna would be found, not alive.

CHAPTER EIGHTEEN

I'm truly sorry we haven't talked for the past few weeks. It really helps me, our talking. But soon after I came home lots of things happened in quick succession, the way they occasionally do, making you feel giddy. The main thing was that my father died and I had to cope with that, which was especially difficult when I was already on an emotional seesaw.

But, no, let me try to tell it in sequence.

I lingered three days in the seaside town, taking lonely walks and doing the sort of thinking I normally avoid. On the first morning I asked directions to Marks & Spencer and bought a couple of T-shirts, extra underwear and tights, plus a travel bag to carry them in. It isn't where I normally buy clothes but it felt safe and familiar and, besides, I don't think the town has my kind of shops. Then I chose snacks for a picnic lunch, which tells you how my frame of mind had improved since the night horrors afflicted me.

There was a young mother and a child, a boy of about five, ahead of me at the check out. He reminded me of my Mikey the way he was springing about, chuckling to himself, never still, like a clockwork toy that's always fully wound. Mikey used to scale anything, jump off anything, totally fearless. Well, this lad was the same. Not facially alike, I don't mean that.

He turned round to me, grinning the happiest of grins.

And his mother flung out an arm and snatched at him, snarling: 'Can't you shut up, you little devil. How many times have I told you?' She slammed his face into the side of the check-out counter. Next he was crying and she was shouting at him and punching him, and she pushed him ahead of her through the check-out, but shoving so hard he fell over and whacked the other side of his face on a stool.

Yes, it was a spiteful attack and it seemed to go on and on, the shouting, the crying and the hitting. But the worst of it was nobody tried to save him. There were three women close at hand: the check-out girl, me, and the customer finishing packing. None of us said a word. We pretended nothing was out of place.

I suppose it was shock at the inexplicable eruption of violence, but I suspect there was a nasty fascination, too, as we wondered whatever his mother might do next. She broke off while she was served and then went briskly towards the door, with the boy bawling and running after her. I didn't see the rest because I was busy paying for my blouses and things. The check-out girl didn't catch my eye, nor did the woman behind me. No one so much as breathed out a sigh of relief that it was over. Yes, three of us, probably all mothers, and we didn't say a word to protect him.

The incident left me shaky. If he hadn't set me thinking about Mikey perhaps it would have been different, but Mikey is always painful for me. He was my miracle baby, you see, born after my divorce and harboured as my good secret. I actually remember thinking that one morning when I was bathing him. By then I'd lived twenty years with a bad secret and it seemed only fair I should be compensated with a good one. Yes, Mikey was my good secret.

Lives are made up of these checks and balances, don't you think? Maybe there are people who design theirs, I don't know. My own were thrust upon me: the bad secret by a child I no longer understand and the good one by a young mother for whom I can, *just*, feel a receding empathy. Don't expect me to apologise for what either of them did, whether their actions were beneficial or despicable. They aren't me.

I wonder how many more 'mes' there are to come? One day, perhaps, I'll be an old woman looking back on me as I am today, fiftyish, facing decisions I'm ill-equipped and, probably, ill-advised to take. I wonder whether she'll be scandalised by my decisions or merely bewildered.

But back to the events, the tangled events, that drove me into haphazard activity when I needed to sit on a beach and watch the tide swish in and out. First, I spent a day mooching around doing nothing. The highlight was a hilariously bad supper, in the hotel restaurant, of chicken stuffed with black pudding. Rubbery, tasteless, grey and greasy – it was all of those. My fault for ordering badly but it sounded fairly promising in French.

By then, you see, I was feeling so much better, well enough to risk adventure with a sautéed chicken, well enough to enjoy wine, well enough to laugh at the disappointment. Oh yes, much better. I'd slept part of the afternoon without nightmares or wakefulness. I'd ticked myself off for fantasising about being pursued by a red car and a detective. In other words, I'd returned to normal.

I considered the possible significance of the red car nonsense while I was strolling along the beach early on the second morning. The tide was in, leaving only a narrow strip of sand where one could safely walk without getting sprayed. Consequently, everyone who wanted a walk on the shore was confined to it. I smiled at the idea that we were like pedestrians on a pavement.

A woman with a docile collie mistook my amusement for a smile of recognition, and actually stopped for a 'Good morning' and a 'How are you?' As she didn't risk a name, I decided she was playing safe because she mistakenly believed I'd made the contact instead of her. After a vague conversation we parted, me smiling with greater amusement than before and she, I didn't doubt, frowning as she racked her brains to remember who I was.

Two days ago, I was thinking, I would have happily assumed another name, reinvented myself in any number of forms, but now, rested and comfortable, I was fit to face reality. And that was when the red car rushed into my memory and, immediately, I experienced the sagging feeling that always heralds unwelcome thoughts. Everything misted in doubt.

I sat on a ledge at the foot of a wall, part of the sea defences serving a double purpose as a bench. Dogs and strollers paraded between me and the waves but, of course, with water to watch hardly anyone spared a glance for me. There was minimal risk of anyone else misreading my expression and claiming an acquaintance. Uninterrupted, I thought about the red car, or rather what it symbolised.

In essence, it meant my grip on reality had slackened, and not simply because I was overwrought as a result of Meryl Aylard accosting me and CJI investigating. My dark suspicion was that my mind didn't work in the same manner as other people's. Never had, in fact. You see, my mother was Rita, the wild girl of the Foley clan. I'm the daughter of John Morden whose mind was crippled by the war and the personal disaster of murder. How dare anyone be surprised if I am, occasionally, less than wholly rational?

The family, both Foleys and Mordens, were kind to me, in their ham-fisted way. They moved me around in search of a safe haven. They cleared their box-rooms for me and laid an extra place at their tables for me. They watched over me and they watched me. They were waiting, no doubt in trepidation, for me to explode.

Rita was explosive. John collapsed in on himself. What might *I* do? Not *nothing*, surely not that. They weren't prepared, any of them, for that.

I decamped as soon as I was able. They were friendly and protective, and two of the aunts possessed what they proudly called a strong sense of family, by which they meant a strong sense of duty towards family members. I needed, desperately, to escape from their miss-nothing eyes. For the best part of ten years the family watched me, and then I dropped out of view.

They couldn't peer at me any longer, weighing up my

words and behaviour and guessing whether I was going to crack up. *They* couldn't but *I* did.

Every outburst, every reaction that might be an *over-reaction*, is measured against what ordinary folk do. I'm forever taking mental litmus tests, wondering how 'normal' I am, or was, or might become. And this, in itself, scares me. Lonely introspection doesn't help towards understanding. Actually, it makes it harder because if, say, I believe on Tuesday that what I did or imagined suggests mental instability, I may decide by Wednesday that I was wrong, but I won't know which conclusion is correct.

I suspect distortion in everything. The truth, if there is a single immutable truth such as June believes in, is buried irrecoverably deep. I'm afraid that if I devote myself whole-heartedly to searching for it, I'll find reasons to blame myself. I imagine you think that's feeble. Maybe so, but, don't forget, the way I lived with the secret was to swing down a shutter in my mind. I did it efficiently. Isn't it possible that if I hadn't, my family's fears would have been realised? Break down. Crack up. Split it anyway you like, I would have been destroyed.

Human beings have the most tenacious sense of self-preservation, I think. Apart, I mean, from the black days or, more likely, nights when enough seems enough, the future seems a void and it makes perverse logic to end our physical existence. Except for those moods, we, as a species, are adept at inventing means of survival. Mine you know about: the shutter, the turning away from the family, the restlessness that drives me on in a subconscious search for the best place for me to be and the best life for me to lead.

Sitting on the wall, I asked myself whether I was bold enough to talk about these fears. We live in an age when talk is everything, don't you agree? Look how readily that stranger on the beach opened a conversation. Given she believed I smiled at her, all that was required in return was another smile. But, no, she had to come to a stop and talk. People, most people, find it so easy. They swing into your life on a tide of talk and keep it flowing. Anyway, sitting on the wall was the first occasion I faced the fact that unless I talked about my fears of instability, I might as well not be telling you the rest.

It's surprising, isn't it, how little research has been done into the ways children survive trauma? When I heard about your work I thought: 'Hooray! At last someone cares!' And this in a century when half the population seems to undergo therapy and the other half seem to be counsellors. What explains the lapse? A thread of guilt running through society, as there rightly is when children suffer?

If my personal experience is anything to go by, it wasn't the dearth of professional help that counted but the lack of any help whatsoever. No one encouraged me to talk about my mother's murder, but I don't blame an ordinary family for taking the contemporary view of 'Least said, soonest mended'. They did what they thought was best.

Besides, in my heart I know I would have blocked any attempt to get me to talk. Professionals would have failed with me, too, once I'd developed my survival techniques. I realise I didn't come out of it too badly, compared to other traumatised children. I didn't take up a life of crime or abuse my own child or suffer mental breakdown. Of course, I didn't heal, either.

While I was walking back to the hotel for breakfast, there was a little chink in the curtain of memory. I think a girl in wellingtons, splashing in the surf, started me off although exactly how I can't say. She didn't look like anyone I used to know, any more than the boy whose mother attacked him looked like my son. There was something, though, that caused my mind to fill with a playground scene.

A dull day in the country and I'm walking across the playground of a Victorian school. I'm wearing a thick hand-knitted Fair Isle cardigan made of reused wool, and a navy skirt run up by one of my aunts from the cloth of a discarded naval uniform. Luckily, my aunts are skilled at that sort of make do and mend and, as other children are similarly dressed, I don't look out of place. As a matter of fact, the village knew my skirt long before I did. A hand-me-down, it was made for one of my older cousins and has hung around the family ever since.

Everyone, though, is staring at me. Everyone. The children whose games slow to a stop. The two teachers in the gabled porch. The caretaker who's bent half-way to the ground because he was about to pick up a lost shoe when I came into view. They stop. Their eyes scald me. I decide to keep going until I reach the porch and the teachers.

It's a sensible idea because teachers know it's wrong to stare, even if no one else can resist, and they recover their normal expressions before I reach them. One, Miss Daltry, steps back and gestures for me to enter the building. The other, whose name I'm not sure of because I haven't been at the school long, goes out into the playground and claps her hands and shouts at the children to run around and keep warm which, the minute I'm out of sight, they do.

It's the morning of the day of the hanging. The fog has almost evaporated, reduced to an indistinct presence down by the river, but the sky lies heavy and grey upon the village. The sky looks the way my heart feels. Leaden, aching, burdened with misery.

I'm late to school because I tried to wriggle out of going but my aunt insisted on it. She sent me out of the farmhouse with a note for the teacher to say I'd been sick, which was a lie. The family were convinced the day should be treated as a normal one. Nobody, they believed, knew I was the daughter of Rita Morden. My name had been switched to Foley, no connections would be made. I believed them until I walked into the playground and brought the school to a standstill.

Who told them? My cousin Lucy, without question. My priggish, sanctimonious, cousin Lucy who's useless at keeping secrets. Whatever my faults, I'm good at that.

All day long I was the object of savage curiosity. Boys, who'd never come near me before, appeared by my side for a closer look. Girls, who were usually friendly, backed off. The girl who was scandalous because her parents were

229

divorcing, took her turn at being scandalised. Teachers couldn't help their eyes flicking in my direction when they were supposed to be chalking on the board or ringing the bell or any of the usual things they did.

They hanged Dennis Aylard that day and my world tilted.

When I tell you I suddenly remembered that playground scene, I'm playing it down. The episode was so intense, I was reliving it. I entered the sore heart of the girl who used to be me. I suffered with her. I became her. Unfortunately, the memories that come to me are increasingly vivid. I'm tempted to call the playground memory a flashback but I'm uncertain where one phenomenon ends and the other begins.

The change, I think, dates from when I realised CJI was closing in on me. Until then, as I told you, I recognised three anniversaries: the day of the murder, the day of the hanging and Sandy's birthday. Apart from that, I banished reminiscence.

When the playground flashback ended – yes, I may as well call it that – I was crossing the road outside my hotel. Without being conscious of it, I'd travelled several hundred yards and launched myself into the sea-front traffic. That's how absorbing my reverie was, and why I'm taking a chance on labelling it flashback.

There was a second's disorientation before I adjusted my thinking and found the answers to 'Who am I? Where am I? Where am I heading? Why am I here?' Immediately afterwards I was plunged into a different sort of confusion, a mixture of relief at regaining control and profound anxiety at it slipping from me.

I hurried up to my room and confronted myself in a mirror, needing reassurance that nothing appeared amiss. Then, tremulous, I went to breakfast. I didn't know, do you see, whether the flashback was a one-off or whether my mind was going to dip in and out of the past. As ever, it was the uncertainty that was most unnerving.

The flashback is the reason I stayed in the seaside town

for another day. I'd been thinking of driving home that afternoon, as I felt so much better, but the absolute inattention
that came over me during the flashback made me wary of
getting behind a steering-wheel. So, instead, I spent a day
visiting a stately home within walking distance, browsing
in a bookshop, strolling along the sea-front, eating lengthy
meals and generally squandering the hours. But it felt good
and there were no other overwhelming memories.

Next day, I went home. Before setting off I made several
telephone calls. I owed my client an apology for breaking our
appointment, but had to leave a message with her secretary.
I rang Susie to say sorry for being away when she needed
me, but had to use her answering machine.

Then I rang my own number to collect machine messages.
To my astonishment, Susie answered me and blurted out
a story about my house being broken into and me being
reported missing. Apparently, she was living in my house
'to look after it'. A good thing she couldn't see my face
giving away that I understood perfectly she was there to
protect herself. Susie had found a bolt-hole. My place had
always been one for her but how much better it must be
without me around!

When I came off the line I was laughing at the sheer
absurdity. Then I quietened to a sardonic smile as I wondered
how long it would take me to move Susie back to her own
home. I planned to be grateful for what she'd done, to pay
thorough attention to her troubles, and to be resolute about
encouraging her to go home.

Before leaving town I bought her a present, a pretty jug
made by a local potter. It was an attractive but unmistakably
domestic piece, the kind you hang on the hook on your
own dresser in your own kitchen, not leave cluttering up
a friend's. Perhaps I was hoping it bore its own discreet
message.

Several hours later, Susie opened my door to me. She
looked stricken but what she was chattering about was
my key no longer working because she'd changed the
broken lock. I dumped my travel bag at the foot of the

stairs. I was looking around, partly to spot evidence of the calamitous break-in and partly to discover what was bothering her. New locks and old keys weren't an adequate explanation.

I brought her flurry of speech to a halt, saying: 'Susie, what's *really* the matter?'

She battled to stop twisting her hands, a habit she had when over-wrought, but once they were clasped in front of her, they jerked as she spoke.

'Anna, there was a call for you this morning from the Cliffway Nursing Home. Your father . . .'

I reached a hand to the bannister rail and sat down heavily on the stairs. Before my face, Susie's hands struggled to be free. I shut my eyes.

'What did they tell you?' That wonderfully calm voice came to my aid, yet again.

'They asked you to ring. They said they had news about your father. I asked . . . Well, to be honest, Anna I didn't realise your father was alive . . .'

'Can you remember exactly what they said?'

'Only that there was news and they wanted you to telephone.'

I forced the issue. 'Did they say he died?'

Quickly she insisted not. 'Oh no, definitely not. But they didn't want to tell me anything and I couldn't persuade them to elaborate.'

I sucked in a deep breath. 'Well. I'd better ring them.'

When I'd slumped she moved closer to me, and now I waited for her to step away before I could rise. 'Look,' I said, getting up and smoothing my skirt, 'why don't you pour us a drink while I make the call?'

Her eyes slid to the clock, visible through the kitchen doorway. I couldn't care less about her rule never to touch a drop before six, and I ignored her unspoken objection.

'There's a bottle of red in the cupboard,' I said, and went into the sitting-room to telephone.

Two minutes later I'd spoken to the administrator at the nursing home and been told my father had passed away the previous night in his sleep. Yes, she actually said 'passed away'. You'd think a nursing home full of geriatric patients would face the reality of death, wouldn't you? The unsatisfactory 'passed away' hung between us for a moment, and then I produced what were, in these circumstances, the usual questions. Had he been ill? Had he been alone? Had he been lucid in his final hours?

The woman I was speaking to said no in answer to everything. I was left with the impression of a frail octogenarian, whose mind had long gone, falling peacefully into the deserved long sleep. His mind had disappeared years ago, now his body had softly followed.

When I came off the line I was unprepared for Susie advancing on me from the doorway, a brimming glass in her hand. I'd forgotten she was there, and when I saw her my first foolish thought was that it was too bad she refused to learn to pour wine properly.

My calm voice announced to her: 'He's dead. His heart failed during his sleep.'

She wrung her hands, hating being the bearer of my bad tidings although, goodness knows, she never minds bringing her own to me.

'Anna, I'm sorry. I did hope it wasn't that, but when they said there was news . . . Well, I didn't honestly see what other news it could be.'

She rambled on like that. I acknowledged her sympathy with a half-smile and a nod, then turned away to the window. I wished so much to be alone. To have anybody near me, no matter how loving and sympathetic they were, was intolerable. I've always dealt with things alone, and being alone is what I know best.

I lifted the wine to my lips, balancing the glass carefully lest it slop over.

Behind me she said: 'Oh, you'd better ring your cousin June and tell her you're back.'

The wine splashed, trickled down my hand and onto the cuff of my blouse. My voice rose an octave. '*June?*'

Susie was instantly on the defensive. 'I rang her while I

was trying to find you. I rang practically everybody whose phone number was in the house.'

I was gaping at her, horrified at what she'd done. She ran on and on, justifying her actions which, to me, seemed wildly inappropriate. I was an adult who went away unannounced from her own home, but within twenty-four hours Susie saw fit to inform the police and everyone whose telephone number was in my house. Oh, Susie! Oh, *God*.

I didn't argue with her. I think my expression said as much as was needed. Snatching up the telephone, I got through to June and announced I was back after a short break for sea air.

June was bemused. 'Anna, dear, your friend Susie said you disappeared. It was all rather odd.'

I said 'Yes. Well', in a tone that conveyed the friend in question was beside me and we couldn't delve into that right away. I was steeling myself to break the news of my father's death but June spoke again.

'I'm glad to hear everything's all right. Except the house, of course. I gather that's quite a shambles.'

'Is it?' So far I'd spotted only chipped paint around the replacement door lock. 'I haven't looked around yet.'

'Ah.' I could virtually hear June revising her opinion of the friend Susie. Then: 'Her telephone call came at a most unfortunate time, I'm afraid. Gillian Spry was with me.'

A sinking feeling. 'Did she realise what the call was about?'

'Yes. I haven't quite got the hang of my machine and I've accidentally asked it to broadcast to the entire house.'

I replied with a lame: 'Oh dear.'

Then I asked about her session with Gillian. Before I'd done my vanishing act, June had told me she intended to speak to her about the Rita Morden affair. I don't know why I didn't mention my father instead of going on this tack. I think it was to do with wanting to know the worst about June and CJI and put it behind me. One thing at a time, that kind of thinking.

June said: 'Anna, I wish we didn't have to talk about

this on the telephone. Why don't you come and see me. Tomorrow?'

I felt a surge of irritation. She knew I'd returned half an hour ago from a three-day jaunt, my house had been burgled, and I had to inform the police and everyone else I'd resurfaced. She was being sillier than when she demanded visits, forgetting I worked.

Swallowing my annoyance, I insisted: 'That won't be possible this week. I'm only just back.'

She said 'Oh yes' and 'Of course' and repeated that it was difficult to talk about certain things on the telephone. I couldn't imagine what she planned to say to me whenever we came face-to-face. In my experience, what's awkward on the telephone is awkward in every way. I suggested that.

June said: 'Yes, that's quite true.' And then she managed to tell me what she'd been withholding. 'Anna, about the *In memoriam* notice and the flowers on the grave . . . I've discovered who's behind that little remembrance.'

This was the last subject I expected her to raise or, indeed, to be too embarrassed to discuss until we were in her sitting-room with dry sherry to hand.

'Really? Who?'

'You recall Mr Tompkins?'

'The neighbour who walks Frisky for you?'

'Yes. He has a sister . . . No, I'm telling it the wrong way round. What I mean is I didn't know the woman was his sister. She was at school with your mother. In fact, you could say she was one of the true friends of Rita Morden. But . . .'

'Yes. Go on.'

'Oh dear. Well, the sorry tale is that I fell out with her. Her name, by the way, is Alice Carpenter. I don't suppose that means anything to you. She introduced herself soon after I moved back here, and she began visiting me.'

I said I didn't know the name.

June said: 'I remember her slightly when she was young, with Rita, but I knew her only as her friend Alice. Anyway,

the awkward thing I'm telling you is that we had a disagree-
ment and I gave up seeing her.'

The butcher, the baker, the greengrocer and the friendly
neighbour called Alice. Yes, I could well imagine the
suspicion and the falling out. I decided not to ask what
Alice was supposed to have done that caused her to be
banished.

After prompting, June clarified the story. She hadn't
connected the friendly neighbour with the Alice who was
my mother's girlhood friend. Neither did she appreciate
the neighbour was the sister of her other neighbour, Mr
Tompkins. However, the kindly Alice took pity on crabbed
June and persuaded her brother to offer help. June, believing
the offers originated with Mr Tompkins, accepted and had no
idea the dog-walking and various other tasks were actually
undertaken by his sister. So far so good, until the notice in
the paper and the flowers by the gravestone.

It's a small town. Questions in the newspaper office led to
talk in the Red Lion. Alice was concerned that June's family
was upset and her attempt at discretion, by concealing her
identity, had backfired. Also, she knew June lived in the
town and not in London, as June led the newspaper staff to
believe. Alice decided the best course was to make a clean
breast of it. She went round to June's house with a bunch
of conciliatory flowers and owned up.

June, after indignant disbelief, had accepted what had
been done to her and that it was done with the best motives.
A friendship was being repaired.

'There doesn't seem,' June admitted, a mite grudgingly,
'any reason not to let her walk the dog and fetch things.'

I grasped why she remained reluctant. 'You're afraid it'll
mean conversations you don't want about the murder.'

'Exactly.'

'That's tricky.'

'Yes, especially as Alice led the campaign to save Rita's
stone when the churchyard was being cleared. However
much she angers me, I have to admit she has a good heart
and she's done our family some service.'

Briefly, I wondered whether Alice Carpenter knew anything June or I didn't about the murder. Mind-reading, June
touched on the point.

'There's one thing we have in common, apart from living
in the same street and having an interest in the murder. We
were both away when it happened.'

I realised I was letting the conversation run down without
telling her about my father. I suspected I'd let it go so far
it would be ridiculous to mention it now, and instantly
recognised it would be worse not to.

'June,' I said, in a changing-the-subject tone. 'I have sad
news to share with you. My father died last night.'

I paused to let her ooze sympathy but there was a curious
silence on the line. I often wish I'd seen her face.

I started to amplify, relating my call to the nursing home.
Then she began to react. Regret. Sympathy. Condolences.
The usual.

I came off the line thinking how false she sounded.

For the second time, Susie startled me simply by being
there when I'd overlooked her. I drank off the wine and
refilled my glass. She shook her head when I held the
bottle aloft, offering more. I pulled myself together and
encouraged her to lead me through sensible discussions
about undertakers and people who ought to be notified of
John Morden's death. She knew more about the matter than
I did because she'd done it not so long ago. I softened and
became genuinely grateful to her for the trouble she was
taking, and had been taking since the lady vanished.

It's interesting how you grow used to neglect, to making
do with second best because everyone else is ahead of you
in the queue for care and affection. The result is it's hard
to react properly when you receive the real thing. You just
have to keep on plugging away at it, hoping you'll discover
the knack and, meanwhile, nobody will notice. I always find
it easier to be the one who gives or withholds than the one
who receives. It allows a modicum of control. When I choose
to blame my family for this, I cite their flair for selfishness
and sacrifice.

June was up to something. Realisation came late that evening, with Susie snoring lightly in my spare room and me sitting up in bed, awake and finishing the final glass of the second bottle of red. Puckishly, I'd opened the second one to rattle her. I didn't care whether I drank any more myself but the imp inside me liked to tease her.

I'd sipped through the evening while making a series of telephone calls, including a second one to June to ask whether there was anyone in the family we'd left out. She was far better at names and addresses than I was, I having given up family, as you know. June shared the chore of spreading the news. During this second call she sounded brisk, businesslike.

Later it occurred to me she was compensating for the effect of several glasses of tongue-searing sherry. The notion came while I was in bed and I laughed aloud, then checked for fear of disturbing Susie. But my thoughts weren't on my house guest for many seconds. June claimed them. I became certain she was hiding information or playing a trick on me.

'I am not deceived,' I said, wagging a finger at an imaginary June in the room.

I was, though. I'd allowed her to pass off that tale about Alice the true friend as if it were what she hadn't dared speak of a minute earlier. Mulling it over, I convinced myself there was another story, one she genuinely couldn't risk without us being in the same room. But what? And then there was her peculiar non-reaction to the news that John Morden was dead.

Since then I'd broken the news to a handful of people and none of them were stunned into silence. Why should they be? The man was ancient and had been sick for most of his life. Only June was taken aback and it wasn't as if she was close to him. He'd been her aunt Rita's husband for a few years while June was a teenager. She'd told me herself she was eighteen when Rita was killed and John went into hospital for the first of many spells. He never lived in the town again.

The puzzle kept me awake for hours, that and the wine, plus the coffee downed to suit Susie who didn't have trouble sleeping after a dose of caffeine. I niggled at it but couldn't turn up anything that explained June's shock. In the end, I decided I wouldn't be satisfied until I'd asked her. With that settled, I eventually floated off to sleep.

The following morning I staggered out of bed to answer a persistent ringing on the doorbell. With my dressing-gown clutched around me, I peered into the face of a crisp young woman who appeared to have come straight from her hairdressers, pausing only to perfect her make-up.

'Susie?' she asked, turning on a professional smile.

'Who wants Susie?'

'I'm from Victim Support, Susie.'

I echoed victim support at her. Her smile didn't falter as she declared she'd come to help me through my difficult experience and invited herself in. I suppose I fell back as she advanced but, however it came about, the next thing I knew we were both in the hall and she was closing the door and shooing me into the kitchen.

The kitchen was untidy. Two dead wine bottles stood sentinel over last night's supper dishes. Miss Victim Support took it in with a glance, summed me up and busied herself making a pot of tea. She whipped out a chair from the kitchen table and told me to sit down. I did, thinking: 'What the hell, she can make me a cup of tea if she fancies. Anyone can, I'm not choosy.'

While the kettle was boiling, and after the cups and saucers were lined up alongside milk and sugar, she talked about my scary experience and how important it was to come to terms with it rather than be turned into a victim. She recited patter about victim psychology and fighting back and not letting it ruin one's life. The smile was unwavering.

'Crime,' she said, with an evangelical glow, 'is a terrible fact of modern life. And crime in which you're physically harmed is especially hard to live with. For many victims, it's easy to be tough at the time but those can be the very people who feel the effects long afterwards. Luckily, there are effective ways of helping you get over your experience. I mean counselling, of course.'

Oh, of course.

I asked: 'What's your name?'

The glow faded a fraction as she realised she'd left out a line of patter by omitting to give me her name.

'Julie. Call me Julie.'

'Well, Julie . . .'

But the imp persuaded me to hold back. At least if Julie was here making me tea she wasn't pestering anyone else.

Overhead, a few minutes later, while we were embarking on my first session of counselling, footsteps sounded, a shower was run, doors opened and closed, and then Susie ran downstairs. She trotted into the kitchen looking all the things I wasn't: refreshed, perky and rosy-cheeked.

'Susie, here's Julie to see you,' I said. And stood up and went out, leaving them to it.

Upstairs, running a comb through my hair before I showered, I heard the front door shut forcibly and a pair of high heels stalk down the alleyway. Susie raced upstairs howling with glee. I hadn't heard her laugh like that for years.

We enjoyed ten minutes hilarity at Julie's expense and then I shut myself in the bathroom. As I waited for the hot and cold water to adjust to temperate, I indulged my own private thoughts about Julie and her ilk. Where had they been when I needed them? They weren't there when my mother died, and they weren't there when my life fell apart the second time. How ridiculous that they should barge in on me now, eager to advise Susie whose hair had been pulled when her handbag was stolen.

I did the rest of my laughing in the shower, where it was secret. The funniest bit was imagining her face if I'd 'opened up' to her, a process she described as a crucial step to recovery.

'Let's just take it from the beginning,' she'd said. Her voice was cajoling, her eyes shining in anticipation.

But what if I'd done that, casting us back to the warm spring evening when my mother was murdered?

CHAPTER NINETEEN

Ann opened the sash window and scrambled onto the flat roof below. She was barely through when there was a flurry of black-and white fur and next door's cat whisked into the bedroom.

'Mabel!'

Ann hesitated, not liking to leave her in there but knowing eviction was useless because the window had to remain open. It was dark in the room so she couldn't see what the cat was up to or whether the bedroom door was shut. She believed it was shut because she usually closed it for privacy although there was no means of securing it.

Turning away, Ann went on hands and knees across the roof, then used a drain-pipe to reach the ground. It was easy because the sill of the pantry window jutted out exactly where a foothold was needed, and Ann had done this several times.

Checking nobody was watching, she crossed the path at the side of the house and entered the deep shadows by the boundary wall. In a moment she was through the door of the dilapidated greenhouse and hurrying the length of it. At the far end a missing panel made a convenient escape hatch. She ran into the adjoining shed.

Sandy complained to her from the darkness. 'You were ages.'

Gasping for breath, Ann said: 'He kept talking.'

'You say he never talks to you.'

'Well, he was. He was going on about the party and the jazz. He hates jazz.'

'Where's the watch?'

Ann felt in her pocket. Her mother's watch was a fancy bracelet with a pile of diamond chips around a miniature timepiece. Ann couldn't find it.

'It must be here. I had it before I climbed out of the window.'

Sandy's sigh expressed the utmost exasperation. 'You've lost it. You're always losing watches.'

There was a sound like the sundering of the sky. Both girls squealed.

'It's only a firework.' Sandy was first to recover.

Ann, with hands clapped over her ears, cried. 'Oh, I can't abide bangers.'

'Perhaps it's only one. The others weren't like that.'

They looked through the shed doorway towards the garden, the bonfire and the firework party. But the trunk of the great tree blocked them and they had to imagine the people milling around on the far side of the lawn, near the fire and the trestle tables of food and drink. Only the jazz, belting from a console radiogram by an open window, was real.

Sandy was brisk. 'You'd better get ready.'

When Ann dithered, she took her arm and steered her out of the door. Ann, pushed into action, shinned up the trunk, along the branch and onto the shed roof.

Out of the shelter of the buildings and the wall, she noticed the breeze for the first time. Because there wasn't much foliage, she had a view of the party, too. A string of bulbs, slung from tree to tree, illuminated that side of the garden but where she was there was practically complete darkness. Nobody could possibly tell she was there.

Suddenly the sky was lit with soaring yellow stars. They spread out until they filled her view but in another second they were falling, fading, being blown sideways by the wind. She knelt and waited for pinpoints of light to fall softly on her but, somewhere between heaven and earth, they had died.

She clambered across the roof, feeling around. Another firework took off and in its purple light she found the branch Sandy had left there. It was thicker than Ann expected. She hefted it in one hand but it was too long and heavy for her.

Crouching at the edge of the roof she whispered. 'Sandy?'

A pale blob of face appeared in the doorway below. 'What?'

'The stick's too heavy. I can't pick it up.'

'Of course you can. I did. How do you think I got it up there?'

There was a pause while Ann reflected that Sandy was older, bigger and stronger. Then she said: 'I thought it would be a little one, like the one you showed me on Saturday.'

On the defensive, Sandy snapped back that the lighter one had since been collected for the bonfire, and she'd had to go looking again. 'Go and have another try. Use both hands.'

'But . . . .' Ann broke off as the pale face disappeared into the shed.

She lifted the stick with both hands and made sweeping movements. It was awkward but she supposed it would have to do. She set it down and began to go through her pockets carefully, seeking the diamond wristwatch.

She didn't understand why they needed the watch. Sandy had said: 'Bring that watch with you.' Ann hadn't refused but her questions had been rebuffed with a scathing look, as though Sandy was fed up with having to explain the obvious.

Ann gave up. Her pockets were empty, except for a neatly ironed cotton handkerchief. She wiped her hands down her skirt and went to sit cross-legged near the edge of the roof and watch the party.

The wind was carrying people's voices towards her. They were neighbours and friends and people she'd never seen before. There were no children and, since the fireworks began, the couple of dogs who'd come along had been taken indoors. Ann thought of Mabel who'd also retreated from the bangs and flashes.

Silver stars showered down. Sandy hissed from below. 'Don't sit on the edge, you'll be seen. Whenever there's a firework, it's like a big lamp being switched on out here.'

Ann wriggled away from the edge. She didn't like being up there alone. She hadn't thought about this side of it when Sandy was making the plan. The loneliness. The doubts. The risks. If she were on her own, truly on her own, she would go home, she thought. But she wasn't truly alone because Sandy was at the foot of the tree. She couldn't go anywhere or do anything without Sandy knowing and approving.

Once the silver stars vanished, Sandy whispered: 'Was it okay with two hands?'

'Yes.'

Once the word was out Ann felt foolish, realising she could have said no and put an end to it. Instead, she'd made it sound all right.

There was a screeching, a terrific crack, and a handful of red lights flew through the night. As the noise died, Ann discovered she'd rushed in panic to the far side of the roof, and might have overstepped it and fallen through into the greenhouse. She was desperate to get off the roof, and she began working out what to say to Sandy so that Sandy would allow her to. Confessing she was scared wouldn't do. Sandy was seldom impressed with that.

Ann wondered what the time was and whether there was much longer to go. She seemed to have spent days, clock-watching, waiting for the right moment to say this or do that, noting when Rita was telephoned and when she came in and when she went out.

It had been a busy week for Rita. Apart from her business meetings and two parties she'd had to attend for business reasons, she'd had rows with three people. Ann, who didn't count; her husband, whom she argued with frequently, so that wasn't especially important, either; and Dennis Aylard.

Ann didn't know what her mother and Aylard had argued

about but she'd caught the tail-end of an angry conversation on the telephone. Sandy, quoting the Red Lion, had assured her it was to do with Dennis Mallard's scheme to run away with Rita. She didn't say whether he was dragging his feet over it or whether Rita was, and when Ann pressed for details she got Sandy's heavy, impatient sigh.

Somehow or other – by the time she was on the roof with the stick she really didn't know how it came about – it had been settled that the row should be used to bring to an end Rita's affair meetings. Sandy was brimming with clever ideas, Ann's role was to watch the clock and tell untruths.

Sandy coached her. 'Say he telephoned and said he wants to meet her by the back gate.' And: 'She'll think *he* did it, because he's furious with her. Then she won't go with him any more.'

Another violent explosion left Ann trembling and sobbing. But before the echo disappeared, she heard Sandy's signal from below. Three thumps on the main beam of the shed roof.

Nerves frayed, Ann leapt into rehearsed action. While green spangles were snatched by the wind and flung across the sky, she was grabbing the stick, straddling the branch of the tree, and poised to strike.

She heard Sandy's '*Now*', swung the stick, made contact, overbalanced and dropped it. In the darkness below, Sandy swore. Ann tumbled down out of the tree. As she stooped for her stick, a whacking hand brushed her face and this enraged her. She lifted the stick in both hands and swung wildly, hitting the ground, the trunk of the tree, just lashing out and hitting anything in her way, thumping and bashing and whacking, and all the while there was the ear-splitting noise of a Jumping-Jack cracker and the yells of the people it pursued.

Ann dropped the stick again. Sandy dived for it. Ann watched her lift it and bring it crashing down, as though Sandy was showing her the correct way to do it, purposefully, with direction and control. Ann didn't want the lesson. She tipped her face to the sky. It was full of golden stars. They were falling, falling, falling.

The next thing she knew, Sandy was panting, standing over the prone figure on the path, the stick loose in her hand.

'Sandy?'

For a few seconds there was nothing but the panting. Then Sandy's grip tightened on the stick and she looked around, alerted by a new noise.

The sound was the rattle of raindrops, the abrupt start of the storm. Sandy threw the stick down, barked orders at Ann. 'Quick. Over there.'

She snatched up the head end, leaving Ann the feet. The body was heavy, they didn't manage to raise it clear of the ground and moved it very few yards. One shoe fell off. Ann fetched it and replaced it on the foot. By then Sandy was shooing her back to the house. The rain was teeming. Giggling guests were scurrying indoors. A safety-conscious man remembered to switch off the chain of lights. And in the darkness Sandy Minch pushed the bloody stick into the bonfire.

Soaked and filthy, Ann went back up the drain-pipe to her room. The wind through the open window had blown open her bedroom door and Mabel had quartered the house, scavenging until Ann's father chased her out of the kitchen. He followed the cat upstairs to see how she'd got in, and on the landing he met Ann.

CHAPTER TWENTY

Richard King was clearing his desk. He'd met an intriguing brunette at a party over the weekend. Romance was in, sloth was out.

Gillian Spry, arriving early but not enough to be first, took in the implications at a glance but asked with casual irony: 'Leaving us?'

'If only.' He crumpled a paper bag and several sheets of paper, then hurled them at his waste-bin. It was full and they rolled off. In his new tidy mood, he dived to pick them up.

Gillian smothered a giggle which he missed because of the noise he was making jamming his foot in the bin and trampling down the rubbish. She hadn't a clue who his new love was but she was exceedingly grateful to her. All last week she'd been wondering how much longer she could tolerate the rubbish tip which had previously been Richard's desk. Three times she'd caught herself staring down on pedestrians' heads rather than face the mess in the room.

The rubbish was crushed, the foot was withdrawn and the roll of paper was dropped into the bin. He ran an eye over the rest of the squalor and looked puzzled by it. 'This is as bad as clearing out the fridge.'

Gillian, hanging up her coat, had realised months ago that he was oblivious to the eccentric tidiness-strikes that accompanied each breaking of his heart. She imagined herself tracing Miss New Love and having a private word in her ear.

'However much Owlie drives you mad, please be nice to him until we've finished compiling the Winterlea dossier.'

She went to her own shiny and nearly empty desk. A green folder lay on it. With a manicured fingernail she touched it, while raising a quizzical eyebrow in that gesture Richard found impossible to ape.

He said airily: 'The Winterlea dossier.'

'Oh. Good.' She sounded uninterested, teasing him.

He declined to rise to it and said in a throw-away manner: 'Just thought you'd like to skim it, if you have a few minutes to spare.'

She shot him a broad smile and opened the file. Miss New Love and Marcus Winterlea within five minutes! Oh dear, the rest of the week could only be a let-down.

After she'd read it and they'd wrangled for a while, she caved in.

'Fine. I'm persuaded. Number One: We have ample evidence against Winterlea to make our typical public fuss. Number Two: We play down the Rita Morden affair because the likelihood is that June Foley's information was correct and, even if she was lying or just plain wrong, we have neither resources nor reason to pursue it. Number Three: When the Aylard family approach us, as they surely will when the Winterlea story breaks, we give them a nod and a wink but nothing specific.'

'Number Four,' he added, in the voice of Mr Justice Sniffle. 'We give three cheers for British justice without which you and I would be out of a job.'

She contrived to look scandalised. 'Cynicism? So early in the week?'

'Sunday,' he argued, 'is the first day of the week. Where were you when I was slaving over the Winterlea dossier yesterday?'

She grew slightly pink with suppressed laughter, partly

at their banter but also memories of a delightful day spent mainly in bed with her fly-about lover.

'I delegated,' she said serenely. 'It's what you do when you're the boss.'

'And you wonder why I'm thinking of leaving?'

The thought of leaving had genuinely crossed his mind. He couldn't stay there for year upon year as Gillian did. Success came too slowly and too seldom for him. He opened a clean dustbin liner and began chucking papers in.

'Oh, another thing, Gillian. A special cheer for Stephen Kuyper who's accepted a contract on the measliest terms. I can't understand why, unless it's because he has a crush on you.'

She smiled the sweetest of smiles. 'Actually, it's on you.'

Then she savoured the split second of doubt before he realised she was joking, too.

Richard dropped a notebook into the bag, wished he hadn't and groped for it. His glasses fell in and he couldn't see to find them, what with the bag being black and the glasses dark-brown.

Head in bag, he made a muffled appeal. 'Gill, could you help?'

She was suddenly engrossed in the Winterlea file. 'Hmm?'

He emerged, upended the bin liner on the floor and knelt. Gillian flew to the rescue, snatched up his spectacles before he crawled on them. It was unthinkable for him to break this pair, not now she'd grown used to them and Miss New Love had fallen for him wearing them. Supposing he replaced them with a completely different sort? Romance might be out and sloth might be back in. With relief, Gillian handed them over.

'Thanks,' he said. 'I'll reward you with a cappuccino at Giovanni's, if you like.'

She correctly interpreted this as meaning they'd forgotten to replace the office coffee finished on Friday. 'Excellent. Now?'

'No, let me finish this first.' He kept hard at it, sifting layer upon layer of old papers and throwing them away.

A quip was on the tip of her tongue but she decided not to tease. Instead she went and stood in a shaft of sunshine by the window. Passers-by on the pavement below were wearing thin jackets or cardigans. There were scarcely any hats and certainly no umbrellas.

She ran over the Winterlea business in her mind, checking and re-checking they hadn't missed anything. Richard's report seemed excellent. They had strong evidence against Winterlea in the Dancing Doll case and the Dormer, Johnson, Middlemarch, Restoril, Helmdon and Bacton cases, and less conclusive evidence in two others. There was really no reason for them to get further embroiled in the Rita Morden affair.

She frowned slightly, remembering how they'd tussled about it. As far as the Winterlea dossier was concerned, Richard had been right and she'd been wrong.

Her own feelings about the case troubled her. '*I ran away with the suspicion that Anna was hiding information, and had been since the evening of the murder. I wouldn't let go of the idea that all eight-year-old girls have sharp eyes and sharper minds. Heaven knows why I clung to it.*'

Another thought struck her. '*I ought to be relieved there wasn't anything in it. Supposing we'd discovered she covered up for her father? Or, horror of horrors, supposing we'd found she and Sandy Minch killed Rita Morden? What on earth could we reasonably have done with the information? They were children when she was killed and they haven't grown up into criminals, so how would we have handled it?*'

She imagined the battles she and Richard would have fought over it. '*I can't be sentimental about children, the way he is. What was that line he quoted at me the other day? Oh, yes. "Hold childhood in reverence and do not be in any hurry to judge it for good or ill." That's all very well, but if we'd found evidence the girls were*

250

involved in murder we would have been forced to do a spot of judging, wouldn't we? Well, thank God we found nothing of the sort.'

She was still thinking what a relief it was to be in the wrong, when Richard signalled the end of Operation Spring Clean and led her off to Giovanni's.

CHAPTER TWENTY-ONE

June wasn't at my father's funeral, a drab affair with half a dozen wreaths and as many people, including two staff representing the nursing home. After the conventional music and platitudes, I drove to see her.

She'd intended to be there but fell a few days before, you see, and hurt her bad leg. A neighbour, who I gathered was the friendly Alice Carpenter, left a key for me on a ledge in the porch so I could let myself in.

June was standing in the sitting-room, more wraith-like than ever. Her light-green jersey suit hung loosely and a toppling comb was letting a hank of hair fly away. She seemed insubstantial, as if only her solid shoes anchored her to the carpet. When she reached out and squeezed my hand, I noticed she was wearing her mother's rings. They clinked as we touched and afterwards she had to twist them round the right way. They were a distraction and I wondered whether that might be why she wore them, to fiddle with when painful topics were on the agenda.

'How are you, June?' I unbuttoned my suit jacket and plonked my bag on the spindly table by the chair I normally used.

'Oh, I'm mending, I think. I'll be all the better for a glass of sherry, now you've come.'

I smothered a smile at the inference she was a woman who wouldn't drink alone. While I poured, I told her about the funeral. The story was done in three or four sentences, which was just as well because Frisky nosed the door open and came to lick my calves while I was talking.

June said sharply. 'Here, Frisky. Leave Anna alone.'

The spaniel, who'd grown fatter since my last visit, trundled towards her, its swinging tail wafting doggy odours around the room. I handed June her sherry and retreated to my chair, pleased to find it in a smell-free zone.

We caught up on other news, of which there was next to nothing because we'd spoken frequently on the telephone over the previous week. The only item of importance was that June's injury had spurred the local hospital to offer an appointment for the hip operation. Unfortunately, it was months away.

She hadn't, as you might be forgiven for thinking, tripped over the dog. No, she fell on her way downstairs after struggling up to the front bedroom on one errand or another. The whole episode was thoroughly depressing because she lay in the hall shouting until the boy delivering the free newspaper rescued her.

Although I'd planned to, I hadn't inquired why she moved into the house instead of selling it when she inherited. A tactless question under the present circumstances, I skirted it. We talked instead about hip replacement operations and rejuvenation. I topped up the sherry.

It was time, I thought, for us to move on to the other matter, whatever it was. She'd insisted I call on her instead of going home after the funeral because 'there's a matter I must speak to you about, dear.' I didn't doubt it was the one she'd ducked when she reported instead on the unravelling of the churchyard flowers mystery.

'Well,' I said, in a meaningful way once the rejuvenation conversation foundered. I emphasised my curiosity with a face promising full attention.

June put her glass down and twiddled her rings. Frisky flopped his head in her lap. She absently stroked one of his ears. Her mother's rings went chink, chink.

When she spoke her voice was low and serious. 'Anna, I have a confession.'

She allowed the unlikely words to sink in. I tilted my head and waited.

'I've been telling lies,' she said. 'To you and to Gillian Spry. I did it for what I believed to be the best, and perhaps it was. Yes, there's no perhaps, I do believe it was for the best. But my accident, you see . . . Well, it's forced me to accept I may not always be around and you ought to have the information . . .'

I dismissed this with a gesture. For heaven's sake, the woman was in her early sixties, only ten years older than me.

June gave a self-mocking laugh. 'Yes, I'm afraid that did sound as though I have one foot in the grave. I didn't mean to overdo it.'

Frisky pulled his head away, probably fed up with the rings clinking by his ear. June folded her hands in her lap for a second or two but then began patting the rings. I struggled to ignore them and keep my eyes on her face. Whatever her revelation, the slowness of its delivery was maddening.

I expect my exasperation made itself apparent because she steeled herself to tell the tale and dashed on with it.

'Anna, I misled you about what I was going to tell Gillian Spry when I asked her to come and see me. What I actually told her was that your father killed your mother.'

Her words took my breath away. Silence lay heavily on the room for a few seconds that felt like minutes stretching into hours. I couldn't take it in; then I couldn't trust my hearing; then I wanted to ask her to repeat it but my mouth was parched; and then, finally, I ran a tongue over my lips and struggled to put my stupefaction into words.

I managed only a 'Why?' but it was one that bore the burden of several puzzles. Why had she thought it necessary to say anything whatsoever to Gillian Spry; why had she blamed my father; why had she misled me? Why, why, why?

Her answer was swift. 'Because I realised after Meryl

Aylard called me that there's no chance anyone's going to continue believing Dennis Aylard committed murder. His name will be cleared, Anna. Therefore there has to be another culprit.'

'Yes, but . . .' I couldn't finish the sentence because it wasn't what I was thinking. My mind was in turmoil, bursting with questions I daren't ask.

Ignoring my confusion June went on. 'I decided to tell Gillian Spry that John Morden confessed to my father years ago when he was visiting him at the psychiatric hospital.'

'June!' Her cunning amazed me but she misinterpreted my exclamation as anger.

'Sorry, Anna, but that's what I did. And . . .'

Without knowing it, I was up out of my chair.

She threw up a forbidding hand. 'No, don't leave. Please let me go on. You must hear the rest.'

What she was telling me was electrifying. It meant so much more than appeared on the surface, but how was I to ask her about this? How could I reach the heart of it?

I tried to say I wasn't going anywhere, wouldn't dream of it, but what she got from me was incoherence. Back in my chair, I put on my attentive face again, desperate to look relaxed and unconcerned.

She said: 'The other thing I told Gillian was also rather bad but, once I'd set off down that path it became, I'm afraid, inevitable. You see, dear, I had to say your father was dead.'

All at once I understood her shock when I announced his death. 'You must have felt you'd wished his life away.'

'I was badly shaken. Such awful timing, when you think he could have died any day over the last thirty years.'

But I didn't have time for genuine sympathy. 'Listen, June, can you remember Gillian Spry's reaction? Did she believe what you were telling her?'

'As far as I know, she did. She certainly didn't ask any challenging questions.'

Personally, I doubted it was as easy as that to fool CJI. For one thing, they would check the date of his death with the

Family Records Centre. June would immediately be proved a liar on that point and then the rest of her dominoes would collapse.

She broke into my thoughts. 'You're going to tell me she would look it up and discover he was alive.'

'She would, you know.'

'That's why I claimed he went to live abroad and died there. Maybe it wouldn't have worked but I thought it might throw her off the scent.'

'Oh, yes.' I was back to admiring June's cunning.

'Well, now the poor man is truly dead, the problem ceases to exist. I don't wish to sound glad but . . .'

I nodded sadly, the sort of nod that refers to ill winds and silver linings. We exchanged a look of deep, unusual understanding.

Questions were bubbling inside me but there was no possibility of airing them. June would tell me what she'd chosen and nothing further. I would listen to her but was prevented from asking for the full story. That was my predicament and I had no choice but to accept it.

Then she gave me a start. 'Do you realise, Anna, you haven't asked whether it's true.'

I gulped. 'Haven't I? Well, of course . . . I mean . . .'

She was wearing a slight, superior smile. 'No, dear, you haven't. That's odd, don't you think?'

A brief, wild laugh. 'Well, June, I don't need to ask because . . .'

Because which? Because I knew he'd done it or because I knew he hadn't. She'd muddled me. I couldn't unscramble the story quickly enough, and she was watching me with that faint, condemning smile.

My words were rushing now. 'Surely, what matters isn't what I believe but what Gillian Spry believes. Meryl Aylard, too. And Gillian will pass on to her what you said, I'm quite sure of that.'

'I was relying on it,' June said drily.

'So, you see, June, my view really isn't important, is it?'

'No. But anyone else would have asked me.'

I shrugged, tried to make light of it and ended with: 'All right. Let me ask now. Did he do it?'

I hated the way she kept me waiting again. Or perhaps she didn't. Perhaps my mind was conjuring contempt where there was only pity. Either way, it seemed an unnecessarily long pause before June replied.

'No, Anna. He was no more guilty of the murder of your mother than Dennis Aylard was.'

I was ironic, trying to make her look silly for teasing me. 'I'm glad to hear it.'

'But,' she said, 'he knew who was guilty. The knowledge unbalanced his mind. And *that's* the confession he made to my father, not that he'd done it himself but that he knew who did.'

My flying thoughts came to an abrupt stop. My body froze.

June's rings slid around her finger. Her roly-poly dog sighed his foul breath into the room and waddled across to the door. A youth came up the front path and tossed a newspaper through the letter-box. Everything around me was alive and the day was moving on, but I was riveted.

Eventually the dog padded back into the room with the newspaper in his mouth. He dropped it in June's lap. She didn't seem to mind the thread of saliva he trailed across her skirt and left there, glistening. I, on the other hand, felt sick.

Having made a fool of myself once by failing to ask the obvious question, I decided not to do it again. 'June, how long have you known this?'

'Ever since my father came home that day from the hospital. Years too late to save Dennis Aylard's neck, should you be wondering.'

I frowned. 'What he was told mightn't be true. After all, he heard it from a man who was mentally sick.'

'I remember my parents arguing that through. Eventually, they came down on the side of believing him. I sat in this room with them and heard them going over and over it.

258

They never changed their minds. John couldn't possibly have killed her himself, but he was protecting the person who did, and it drove him mad.'

I put the unavoidable question. 'Who?'

June slowly shook her head. 'He didn't say. That was rather the point, wasn't it? He was determined to keep the secret. As far as I know, he did to his dying day.'

Very calmly I reminded her he talked an enormous amount of nonsense during the increasingly long periods when he lost touch with reality. Whatever he said, it was rash to believe it.

June was silent for a moment. Then she looked at her wrist-watch. 'You'll appreciate I'm not cooking for you today as I can't stand for long on this leg.'

I offered to do whatever was necessary.

She said: 'Don't worry, it's in hand. A charming Indian family have opened one of those baltic restaurants in the square. I thought we'd ask them to deliver our supper.'

Balti, she meant *balti*.

'Yes, that's a good idea.' I sounded remarkably enthusiastic.

'The menu is beside the telephone.'

We browsed and made a haphazard selection of king prawn and chicken balti dishes. Then it was her job to telephone the charming Indians.

I went through to the kitchen, put plates to warm in the oven and arranged cutlery and napkins on the table. After that I took the rubbish bag out to the dustbin and hovered in the garden for a few minutes, relishing the opportunity to think things over without being under scrutiny.

A light breeze was fanning the blowsy, overgrown roses. I pretended to be admiring them, but naturally I was fretting about what June said. She knew, that was the inescapable fact. Oh, not the intricacies, but anyone who thought about it for two seconds would realise there was only one person John Morden would have protected.

She'd known for over forty years and on the day of his funeral she told me so. What now?

I shut my eyes. My head filled with roses, and they became the scents of a distant summer. It was Sandy Minch's tenth birthday and I was walking to the shops with her because she'd been given a ten-shilling note. She promised her mother she would spend only half a crown and put the rest in her Post Office savings account. I thought she was going to spend at least five shillings, maybe eight.

We cut across the park, and that's when we stopped by the rosebed and talked. This wasn't planned but the parky was having a row with a gaggle of big boys who were kicking a scuffed old football. We were nervous of being dragged into it. Those boys were always rude to us. If they caught us, they called her Sandy Pinch, nipping her as they said it. They knew her because she used to be in their class at school. 'Before she was kept down for not keeping up,' as the smartest of them taunted.

To avoid them we lingered by the roses. This was a mistake. Every rose-bush had a metal plate in front of it saying it was planted in memory of someone or other. Most of the people whose names were there died during the war. I tried to ignore the names and dates and concentrate on the flowers.

Sandy wasn't taking much interest in the flowers. She stood on one leg and bent the other one up behind her. The hand that wasn't clutching the savings book and the cash gripped her ankle. She bobbed about until she got her balance.

'I wonder if anyone will plant a rose in memory of Dennis Mallard,' she said.

I felt a flush of revulsion. 'They aren't going to hang him. You said they'll find out they were wrong and then they won't do it.' My voice was pleading. She didn't look at me.

With a careless shrug, she hopped a couple of steps away. 'They'll have to do what the jury says, and if the jury says Dennis Duck did it, they'll hang him.'

When she called him Dennis Mallard or Dennis Duck he didn't seem real or important. When we talked about 'it', it didn't sound like murder.

Stupidly I repeated myself. 'You said they won't.'

She withered me with a look. 'If they don't hang him, they'll hang whoever else they think did it.'

I stared, at a loss.

She said: 'You can't go and tell them he didn't do it, can you?'

And when I still didn't answer she grabbed the collar of her blouse, yanked it up at one side, rolled her head back and stuck her tongue out, making choking noises.

Just as suddenly she was back to normal. 'I don't *think* you'll tell anyone, will you Ann?'

I jerked away from her and cried. My tears splashed the roses.

When I sniffed to a stop I found her standing there, hands on hips, waiting. 'And you'd better give up doing that, too,' she said.

My handkerchief was soaked. I dried my eyes on the hem of my skirt. I started to argue but she cut me off.

'We all have to make sacrifices, Ann.'

And that's how we came to sacrifice Dennis Aylard.

Sandy set off down the path with a hop and a skip. Bleary with unshed tears, I stumbled after her. Strange though it sounds, that was our last conversation about anything, ever. Before I caught up with her, I heard a voice calling me and turned back. Although no one had told me, my family had decided I should leave the town and the aunt I was going to live with had arrived to collect me.

I opened my eyes and focused on the roses in June's garden. Leaves were spotted with mould, petals were distorted because worms had chewed into the buds. But the flowers were acceptably roses, their perfume untainted. Unless you looked closely, you wouldn't know they were damaged.

Flash-back. Another summer. Another crop of roses. This time they're climbers, tethered to a trellis. I'm sitting on Kate's patio and she's telling me about her latest love, a cellist she fears is two-timing her. Mikey is a brazen flash of colour running around us, through the flat and back to the patio. He tries to scale the trellis but his foot slips and snaps off a stem of yellow roses. Kate looks incensed but it's a momentary reflex and when she speaks to him, politely asking him not to hurt her flowers, she doesn't sound upset. Everyone makes allowances for Mikey. He's too quick, on a different plane from other boys.

Behind her back Mikey pokes out his tongue and then spins away through the door into the flat. Kate takes up her story again, about the adorable cellist and her reasons for suspicion. I'm putting on a show of interest, hanging on every nuance, but I know we're both listening for Mikey. He should have completed his circuit and been back on the patio by now.

When the door to the street slams, we're on our feet and running before the echo dies. She's first through the house because her chair is nearer. She flies down the front steps to the pavement. I cannon into her.

There's a lorry slewing towards us, locked brakes howling. A vivid object is flying through the air. Kate understands immediately but I won't. For days I won't.

I live in a cloud of cottonwool until about a week after we bury Mikey. Then I wake up one morning and think: 'I've lost my good secret. Now I have only the bad one.'

I always linked them. Before he died, I regarded Mikey as the good secret that cancelled out the bad one. After he ran under the lorry, I persuaded myself it was a divine balancing of the books. I'd taken a life and I'd lost one. No doubt that's illogical but it helped me survive Mikey's death because it allowed me to believe there was a reason. If I hadn't been able to see any purpose in it, I don't think I could have come through.

A couple of months later, Kate showed me photographs of the funeral. She'd asked a friend to take them because she knew I wouldn't remember anything of the day, and that the time would come when I needed to. The coffin was pathetically tiny, the flowers were glorious. Roses. Lots and lots of yellow rosebuds.

Well, I must tell you about June and what happened after I went in from the garden. She said she'd ordered the 'baltic' without a hitch and there was time for another glass of sherry before it was delivered. I fetched a new bottle from the kitchen. When I carried it into the sitting-room she started talking about her operation again and how difficult it was for her on her own in that great big house.

I know I can be slow sometimes but it took me half the evening to work out that June had dropped the subject and wouldn't revive it if I didn't. Of course I didn't. So, we're back where we were months ago, avoiding talking about the family tragedy.

My house is on the market now and Susie is living there 'to look after it' until it's sold. June is delighted to have me under her roof as companion and helper. Yes, I know she's taking advantage of me but I can face that for a while. I expect to be here until she has her operation and becomes mobile. After that, who knows? I am, as she mentions now and then, entirely free.

I walk the dog, who's lost a few pounds since I've been feeding and exercising him, but we don't go into the churchyard. I take him on long strolls through the medieval town and into the country. It gives me time to think.

I think about everything, including what I did and what happened as a result. I've gradually remembered a scattering of details, although the important things remain a mystery. The butterfly fails to understand the caterpillar. I can't even say whether I was a truthful child.

Sandy's hold over me is plainer now but I won't put the blame on her. She bewitched me but that's no excuse. There are lots of days when I can't believe any of it happened. On others I'm convinced Sandy pushed me into it, or that she did the deed while I was a petrified onlooker. On the cruellest days I suspect I did it entirely by myself. These last are the days when I'm glad I can't re-enter childhood to check.

I envy June her certainties. She settled on an immutable truth years ago, and for her the past is unthreatening entertainment. Strong-minded woman that she is, she's secured her future, too, with me to take care of her.

Ah, but does she see it that way? The remarks she makes

and the way she looks at me, suggest she thinks *she* is protecting *me*. As ever, we view the picture from different angles. Which doesn't mean, of course, that either of us is wrong.